WAYWALKERS

By Catherine Webb

Mirror Dreams
Mirror Wakes

Waywalkers

Coming soon . . .

Timekeepers

Praise for Catherine Webb

'Assured, well-sustained and engages directly with the
reader . . . If I were a teenage fan of Terry Pratchett
or Philip Pullman I would love *Mirror Dreams*'
SUNDAY TELEGRAPH

'A Brilliant book!'
WHS ONLINE

Recommended
TEEN TITLES

'*Mirror Dreams* is a splendid book . . .
I want to read the sequel. Now'
THE ALIEN ONLINE

WAYWALKERS

Catherine Webb

www.atombooks.co.uk

An *Atom* paperback original

First published in Great Britain by Atom 2003

A CIP catalogue record for this book
is available from the British Library.

ISBN 1 904233 21 X

Typeset in Cochin by M Rules
Printed and bound in Great Britain
by Bookmarque Ltd, Croydon, Surrey

Atom Books
An imprint of
Time Warner Books UK
Brettenham House
Lancaster Place
London WC2E 7EN

Contents

ONE

The Linguist

'An eagle scared of heights.' That was how one col-
league summed up Sam Linnfer. 'Probably has a
mad wife in the attic too.'

Like all rumours, in time this comment circulated back
to Sam, whose boyish face split in a grin of delight.

If there was one thing Sam liked about working as . . .
whatever he was, he enjoyed the mystery accorded him
by other people. It gave him great satisfaction to take the
same trains, eat the same meals, wait at the same bus
stops, and still be above it all, if only in the wild, fantastical tales told by everyone around him.

Though Sam was indeed different, everybody
throughout the university somehow managed to know
him. His sparky smile and disregard of authority
endeared him to the undergraduates, and certainly he
was bored at the very idea of the life led by the dons, as
they ambled through a daily ritual whose high point
seemed to be exchanging Latin puns while dining in hall.

But neither did Sam truly resemble a student, for despite his seeming youth he had an air of command, one that came from a long, unsung history.

He mostly wore black – a black coat buttoned up around a baggy black jumper, worn over a shapeless black shirt. Sam wore bad clothes as a kind of protection, which no one had yet penetrated. People speculated, most of them inaccurately, on exactly what shape he was beneath all those layers. The idea that he wore black from vanity never survived a first meeting: with these clothes went a pair of terrible old trainers, and a scruffy blue and grey scarf hand-knitted for him by some person unknown. The whole effect was finished off by cuffs that were never done up, shirt buttons that didn't match and sometimes a jacket, haphazardly patched, that gave him the look of a fashionable scarecrow.

To round off this character, whose contradictions so attracted other people. He had thick black hair, and eyes so dark that they too seemed black. Not that many had met Sam's eye for long enough to confirm this, since his gaze was something of unrivalled intensity. Though his voice bore the slightest accent, no one was sure where that accent came from. Some said his speech was northern; others held that there must be a touch of Gaelic in him. At one point he was credited with the ghost of a Welsh accent, so it became rumoured that Sam Linnfer had grown up in the wild Snowdonian mountains. A few who cherished difference in any form said he had to be a gypsy. Sam himself, when questioned on his past, was devious.

Compounding the mystery, Sam also showed a flair for unexpected languages. On one occasion a distinguished guest was visiting from India on the kind of freebie trip that academics love to call 'research'. Sam, overhearing him stumble in conversation on a word in English, was not only able to supply the correct term in Hindi, but added some word-play of his own. By the third time something like this had happened, always in some language from far away, it was a subject of gossip for days.

Sam had seemed at first to have no official job within the university. He'd given no seminars and supervised no papers. But when, in a lecture one day, an overworked head of department had been asked a difficult question about traditional Gaian worship, Sam was the one who answered it. There started an unusual relationship by which Sam, for unlimited access to the university's facilities, helped write papers that would otherwise have taken many weeks more. Departments specialising in ancient studies or remote cultures began calling upon his huge knowledge, counting on his readiness to find out some elusive fact in a frenzy of activity.

His movements acquired a pattern, if not a purpose anyone understood. For five days every month or so, Sam caught the train up from London, ate at high table, and sat in the library writing in unfamiliar languages from forgotten books. Over the rest of the month he could have gone off-planet.

So he had a token job. He didn't earn much, as a part-time college librarian whose speciality no one quite knew, but he'd never shown much interest in the size of his salary. Of the favours he'd been offered, from easy money through fancy job titles to things the most publicity-seeking lecturer might sigh after, Sam had turned down even the best. At one point he declined a chair, saying he didn't want to be tied down.

'Dare I ask, Linnfer, what it is exactly that you do?' the Master of the college once asked. 'When you're not researching, that is.'

'Ghost-write the papers of idiots who can't be bothered to write them themselves.'

Taking Sam at his word, the Master brightened. He loved nothing more than getting ahead of a rival in 'their' field, as though a subject could be owned by whoever studied it. 'Anyone I know, or aren't you allowed to say?'

But Sam didn't answer. Not from discretion – no, this time he kept silent because he hadn't just wiggled out of answering a question; for once, he'd told a direct lie. Not that he felt guilty. Some truths were much, much more damaging than the odd small lie.

And no: there was no mad wife in the attic, nor ever had been.

It was late one rainy February evening that Sam trudged up the stairs to his flat, started digging in his pocket for the key – and froze where he stood.

The flat was in one of those huge scruffy terraces around the edge of Camden which have been climbing up-market for forty years but somehow still have leaky taps. The woman who claimed rent from him every week was in her eighties, deaf in one ear and hardly knew Sam's name. She still called him Mr Samuel, even though he'd been in the flat for three years. But her failing mind, bordering on senile, served perfectly. Sam wanted unreliable witnesses to his movements. If for nights on end he wasn't in the flat, Mrs Dinken was the ideal person to say he had been, all the time believing it to be true.

But tonight, audible to few creatures but Sam himself, something was moving in the flat. His dark, dark eyes had seen a faint glow from underneath the front door, suggesting that somewhere inside a light was burning. He knew he hadn't left one on. Staring at the door again, his eyes grew distant and for a moment he seemed to be listening to an inner voice. At length his look of concentration converted to a scowl. He found the key and thrust the door open.

The intruders wore such plain, ordinary clothes that Sam identified them immediately for what they were. Policemen.

One of them brandished a warrant card. 'I'm sorry about this, sir.'

If he was making excuses even before Sam had entered, it had to be bad.

'What,' asked Sam in a very calm, controlled voice that aged his young face and gave him a gravitas quite beyond expectation, 'are you doing in my flat?'

'If you could just step inside, sir.'

Seeing no alternative, he entered the small, slightly musty sitting room with its piles of unopened mail, unread newspapers and magazines, and empty coffee cups growing interesting moulds. For all the squalor, though, there was a feeling of organisation about the place, and a sense of homeliness.

There were two of them. Without a further word they indicated that he should go through and sit down at the kitchen table. One of them, the older, sat himself opposite Sam as though about to conduct an interrogation; the younger leant against a worktop with a languid ease that Sam found somehow offensive.

'I'm sorry to have to trouble you, sir –'

'But –'

'The matter *is* delicate.'

Sam pulled off his coat and shoved it carelessly over the back of the chair. 'Tell me what you want.'

As the officer began to talk, Sam Linnfer resigned himself to a bad night.

TWO

Friends and Family

Freya Oldstock, the man had said. Was it a name that meant anything to him?

On his guard, Sam made a show of thinking about this. In fact his memory made an instant match, though down the centuries Freya had used many names.

'We did know each other. Years ago.'

'Close, were you?'

'I liked her, certainly. I think she liked me too, but neither of us felt we had to be especially forthcoming.' *Because when I knew her, talking was the last thing we did.*

Already, taking hold like the brief numbness after some bad injury, there was the sense that what came next would be bad indeed.

He forced himself to say, 'Why?'

Seeing the look on Sam's face, pale and slack, the policeman did his professional best to use tact. 'Sorry to be the one to tell you . . . her body . . . discovered yesterday . . .'

Sam's thoughts had exploded in several directions at once.

Freya's dead?

What should I be feeling?

What should I be saying?

Freya, I'm so sorry . . .

Who'd do this?

He had to ask them to repeat themselves before he could take in anything much – the time, the place. Part of him, as if looking on at his own shock, supposed most people must respond like this.

She'd been found at her cottage in the Devonshire village of Holcombe. Stabbed. He had the presence of mind to ask, 'What sort of weapon?'

'A strange one, sir,' the older man said, watching him even more closely.

Of course it was. You think a conventional weapon would kill Freya?

'Strange . . . how?'

The two policemen exchanged the briefest of glances. Sam felt the atmosphere turn unforgiving

'Traces of bone were found in the wound. Not her bone – we couldn't find a DNA match.'

That's because she was stabbed with one of the few weapons that are good at killing us. The bone of a dragon would hardly have DNA on your record – not a dragon-bone knife. Oh Light, that means it was one of us who did it . . .

They were waiting now, to see if their silence would make him blurt out anything more. From grief, from confusion, from dread of a danger beyond anything they suspected, he couldn't help himself.

'So why have you come to me?' It made it worse that he couldn't meet their eyes. Something about the presence of the law made him feel guilty even when he knew better.

He tried to forget that it was Freya who lay dead, tried to freeze over and think logically. *What would they know about her, about me? She's dead; nothing I'm able to do can bring her back. I must look after myself, she'd understand that.*

'This letter' – placing it in front of Sam – 'was found. In two envelopes. The first was addressed to someone by the name of Luc Satise, the one inside to Sam Linnfer. I think the idea was that if it didn't find Luc Satise the first envelope could be torn off and the second one used to get to you.'

Sam took the letter warily, as if Freya might attack him from the hereafter. It was in a neat, precise hand, definitely hers, but the text was faded by much application of chemicals. Apparently the police, having tried to analyse its purpose, saw delivering it as just a fall-back.

Dear Sam/Luc, it read.

I'm not sure whether Sam or Luc, or either, shall receive this. But it's important that I meet you. I need help, and you are the only ones who haven't been corrupted. First the old hammer, and now the head of my house, is turning, and I can do nothing to stop them. I would write more, but I fear even this is too much. I hope that by contacting you, as another prime, in this way I will not be intercepted, but I'm afraid it may already be too late.

Meet me at the usual time in the Grove. If I'm not there, assume the worst. We will talk more.

Freya

'Does this mean anything to you, sir?'

'No,' he said firmly, eyes not moving from the letter.

'The Grove is a pub in Hampstead where we used to meet, but that's all I know.'

'No idea who Luc Satise is? Or "the old hammer"?'

'No.'

'Or "the head of my house"?'

'No.'

'What does she mean by a "prime"?'

'Her quaint way of saying someone she liked. "Primes" were people high in her esteem, "seconds" were those she liked well enough but not greatly, "thirds" she could tolerate, "fourths" she didn't trust, "fifths" she couldn't stand.'

'And what do you think she meant by "*another* prime"?'

'She often said she was her own best friend. A strange lady, Freya.'

'Strange indeed, sir. Writing cryptic notes to two people but sounding as though they were one. Categorising people. A secretive person, was she? Perhaps not a . . . regular citizen?'

For a panic-ridden second Sam thought they'd found it. Just as quickly he discarded the idea. No. They wouldn't have had time to search his flat properly, and even if they had it was well sealed with things the police would never understand.

He was careful to control his voice, though, as he said, 'What do you mean?'

'When we searched her house' – Sam winced at the thought of intruders digging through Freya's neat, fragile possessions – 'we found several bizarre items. A collection of books – and several charts – in unfamiliar languages, and a kitchen full of unidentified herbs and odd-looking knives.' He leaned forward and added, '*Three* passports: British, Swedish, and Russian. All dated the same year.' The man's little eyes, made narrower by his intent on the hunt, wrought havoc on Sam's nerves. Of all people, Sam didn't need to hear the words 'highly irregular'.

'And none of them had been revoked.' The man sat back, patience itself, waiting for Sam's response.

'Certainly she was a British citizen, as well as Swedish at one time. I didn't know about the Russian passport, but I suppose it was possible.'

'Legally, sir, it wasn't at all possible.'

'Oh.' He gave a nervous laugh. 'Shows how much I know.'

'And the books, sir?'

'I beg your pardon?'

'I hear you're quite the expert on unlikely languages.' That grating phrase – 'I hear' – implying that the officer knew Sam from within a shared circle of friends, rather than as a stranger.

'She was very good on old Scandinavian languages.'

The questioning was contrived, as he soon realised, to catch the subject off guard at every turn. At one moment, ancient languages; the next, back to the letter; then his past with Freya. Here Sam had to tread more carefully. He had no idea what other leads the man had. If he told one story, he was pretty confident that someone else would tell another.

'We studied in roughly the same field. One day we met in a library looking for the same book, and we've bumped into each other now and again ever since.'

He knew they weren't buying it.

'We're told that Ms Oldstock seemed a sensible woman. Why do you suppose she'd write a note which no one could understand, and send it to you?'

'I don't think it was intended for me. Probably this "Luc Satise" was supposed to get it. I was second choice.'

'But from what little we can understand, the matter was important. Why, if she wasn't certain it would get to Mr Satise, would she try and contact you? I thought you weren't close.'

'We weren't. I've no idea why she acted as she did.'

'Do you know any other of Ms Oldstock's . . . acquaintances?'

'No. She never introduced me to any of her friends.'

A dangerous answer. Sam felt like a man standing on one leg, not sure what forces were about to shove him or from which direction. If 'other acquaintances' were involved, again he had no idea what testimonies might contradict his own.

Meanwhile with every plausible reply he made, the younger man seemed to get more annoyed with him. Taking the letter, he thrust it at Sam. 'So what can you tell us about this bit – where she seems to suggest she's being watched? Are you sure you can't think why someone might want to watch Ms Oldstock?'

'Yes, I am. No, I can't think.' He had to stop himself from pointing out how often they'd now asked him this.

'Was she given to paranoia?'

'Definitely not!'

The older man opened his mouth to ask a question, and seemed to think better of it. Finally he stood up. 'I'm sorry to have troubled you, sir. If anything comes back to you, please contact us.'

Sam gratefully rose with him. In his relief he found it hard not to gabble. 'I'm sorry about Freya,' he said, as much to himself as them. He remembered to add, 'I don't suppose you know who's arranging the funeral?'

'Family, sir.'

Family. Great.

As the police were leaving, the senior man turned in the doorway. 'Just one small thing, sir.'

'Yes?'

'Where were you the night before last?'

Faced with such a grotesque implication, somehow Sam managed to restrain himself nonetheless. In angry, clipped tones, he replied, 'At my university.'

It showed how well the coppers had done their research that the man didn't ask 'which university?' He merely smiled, rapped off a cheerful 'goodnight, sir', and led the way down the stairs. Behind them Sam slammed the door, harder than necessary.

Only when the sound of their footsteps had retreated from the house did he lean on the door and close his eyes against involuntary tears.

Damage Control

Though he'd mastered himself and calmed down, Sam didn't go straight to bed even though the night would soon be growing old. Having opened the windows to let in the cold February air he sat for a long time motionless at the kitchen table. His face would have been expressionless, but that his reddened eyes were narrowed against the glare of bright memories.

Freya had been killed with a dragon-bone knife. Dragon bone meant someone who knew what Freya was, and was strong enough to approach her and do the act. Before she'd died she tried to arrange a meeting with him. Was that connected to her death?

But who would want to kill Freya? She had no enemies. Not now. In the past, yes, but the war is over . . .

The involvement of the police was a new kind of problem. Whenever there'd been something like this before – and, yes, things like this had happened – the body was tidied away by relatives or friends well before the police could get stock of the situation. By the time officialdom woke up to any of what had happened, every record of the dead person's life had been erased.

But not now. This time, family hadn't responded to the disaster. Because of the . . . corruption reported by Freya just before her death? Even the old hammer is corrupted, she'd said. Sam felt his guts churn. The old hammer and he were not famous for being friends. It seemed there'd be little help there, in finding out what had happened.

Besides, how to do so without the police knowing? He was certain his performance hadn't been good enough to shake them off. Murder was murder, and he must be almost the only lead. *For that matter, maybe the only suspect.*

Rising, he padded into his bedroom. He knelt down beside the bed, pushed a frayed red carpet to one side, and laid his hand on a floorboard. There was a flash below it, as of a spark rising from a fuse. When the light had faded he pulled back the board and extracted several items, including a long slim object and a shorter narrow one, each wrapped in well-oiled leather, and a shoebox fastened with string.

From this last he produced a wad of fifty-pound notes still in its banker's slip, and five well-thumbed passports: American, British, German, Swiss and Canadian. Each was stamped with place names from Greenland to Egypt, Nigeria to Tibet. Two, the Canadian and the Swiss, were issued to Luc Satise. The face that stared out from these with traditional passport-photo stoniness was Sam's own, albeit unusually hard and expressionless. It was remarkable, he mused, how passports made everyone look like a crook. The German one was issued to Sebastian Teufel; the other two were Sam Linnfer's.

From inside his wardrobe he took out a travel bag, fully packed. He always kept it ready lest one day, leaving in haste, he forgot something whose importance meant life or death. He also lifted out a box, from the very bottom of the wardrobe, containing Ordnance Survey maps and a *London A to Z*. The street guide he opened at the end of its index, where a neat hand had written the heading, 'Portals – Hell'. Below were a series of names. Hyde Park. Camden Market. The Embankment. Mare Street. A further three entries under 'Portals – Heaven' were in the same hand.

Sam was reluctant to use any of these; as a method of travel the Waywalks that lay beyond were exhausting and often inaccurate. If he could reach a destination instead by Intercity, he'd do it however appalling the price. But it was always good to know where the serious escape routes lay.

Next he made a phone call.

'Hi, it's Sam.' It wasn't his usual name when talking to this person, but he knew it would be recognised. He also knew that if he started saying, 'Hello, it's Luc' his troubles could only get worse. There might well be a tap on his phone, especially if he was a suspect. *And even if the police don't listen in, others may try.* Sam didn't trust his own story to hold.

'Sam? As in —'

'Adam, thank God it's you!' he exclaimed, forestalling the other's words.

Adam cut short what he'd been about to say, on recognising his own alternative name. Also Sam had pointedly exclaimed 'Thank God', when on principle he abhorred saying any such thing. Clumsily Adam grabbed at these hints. 'Oh. Yes. Hi, Sam . . .'

There was no right way Sam could give news like his. 'Freya? *Dead?* How?'

'I can't talk. Can I see you in the King's Head, usual time tomorrow? Bring your wits.'

For all that Adam might want to say, 'Oh sorry, how are you for the day after?', he didn't dare. When Sam Linnfer asked if you could meet up, that's what you did. It was a matter of respect and rank. If he said 'bring your wits' it made the situation doubly bad.

And the question that besieged both of them. *Who would want to kill Freya? She hadn't an enemy in the world, in any world.* A silly thought. Of course she had an enemy – she was, after all, dead.

But Sam knew as he rang off that by tomorrow, while losing all pursuers, Adam could be trusted to have discovered everything he could concerning Freya's death. And Adam had eyes everywhere, so the rumour went. *Always rumours. And how proud some people would be to realise that the most fantastical ones were right.*

He went into the kitchen and dug around behind a large biscuit tin full of stale flapjacks foisted on him by a friend who fancied herself an excellent cook and who he hadn't the heart to enlighten. It was cooks like that, he reflected, who made you wish for a handy dog under the table. He pulled out a fat address book from behind the tin and flicked through it. Some addresses were in English, but most were in an archaic script that would have multiplied the rumours at the university many times over. When in Europe he claimed it was a form of Hindi; when in Asia, he pretended it was written in Scandinavian runes.

But language aside, it was simply an address book. Finding the entry for Freya Oldstock, he scribbled it on the palm of his hand. He didn't want to be caught with the book in his possession – too many names in it would rather stay private.

That done, he consulted his map for the area, marked at strategic points in two colours. Blue for Heaven, red for Hell. He ran his finger round the village of Holcombe, knowing he didn't have to look far. Freya would almost certainly have had her home near a Portal. It was in the blood of everyone in his family. You were either as far away from a Portal as possible and damn quick on your feet when you needed one, or you lived close by, ready to run straight through it. Because evidently in this world anybody, even innocent Freya who just a while ago was friends with everyone, had enemies.

When the clock struck twelve, Sam Linnfer finally put his head on the pillow and fell into a dreamless sleep. Outside in the street, there was the sound of a cat mewing. In the distance, the roar of a main road and the wet rush of a bus. The wheels of the bus sent a sheet of water up from the little lake around a blocked drain, to soak a group of drunken youths emerging from the nearby pub, so saving maybe three hours' worth of sobering up. The V Shop across the road played its endless silent songs and films on the never-dying TV screen in its window, and New Look squatted uncomfortably between the shoemender's and the newsagent's, which even at this inhospitable hour was still open, the family that owned it working constant shifts to try and pay off who-knew-what debt. Only two of the five children spoke English, and the husband kept a very old guard dog with yellow teeth and a famous temper. Outside the shop was a stand that sold strange bent vegetables that looked like some kind of religious symbol, and which only one ethnic minority in the whole world could cook properly to get that particular dead-dog taste that was so prized.

A raven flew down the street, and this was unusual in several ways. Firstly, Camden is not famous for its ravens; the dustbins full of McDonald's packages tend to attract, at best, a scrawny breed of pigeon. This raven was sleek, a gleaming shade of black. It flew along a dead straight line, keeping below the house tops and following the street itself – as though it had been given directions and needed to see the street signs to know where it was going. Once it overshot a turning and had to spin round, disobeying the traffic system in a way to make a traffic warden weep. Somehow it managed to navigate from Tufnell Park station to Camden Road and along a canal, until, looking, it must be said, slightly lost, it hit the street where Sam lived and banked sharply, almost colliding with a lamp-post. Flying down the quiet street, it looked this way and that until it reached his house. It made for a window ledge, sensing its target.

Then something happened. The raven itself was not thinking as such, but behind those unblinking, beady eyes there was an acute consciousness nonetheless, a light that most people wouldn't expect to find in a brain the size of a walnut, and one that fed hungrily on the images the raven sent back to it. As the raven's feet touched the window ledge, however, something seemed to change. There was a tingle through the creature's body. Silver sparks flashed across its eyes. The grip on its little mind slipped, faltered, was shoved away. Then the raven was once more a raven, taking off in panic, completely disorientated and with no memory of what had just happened.

In the bed, Sam rolled over and opened his eyes. He felt no surprise that someone had tried to spy on him; indeed he'd been expecting it, which was why he'd taken such careful precautions. His landlady, dotty as she was, hadn't noticed the many hours he'd spent drawing symbols throughout the house, that sparked occasionally during thunderstorms even though not connected to the mains. It was inconvenient, he decided, before drifting back to sleep, that his defences had been activated, but it would have to be tolerated.

For now.

FOUR

Adamarus

There are many King's Heads in London. But for Adam there would really be only one. It was the cheerful pub of that name down one of the many alleys off Fleet Street, and was usually full of journalists spending freely on doing what journalists do best. In the secret square where the King hid his Head, a board declared that this was 'an authentic pub, lunch served'.

Adam had been sitting in a corner nursing a pint of beer for half an hour, and now eyed those same lunches eagerly. He was small and slightly podgy, with clammy hands, a freckled face and ginger hair. The thought of meeting Sam made him nervous and he was finding it hard to keep still.

When the door was indeed darkened by Sam's black shape and Sam came in shaking rain from his coat and headed arrow-straight across the room, Adam saw in him a man going to war. There was the travel bag, and the oh-so-convenient coat with at least three pockets that only special eyes could see. The coat's sleeves were baggy, and as Sam took it off Adam observed that his jumper also hung loose.

So. He was ready to draw the weapon no one expected, hidden in its sheath, for the first time in years of respite. And yes, across his back was a narrow plastic wrap, slightly longer than a bag of golf clubs. Full-out war, then.

All of which made him more nervous, so that as Sam sat down and greeted him it was all he could do not to burble, '*I* didn't do it!' Sam inspired in Adam, and in spirits like him, an awe that those who didn't know The Truth, capital T, capital T, would never understand.

'I don't suppose you know anything?'

'I asked around last night. Had a chat with some people in Devon.'

'Go on.' Sam wasn't interested in the how of the matter. For now he just wanted to establish the what and the why.

'It isn't nice.' Adam told what he'd heard in a night's frantic telephoning. A neighbour claimed to have seen a man go into Freya's house the afternoon before she was found dead. But he hadn't left for several hours, according to the neighbour, who claimed she'd been gardening. She was evidently the kind of woman, recently retired, who liked to stick her nose into other people's business.

'And she described the man as dark-haired, tall. Elegant.'

'Dark hair?'

'Very dark. And extremely dark eyes. That struck her even from the next garden.'

'Damn.' Sam caught Adam's satirical look and added,

'I do have an alibi, in case anyone thinks it's me. And I am not "elegant".'

As a cue for what he termed 'the grisly bit', Adam frowned. 'Whoever killed her knew her very well. And she must have been extremely pleased to see him. That is, before he stabbed her with a dragon-bone blade. What I mean is, whoever killed her did it in the bedroom.'

'Someone she knew as a lover?' Sam asked.

'Almost certainly. At least we know it wasn't one of her lot, since he didn't have blond hair and blue eyes.'

No, thought Sam. *Dark hair and dark eyes put him in the younger set. One of my lot. So who would she know well enough not to suspect? Enough to love, even? But then, Freya's loved so many. Even me, in her own quaint way. Prohibited love always had a certain attraction for her.*

Privately Sam began listing Freya's many lovers in his family. *Primes – apart from me: Seth, Jehovah, Thor, Helios, Apollo. Seconds: Gawain, Jason, Mark. Two of whom are dead. Thirds: Rhys, Alrim, Saul. Numerous others who don't know who it was they loved. And after that I lose touch. Shit, with that on my record –* remembering the raven – *no wonder I'm under surveillance. The only prime around with dark hair, dark eyes, a reputation for swordsmanship and a ruthless inclination towards survival. Seth and Jehovah have my colouring – but why would they kill Freya? Whereas I – I'm the ideal scapegoat. And even if I don't have a motive, I've enough history for people to think they perceive one.*

But I wasn't there. I can prove it.

'It's a narrow field of suspects, but a hard one to search. Do we know where any of them are?'

'Rhys, Alrim and Saul are all growing old, being third generation. One of them's seventy and he's already going grey.' Adam gave a disregarding laugh, as though grey hair were something he only imagined. 'As the surviving second, Mark is still under Jehovah's firm wing.'

Sam swore. 'That makes him about as accessible as opening a can of solid diamond with a Swiss army knife.'

'There are others who fit the description, you know. I don't have records on many of them. But there have been a few who've had it off with her.'

'List them, then,' Sam said abruptly. Hearing all those names duly recited, he felt sickened. He hated Adam's crude turn of phrase even more; its injustice rankled. Freya was love, Freya was life. No one could be surprised that she'd had as a lover just about everyone who came near her. And the coward who'd killed her hadn't even had the guts to use his own weapon, instead of dragon bone. Freya had trusted him, too. Freya had never learnt not to trust.

'When's the funeral?'

'Tomorrow evening. Family's wasting no time in getting her back up to Heaven. Her mother is furious.'

Sam rose to go, but Adam shot out his arm to restrain him. He didn't actually touch Sam – he was too intimidated for that. 'It's a closed funeral. Old school only. Just the Valhalla bunch.'

Sam was silent as he slung the bag on his back. Turning to leave, he merely said, 'You've been very helpful, Adamarus.'

The train journey to Devon was a long one. On such a short winter's day Sam didn't expect to arrive before nightfall. The carriage was full: tired-looking business people in suits, a noisy group of students, a mother and her two complaining children. Resisting the temptation to go first class and avoid the incessant whining of children, he sat facing the sunset and watched without seeing as the English landscape rushed past. Large wet fields between the thinning suburbs. The odd farmhouse, brick and timber, then stone, in which the lights burned early. Then the outrage of other cities, huge factories forcing billows of chemical smoke from their metal chimneys. The vast car parks by the stations, the large neighbouring Safeway's and Tesco's. The empty sidings. The burrows torn in the embankments by rabbits.

Sam saw all of this, but registered nothing. His mind was fixed on Freya, and his memories.

Close, were you?

I liked her, certainly.

He'd known her back in the old days; and that was how he'd always remember her. She carried a staff around which ivy coiled, and her long fair hair was crowned with more ivy that twined around her brow. The kindest and most beautiful of women, standing by a river singing her songs to a perfect world.

But when he met her afterwards, she wasn't in that world, and neither was he. It was when the war raging in Heaven was at its worst. And if there was war in Heaven, whether between traditional combatants like Valhalla and Olympus or Elysium and Arcadia, or between such new and unexpected factions as Nirvana or Shangri-La, you could be sure of repercussions on Earth. Sometimes it was simply a matter of war in Heaven tapping the resources of Earth – weapons, manpower – in order to eliminate their enemies' allies there as well as in Heaven itself. More often it was down to basic human empathy. Mortals' awareness was tragically

underdeveloped, but still they could *sense* it when the
creatures of Heaven were fighting – the deaths of all
those angels, avatars, valkyries and seraphim echoed
back to Earth, and in their unconscious way the humans
knew. And they also fought. It was infectious.
Regrettably, too, what they lacked in Heavenly magic
they made up for in sheer destructive ingenuity.

A siren was wailing. The streets were empty, save for
rats running through the collapsed buildings. The sky
was full of smoke and he could hear the rumble of planes
and the distant thud of bombs.

Why had he come here? With the whole world to
wander, why here? What was Sam Linnfer with his
boyish smile, aka one Sebastian Teufel, doing in ruined
Berlin at the height of the 1944 air raids?

He knew the answer already. He'd come because he
needed to convince himself. He'd come because he'd
seen what one country had done to so many millions of
people, and wanted to reassure himself that this place
was still human. He'd come because, after four years of
fighting in France for the French, he'd seen the tables
turn and felt bound to help the losing side. He'd come
because, deep inside, some part of him that still wandered in that perfect world back in the good old times
had known that this was just a shadow of the war in
Heaven. It was his responsibility to lighten this shadow
in whatever way he could.

The air raid receded and the people of Berlin began to
come up out of their shelters. In scenes like these, not so
long ago he'd helped dig bodies out from the ruins of
homes in Dover and London, or kept injured people
alive with a touch of his magic. Even if their sufferings

weren't due to him, they were the fault of his family and therefore a responsibility passed down to him. Helping these people was what he saw as duty. Sam had been neither born nor bred to this ideal. But, like several other human words, it helped justify actions prompted in him merely by impulse.

He came upon a crew of firefighters struggling before a burning ruin. They were trying to work their hose before the blaze caught the few nearby houses left intact. Sam stood across the road, gazing at the fire, his eyes distant. As he stared the flames seemed to shrink. Eventually there were just a few burning embers, which died as he clenched his fists. The whole process had taken him ten minutes of concentration.

Ten minutes of standing exposed and dumb.

'Papers!'

A Brownshirt officer, uniformed, his shiny buttons silly in the ruined street. He was holding out his hand imperiously. Sam dug around and produced his papers. The man flicked through them, looking ready for a fight on any pretext. A single flaw in Sam's documents, one look out of place, and Sam might be forced to get mythological. Which would be embarrassing.

But the papers, as Sam had known, were perfect. Unfortunately though, his look of dowdy submission was badly out of practice, and he peered at the Brownshirt with unabashed curiosity.

Sure enough, this made the man angry.

'What are you doing here, just staring?'

'I don't have anywhere to go.'

Another voice. 'You can come with me.'

The speaker was blonde, tall and wearing a long coat unscathed by any of the hardship around her. But this wasn't what attracted Sam's attention. He'd long ago learnt that outside appearance was only useful for mundane matters. Mostly what counted was the glow he might perceive on the inside. And here he was, seeing a prime in the same street, in the same town. He couldn't quite believe it.

Freya had zapped the charm up to full voltage, and it quickly won out. Within a minute she had taken the unresisting Sam by the arm and was dragging him down the street. 'Where's the nearest Portal?' she asked quietly.

'Bomb dropped on it last night.'

'We're in danger – not from humans. There are people here fighting another war.'

Sam felt his guts churn. 'What are we talking about?'

'There are five Firedancers on my trail. Now that Valhalla's fallen, this was the only place I could think of where Firedancers stood a higher chance of dying than me . . . What are *you* doing here?'

'I'm everywhere in this shadow world. Isn't that the story? These Firedancers – has anyone bothered to send some after me?'

'You don't merit the attention. The battle is for Heaven, not Earth.'

There was the clatter of a roof tile falling. A sound common enough, but Sam's head snapped up; Freya too looked quickly around. A shadow disappeared over a rooftop and suddenly they felt very alone. They were some way off now from the wail of fire engines, and the voices of people clambering out of their cellars to discover that everything they'd called their own was destroyed. Close by was a shattered railway station, carriages still at the platforms with all their glass blown out.

A tape surrounding the skeletal building declared, 'Danger – Unexploded Bomb'.

'They're in the station,' whispered Sam.

'They don't know what you are. They're on your territory now.'

He smiled wryly. 'You expect me to be your knight errant?'

She put a hand up to her hair, fastened in a tight bun, and pulled from it a narrow stick. The bun stayed in place, supported by other means, but looking at the stick the word that came to Sam's mind was: needle. Its end was gleaming and seemed very sharp. The thing was made out of a dark, dark metal, and he had a feeling it would be poisoned.

'Will you?' asked Freya softly.

He made a flicking movement with his right hand, and there was a slim, silver dagger in it. Another gesture and it was gone. 'Why should I help you?' he asked, eyes not leaving her face.

'Because I'm not one of those who's harmed you. Because you know that Firedancers are only used by the bad ones among us. Because it's cowardice, sending Firedancers against a prime. Because no one from Family has spoken to you for far too long.'

Sam considered this. Of course, she could be trying very subtly to influence him with her unique power. But it was rare to be greeted with such open honesty, especially by anyone from his extensive family. For too long he'd not been spoken to in such a reasonable, friendly way by one of his own. He said, 'Fair enough. Give me five minutes to get into the station.'

She nodded, breathless with anticipation. Though her face was taut and she held the needle tightly, poised to strike, her eyes were sick at what must be done. Sam, on the other hand, was already moving with cat-like determination. He had no qualms about killing Firedancers.

The train was passing over a river. Sam closed his eyes as the hills of now were lost in a flare of sunlight. The sky was pink, with brilliant shadows cast across the belly of the clouds. Back in that bombed-out station, he'd had no need to help Freya. But what made her special was that she'd not cared what the others had said. She'd taken him at face value, and listened to what he had to say. He'd been honoured to risk his life tor her. That was Freya's magic, her greatest weapon. And she'd never realised how recklessly she wielded it.

The station had been deserted. Glass was sprayed across the platform and the fire crews hadn't even begun a clear-up. Twisted metal hung down on all sides, like blackened and burnt lianas in a chaotic jungle. Not a soul moved.

Through a feat of climbing and guesswork Sam had found his way to what remained of a gantry overlooking the station. He heaved himself through a shattered window, landing with the faintest clang on the gantry's metal platform below. It creaked ominously, and somewhere there was the thunk, thunk of bricks falling. But it held.

Edging along, dagger ready in his hand, he peered down into the main concourse, straining to find his adversaries. He pressed his back against the nearest wall and willed himself to hear them. Below, on a floor strewn with fallen tiles, a crater held an unexploded bomb counting the seconds until destiny.

Sam heard it. The faint thump of a boot on the gantry platform. Then he felt it, the faint tensing of metal beneath him as a foot was raised, fell, was raised again. Heading towards him. Five yards. Three. Two. In the shadows someone – or thing – had stopped less than a yard away, breathing fast.

Overhead, something else moved. Too late Sam cursed himself for a fool – Firedancers always attacked in twos. A lithe shape, masked in executioner's red, swung from the torn rafters above and struck, his red feet impacting sharply with Sam's chest and knocking him back. At the same moment his comrade whirled round the corner, gloved hands bright with fire. The flame sprang up around Sam and sought to burn him. As the second Firedancer landed neatly on the platform, which creaked in loud distress, Sam staggered to his feet, shaking himself like a dog to be rid of the fire. He emerged unscorched as it flew from him in drops. Both Firedancers struck at once, each lunging forward with a knife of white bone. But Sam was ready for them. Seeing dragon-bone death stab towards his throat, he raised his arms. Both knives exploded in their owners' hands, turning in an instant to dust.

The Firedancers were unmoved. From a standing jump one leapt three feet into the air and grasped a beam above, swinging his legs to catch Sam's exposed face. Just in time Sam ducked and twisted. With his back to the second Firedancer he knocked into the creature, ramming him towards the edge of the gantry. Again the metal platform creaked. Then trembled. But by now both Firedancers knew their game. As one struggled with Sam, trying to lock his arms and feet in place, the other delivered a ringing blow across his face, then another to the side of the head that sent Sam staggering.

Sparks seemed to fly across Sam's eyes. Then he felt mortar dust crumbling on his fingers, and out of the corner of his eye he glimpsed metal bolts loose in their socket, which in turn strained against brickwork held together by little more than inertia. Willing himself to ignore his attackers he struck instead at the brickwork behind him. Part of the wall exploded outwards, clattered down a rooftop and bounced with a far-off sound into the street below.

It was enough. The socket popped loose, and the platform lurched violently to one side. For a sickening couple of seconds it paused, then slid a little way, and finally turned over and crashed on to the ticket hall below. It was a fall no Firedancer could survive. No man, neither.

At least, no human.

Sam had come to himself in an alien bed. He felt bruised all over and his right arm and leg tingled from newly regenerating. Pain coursed through most of his body. He tried to sit up, and instantly regretted it.

The next thing that struck him was the heat. And the flies – something else he didn't associate with Berlin in the autumn.

'Welcome back,' said a cheerful voice. 'That was a nasty selection of breaks you had to mend there.'

'I'm out of practice with Firedancers,' he said, feeling twice his lengthy age.

Freya hadn't got off lightly either. There were lines down her bare arms where the Firedancers had managed to scorch her, and one side of her face was bright pink.

'Where are we?'

'Spain. I Waywalked us here.'

He nearly fell out of bed with surprise. 'Through the Way of Heaven?'

'Don't worry, no one spotted you.'

'That was extraordinarily stupid!'

'I owed you. You killed their leader.' Freya never seemed to take offence. Everything in her eyes was either light or dark. To her, a Daughter of Time and Love, even the blackest of blacks should be offered a second chance.

That was when the war in Heaven was at its worst. Eventually the Queens had intervened. The official Wives of Time – Love, War, Wisdom, Night, Day, Chaos, Order, Belief – had taken their warring children in hand and drawn up treaties to guard the new borders. For a brief while there was peace in Heaven.

Peace which has been broken by the death of Freya. Only now did Sam feel the full impact of this. There would be feuds in Heaven, some of which would carry through to Earth, as these things always did. But what were the dangers these days, in this time of nuclear and bacterial warfare?

The more he thought, the more desperate he became to know what Freya had wanted to tell him.

It was late when Sam arrived in Holcombe. The village wore isolation like a protective cloak against a hostile world. The hedges in front of the whitewashed cottages were obsessively trimmed, and several homes had contrived to keep a thatched roof. On the one main street the few shops were in immaculate repair lest people gave up and went instead to Sainsbury's and Boots in the nearby market town. Holcombe was a pensioners' village – quaint, quiet and self-consciously remote. Every cottage had a name, and as the bus emptied outside the post office the driver wished at least half his passengers a goodnight, Mrs Walsham, goodbye Mrs Leigh. Sam felt that the village's politeness too was an act of defiance against the outside world.

By the time he'd reached Holcombe's only bed and breakfast, apologising for the lateness of the hour, his voice had already acquired the local accent. Asked who he was, he decided against both Sam and Luc, for fear that either would attract attention.

'Mr Simon Lewiser.'

He paid for the night in cash, and was shown up to a bedroom with a sloping ceiling and one small window. It looked out across a little playing field with a Scouts' hut at one end and, beyond, a landscape of hills and woods, lost in the darkness to all but his extraordinary eyes. No wonder Freya had loved this place. Even from a distance he could sense the pull of a Heaven Portal.

His room was the one you get in any bed and breakfast. A basin in the corner, a large bed neatly made with nylon sheets, woollen blankets and a heavy frilled bedspread. Flowery wallpaper, put up by people thinking not what they'd like, but what – improbably – others might prefer. A frayed carpet bore various stains, from coffee and tea to yellowed substances Sam didn't care to contemplate. On the door with its sturdy lock was a no-smoking reminder and a notice about what to do in the event of fire. Sam didn't bother with unpacking thoroughly, but dug around in his travel bag until he found a very small radio which he turned on at random. A concerned voice informed the world that more international forces were massing in central Asia and that the Israelis had again 'retaliated' against one of their numerous enemies.

To the sound of this stream of disaster, Sam padded round the room. At the door he pressed his hands on to the wood and stood motionless for five minutes, eyes closed. The same procedure was repeated with the window. Finally, turning to stand in the centre of the room for a few seconds, he raised his hands palm upwards.

If anyone had been there to see him ward the room, at each point they might have noticed a glow around his fingers, a silver tinge that faded almost as soon as it had sprung up.

As he went to sleep that night, he wondered what the police were making of his sudden absence. And who had sent the raven?

FIVE

Freya

The address he had was 9 Thomas Strepton Road. What Thomas Strepton had done to have a road named after him, Sam couldn't guess. Actually it was more a deep lane between mechanically cut hedges where the village gave out on to open country.

Freya's house looked just like he'd expected, even from the outside. It had a deep thatched roof, and a garden with nesting boxes and a birdbath. Ivy crawled up its reddish-coloured stone walls. Sam wasn't surprised to see all the windows open. Sometimes that helped to blow away memories as well as the dust. He was more surprised to see absolutely no evidence of police activity.

It was a long time before anyone answered the door. The girl who eventually opened it had Freya's same blonde hair and blue eyes. But she was unlike her, as Sam sensed, in possessing none of the power of a prime.

'Yes?' Her voice was subdued.

'My name's Luc Satise.' Trying to guess at her relationship to Freya, he added, 'Did your ... mother
mention me?'

'Grandmother,' she corrected. 'No, she didn't.'

'Ah.' A show of disappointment. 'Thank you anyway.
I'm really very sorry to hear of your loss, and if there's
anything I can do—'

'Unless,' she said, cutting him short, 'you're Luc
Satise, as in the same man who fought with Firedancers
in Paris.'

He smiled, recognising the test for what it was. 'Berlin,
not Paris.'

She stood aside. 'Come in.'

The inside of the house was also as Sam had imagined.
Polished wood, potted plants, light and space.
Comfortable, quaint, yet reminiscent of the halls of
Valhalla in the style in which everything was fashioned.
He was led into the kitchen, and gratefully accepted a
cup of tea.

Fran, as a second-generation child of Freya's, was
descended from a mortal grandfather of whom, she
claimed, Freya had been extremely fond. They'd had a
number of children, who'd scattered to the corners of the
world and would probably die long after Fran herself.
One of these, a son, had married another mortal, and
she'd been their only child. Both had died in a car accident, and Fran had been returned to her immortal
grandmother. It was then that Freya had begun to teach
her what little Fran now knew of magic, Heaven and
Hell.

She'd never seen another prime, she said, a first-
generation Child of Time, and as she watched Sam her
eyes were intense. Unlike her grandmother, she was

keeping a closed mind about him – and he knew it. He could see the suspicion in her face, and noted with annoyance that she was careful to keep at all times near an opened drawer full of knives.

She had no idea who'd killed Freya, she said, and didn't want to know. Hers was the attitude that, since there was war in Heaven, the best she could do was keep out of it. As a third, with mostly mortal blood, she would be an easy target – especially now she had no one to defend her. And as Sam heard those words he frowned, because there was a bitterness there that seemed to stem from more than just grief. *Grow up, Sam*, sighed a voice inside. *She hasn't had thousands of years on this planet to get used to the idea of death. She's emotional*.

It would have been somebody Freya was attached to, Sam pointed out. 'Did she mention anyone?'

'Everyone. Freya was attached to everyone,' she said, with bitterness again.

Sam couldn't help imagining what many might say about Fran. 'Little weasel. Spoilt when young, forced to grow up, became bitter in the process.' Sam himself took a more moderate view. It couldn't have been pleasant, ageing slower than all your friends but fast enough to look older than your own grandmother. Nor to know that the family she'd been born into was engaged in an intense war, but that if any of them tried to kill her, she'd be defenceless. It must be only a hop and a jump from this to wondering exactly *how* her parents had died – surely it would have taken more than a car wreck to kill her father. It would have required the sort of premeditated violence that destroyed Freya. Thoughts like these had put shadows under her eyes, made her twenty-something face look old, and frozen all smiles into an empty expression behind which constant calculations were running. *Of course you reason you're maybe next in line.*

In the clipped, shrill voice of nervousness, she was saying, 'Freya spoke well of you. She said you were the only prime who hadn't been twisted.'

'Twisted by what?'

'By power. The lure of Heaven and the promise of ruling it for ever.'

Sam said nothing. He knew what was being left unsaid. *One reason I'm not twisted is that I never had the chance to sell my soul. There's an irony. Of all people, I'm the one who hasn't sold my soul – and I'm supposed to be the principal dealer in that currency.*

'Do you know why she wanted to talk to me?'

'She told me she'd discovered something important, but that she also needed help. She said it concerned Earth, Hell and Heaven all at once, and for that reason you ought to be brought into it.' A shade of resentment seemed to pass over her face. 'She refused to tell me what it was, though.'

'Might anyone else know what this urgent discovery was?'

'Not that I can tell. She was hardly ever here.'

'This is going to sound terrible,' he ventured, 'but may I have a look through her things?'

Fran looked ready to say no, but thought better of it. 'She said I could trust you.' She gave a harsh laugh. '"Trust darkness incarnate, he's not such a bad sort."'

In Freya's bedroom her belongings had already been piled into cardboard boxes. Sam felt dismayed by the speed of it. There was still a stain on the carpet where she'd bled to death, though the family had been efficient at removing evidence where possible, as well as getting

rid of the police. The place had been dusted for finger-
prints and a forensic examination made, but Sam knew
they wouldn't find anything.

He sat down in the centre of the floor and began rum-
maging through the boxes, feeling more like a defiler
with each one. Books, clothes, tapes, a bit of stationery.
Nothing of course as unnecessary to Freya as make-up.
Old bundles of letters, already violated by the hands of
police investigators. Her diary.

This was full to only a few days before her death. He
flicked through it. Tenth of January and she had an
appointment with someone called Gail. The name
cropped up a lot, with the last encounter falling four days
before the diary so abruptly terminated. There were also
several meetings with someone described only as
'Historian'.

As Sam was turning to the end of the diary, a shower
of papers fell out. A card declaring that the services of
the local Indian restaurant would give her a taste of
heaven. Receipts for a thermal jumper and jacket, purchased late January. *What was she doing buying thermal gear
as winter drew to a close?* An invitation to a christening, now
never to be taken up. A postcard dated the fourteenth of
February, with a picture of a Buddhist temple nestling
amid high mountains. On the back someone had written
in Cantonese. Sam deciphered the message easily:
'Freya – having a wonderful time here, the food's excellent. Made an exciting discovery yesterday, wish you
were here.' It was unsigned. Turning over the card a few
more times, Sam checked the picture, then the mark on
the back. It was stamped from Tibet.

There were two conclusions to be drawn from this.
Firstly, the card was not just an idle missive from some

dear friend, but contained an important message. Secondly, Freya had been ready to respond to the 'wish you were here' part of the card by going out to Tibet at a moment's notice, hence her purchase of some pretty hard thermal gear.

Following fast came the realisation that, to discover what was so important, he'd have to go to Tibet – in good time, if he hoped to find whoever had sent the card. The afternoon would have to be spent in the local market town, buying appropriate gear for the mountain climate – and, as he went along, rehearsing phrases in every local dialect he could think of, to get back into practice.

'Who's Gail?' he asked, before leaving.

'I don't know. She never told me anything.' The girl spoke the words as though by rote.

'Or "Historian"?'

'Don't know.'

He had a feeling she was lying.

He felt Fran's gaze on his back as he crossed the threshold. For want of any better farewell he turned and said, 'Look after yourself.'

'Am I in danger?'

'Everyone is always in danger. If you're sensible, that danger is less.'

Her eyes were steady and her voice calm as she answered him. 'I'm just a third-generation Daughter of Time,' she said simply. 'Trapped between worlds. Even if I got hit by a truck I'd survive, so there's no need to be sensible in that respect, is there?'

Sam said nothing.

'On the other hand,' she continued, still holding him in her gaze, 'if I do step to one side and forget how little on this planet there is that can harm me, and turn towards the world from where the rest of my blood stems, then what? I find I'm a weakling, a pathetic half-breed. The butt of bad jokes and an object of scorn. If there's danger from this other world, I'm powerless against any of it.' She smiled faintly.

'That's why there's no point in being sensible. Nothing here can harm me, and if harm comes from there, nothing I do can prevent it. It's the blood, isn't it? The blood *she* gave me . . . So goodbye, then.' She closed the door in his face, leaving him alone on the doorstep.

The nearby town was everything Holcombe had striven not to be. Chain stores dominated the main streets, and huge swathes of land were given over to car parks. Sam bought a guide covering the area of Tibet he needed to visit, and even found a picture of the Buddhist temple from the postcard. He also changed some currency – though not much, because, if he remembered, in Tibet no kind of money counted for much.

He wasn't sure what he was going to do when he got there, but he was determined to try something. Anything.

Unfortunately, Tibet meant travelling by Portal. Leaning against the weight from his bag full of newly purchased clothes, Sam tried not to think what difficulties that would involve.

And now it was late afternoon, and he was marching down the road out of Holcombe with the bag and a slim package slung over his back and a thickly lined box attached to his belt.

Sam was following his instincts. Sure enough a convoy

of black cars soon overtook him. After five minutes he caught up with them again, parked in a lay-by. A path led away from the road into woods. It was cold and wet, typical West Country in February. Sam shivered, drew his coat more tightly around him, and began to trudge down the narrow track. His feet squelched in other, deeper footprints. Not a creature stirred.

A mist had come down, as if in respect for the sombre secrecy of Freya's departure from this world. Soon it was so thick that Sam could hardly see his hands in front of his face. He could sense the magic in it. The family had brought down this mist, so that they might not be observed.

As he walked, Sam extended his senses, to touch the minds of the woodland animals. As always the owls and the badgers were first to respond. Through their knowledge and senses he was guided without mishap towards the clearing where a dozen silent figures stood bearing torches.

From just outside, hidden in dimness beneath the trees, Sam watched through the mist that was being burnt away by the twelve torches. Four dark figures lowered a coffin to the ground and stood back. One of the torchbearers stepped to its head. He had one eye and a face worn with scars. Odin himself. When he spoke, it was in an ancient language that even Sam struggled to translate fast enough.

'She was the fairest child of us all,' he was saying. 'Daughter of Love and Time, Princess of Valhalla. Lady of Nature and Life.' There was no emotion in his voice – it was a flat statement. She was the lady of Nature and Life. Statement. She was the Daughter of Love and Time. Statement.

As he stood back, the torchbearers drew their weapons. Some were swords, some axes, singled-handed or double. Cold moisture glistened off the blades, all faces were stony. Sam recognised Thor, the old hammer, caught a glimpse of blind Hector, of Signi and all the rest, faces from his past, memories returning in a rush.

All were crowned or helmeted. Thor had a headpiece that covered most of his face, creating the appearance of an armoured executioner. Hector wore a dark crown with black, withered leaves carved on it. Odin, head of Valhalla, with his one eye, was crowned with spiky iron. A man tormented, if Sam ever saw one. It was Odin's responsibility to uphold the glory of his house, a duty in which he was failing wretchedly. He'd tried almost everything to restore its greatness: diplomacy, war, bribery – even, so rumour said, the odd murder attempt – yet increasingly Valhalla was giving place to the other houses of Heaven. The chance of a Valhallan ascending to the throne of Heaven was now one in a huge number.

The Children of Valhalla began to sing, very softly. A mourning song for the dead. Sam too mouthed the words, knowing every one from some part of his past that he'd long ago forgotten but which now rose in him and filled the world with shadows of things that had been. As he sang he took from the box the slim silver band that marked him too as a Prince of Heaven, one among these. Moisture clung to it, just as it gleamed on his face and hair. He put it on out of respect for the dead, as he joined his mourning with that of Odin, Thor, Hector, Fricka and the rest. Old school. Weak school. But, because of war in Heaven, the kind of people who at a word might kill Sam for the simple act of being who he was.

When the song ended, each in turn went up to Freya's coffin and placed in it some gift, be it spell or treasured belonging. That done, four of them raised up the coffin and turned to face north. Odin and Thor, standing either side of nothing, together raised their hands and drew them apart. Where their hands trailed through the air, white fire followed, writhed like a snake in its captor's grasp, and traced the outline of a doorway filled with thick, white mist. Through this the coffin went with its silent bearers. Then the rest of them followed, pairing one to the other to march in silence through the Portal. Only Odin and Thor remained as the Portal snapped shut.

Thor spoke first. 'Who did this? Why? I don't understand!'

'You will soon, I promise,' said Odin quietly.

'There was no need for her death!'

'But you know *who* made it happen, and why. And it's you who must be our means of revenge.'

Thor hung his head, still radiating anger. 'For centuries I've served you, like all of Valhalla. Other deaths . . . in the end I've always understood why. But *her* . . . my Freya . . .'

Odin squeezed his shoulder in what was meant to be a fatherly way. 'There is proof, of that I can assure you. The correspondence, the company she kept . . . And since you know as well as I who did this, we must strike while we can. *You* must strike.'

'Where is he? Where can we give him the fate he deserves?'

Odin spoke softly, almost kindly. 'We don't know. He's clever. He's running. There are places, though, where he can be found. Gehenna. Pandemonium. London. Paris.

And sooner or later, if we don't find him, he'll come to us. He won't be able to help himself – to stay away from those nearest to her. He loved her too, you know.'

'Everyone loved Freya. *My* Freya.'

'Yes, well, apparently not everyone. And you deceive yourself if you think she was yours. She belonged to no one but herself; that, so it seems, was how she sealed her own fate . . . But you know what to do. Find *him*.'

In farewell, Odin gave Thor a reassuring clap on the shoulder, before turning to march through the Portal. Slouching, Thor watched him go; then he looked around and surveyed the clearing, as if he'd only just noticed its existence.

His eyes narrowed. 'Who's there? Show yourself!'

Sam was careful not to move. He said nothing, his breathing terribly loud. *You couldn't find a rhino, you clod, let alone me.*

'By all that's honourable, show yourself!'

Honour, Thor? You're not bright enough to know what that means. Now, courage – that's a virtue I can bear to acknowledge as yours. Unfortunately, you also have a tendency to overdo it, at a major cost to your brain.

Thwarted, Thor gave a grunt of anger and, in his turn, strode away through the Portal.

Sam watched him go.

Around the Hell Portal there was no mist, natural or otherwise. It was situated a short bus ride from Holcombe, in a hilly expanse of hedged pastures where sheep munched on soaking grass and their wool dragged under the weight of rainwater. Sam, zipped up against the drizzle and shouldering a bulging bag, was already wearing his thermal gear as he trudged across the fields, growing uncomfortably hot. England was rarely as cold as he was dressed for.

'Mud, mud, *муд*,' he sang half-heartedly as he stamped along. Grass was all that grew up here, and for miles around there was no sign of human life. His feet squelched.

Abruptly the land descended into a little dip where in prehistoric times a river had carved its passage to the sea. At its base was a dry watercourse a few feet wide. Sam descended to the riverbed, then began to climb, following it to where the source would have been.

After about ten minutes, with the sky darkening and the wind growing colder, he reached a copse of oak and hawthorn trees. He forced his way in, clambering through a tight growth of branches that would have kept out all but the most intrepid. Inside the copse it was even darker, but gave shelter from the rain. Sam probed for, and quickly felt, the Portal, a shadow gateway standing in mid-air a few feet in front of him. Carefully he turned his mind on to the Portal, by willpower alone forcing it to open for him.

Only the Sons of Time could Waywalk, so he'd been taught. Everyone else lost their way.

He wondered which Portal he should try to open at the other end of his journey. Each Portal led to another, but such was the flexibility of the Ways that you could decide in advance which one. It was an inaccurate method of travel; you'd often arrive miles from where you wanted to be and with no means of reaching your destination anyway. The benefit was that if you took a Portal to Hell, you had immediate access to a Portal leading anywhere on Earth. Nevertheless he disliked Waywalking.

As white fire defined the misty Portal, Sam reached a conclusion. Yes. He'd go to Gehenna, drop off a few things.

He pressed his way into the Portal. Immediately he was surrounded by a pale mist and felt the sudden cold. Shadows stirred and leered around him. He gritted his teeth and began to walk, forcing each foot in front of the other with agonising slowness. It was hard to breathe; he had to take only shallow gasps of air, and each one left him racked with weakness. There was only as much air in the Ways as you brought with you through the open Portal. Stay in the Way for too long, and you would suffocate.

Sam forced himself to keep moving, forced the image of Gehenna to stay fixed in the front of his mind. To lose the image was to lose your way. To lose your way was to die. He stubbornly ignored the leering shadows ahead, but knew he had to keep his eyes open to spot the doorway. Ghostly fingers tore at his face, his hair. Half-perceived voices whispered, pleaded with him for attention, begged him to stop and help them. These were the shadows of people who'd got lost in the Way. Those mortals who hadn't had Time's blood and resilience, who'd wandered into a Portal by accident. Those Children of Time who'd lost their way.

There was a light, burning through the mist. Grateful, seeing his journey's end at hand, he staggered towards it, nearly tripping over his own feet in haste. The white light grew more defined, formed a doorway, a distinct shape. He fell through it, gasping for precious air and feeling dull aches rise in his legs from the strain of the Waywalk.

He had come out in, for want of another word, a dungeon. Gehenna had been constructed around a

Portal, and the demon architects had reasoned, under-
standably enough, that if anyone tried to come through a
Portal they'd better arrive where they could do no harm.

So the room Sam emerged into was chilly, dark,
slightly damp, with plain stone walls and a heavy
wooden door. He considered hammering on the door, but
decided there was no point. After all, he wasn't staying.
Instead he unslung his bag of extra clothes, pulled on a
woollen hat, wound his scarf across his nose and mouth
and took in several deep hauls of breath. Even well prepared as he was for the Tibetan mountains, he stood
facing the shadow with trepidation where the Portal
waited. Practicality dictated that he got his breath back
before attempting the return walk; fear also demanded
that he first consider the pros and cons of his actions.

Which was why for a long time he just stood there,
contemplative, mustering the nerve to face those
shadows once more. Then briefly his courage soared,
and he rushed forward, knowing that if he didn't start on
that swelling of bravery he'd never move at all.

Mist. Shadows. Pressure. Not enough air, burning
lungs, begging, leering shadows. Asking for release,
seeking to lure him off the set path. A reluctance now in
the Way to respond. The image he'd given it wasn't near
a Portal, and the Way was casting around for the nearest
access points. This made the process even harder. He
was covered with cold sweat, his hands shaking as air
became yet more sparse. A light ahead, but oh, how hard
it was to breathe, how easy it would be to let go of the
image, let his eyes drift shut . . .

The realisation that he was losing the battle between
Waywalking and survival started him to new efforts and
he moved on faster, eyes fixed on the light, almost

reaching out to hold it as he tore through the shadows, mindless of the burning in his lungs and the whisperings all around.

He exploded from the Portal, to be smacked into by a sharp wind that screamed around the mountains. Sam could hardly see for the intensity of the snowstorm. He'd fallen into a snowdrift, and lay there for almost twenty seconds getting his breath back, in which time a small bank of snow was already building up around him.

He'd largely forgotten how it was among the mountains in winter – how bitterly cold and dangerous, how thin the air.

Now, chiding himself for lack of foresight, he could barely call on what memory he had for survival, and recall that his destination was nearby. All he had to do was find it. *Don't stop moving. Do that and you'll freeze over. You stop moving and you'll realise just how stupid this whole idea is*.

How he wished he could have prepared in advance, and taken the plane.

The Tibetans know about hardship, and have known for all of their history. Sam, curious to explore Earth in his younger days, had learned Tibetan. He'd set aside a hundred years for mastering every Earthly language he could, but each time he'd been to Tibet he'd taken one look at the weather, the mountains, and the food or absence thereof, and decided to leave as soon as possible. The land itself seemed set on annihilation, being semi-arid in the north and, in the south, part of the huge Himalayas. First came the Mongols, then the Chinese, then once more the Chinese, then the Chinese again, with the Indians crouching on the southern borders and watching to see what happened while testing the odd nuclear bomb, just to make sure it had been properly oiled. At one time under Chinese rule, a sixth of Tibet's population died; the communist regime was ruthless in suppressing support for the Dalai Lama and all his anti-Chinese works. That had really pissed off some of Sam's family, but even they weren't going to take on a sixth of the world's population. The majority of people in Tibet were nomadic, and what few monasteries had survived the attacks of the Red Army were deep in the mountains, where resistance still whispered its message of anti-communism. To little effect.

But the monastery where Sam was headed was not only remote but had long been regarded as an international treasure, accessible at least to his pocket guidebook and the makers of postcards. Even the attentive Red Guard hadn't touched it. Without wanting, for the time, to find proof, Sam suspected that here one of his family *had* intervened.

But to arrive up there in winter, coming out of nowhere . . .

What will they think? Sam pondered as he staggered through the snow, sensing rather than seeing his path ahead. *A European who speaks fluent Tibetan, Cantonese, Mandarin, appearing out of a snowstorm* . . . He already had his excuses prepared. *Please sir, I'm a climber, the storm took me by surprise, please sir* . . .

A shape loomed in the snow, picked out in black and white. Sam saw a colossal wall left over from ancient times when rockets and gunpowder were just for fireworks. The gates were, not surprisingly, closed. The whole city, without electricity or a proper water supply, was little more than half a mile across with, raised up at its heart, the monastery on the card sent to Freya.

Sorted in this city, the card would have been carried down the mountain by donkey pack, transferred to a clunky old van in the lowlands, and no doubt read over by at least five airport officials before being loaded on to a plane, to arrive just before Freya died.

Seeing no other way to gain admittance, Sam hammered on the gate. A hatch slid back and a pair of suspicious eyes took in this stranger wearing none-too-substantial thermal gear bought in Devon. Sam didn't know whether the gatekeeper noticed his pale skin beneath the scarf, but he heard a snatch of questioning in Tibetan shouted against the storm. He yelled back, 'Please! Let me in!'

The hatch slid shut. *They're not going to. Strangers aren't welcome here.* He immediately chided himself for the thought. *They're good people. They'll let me in.*

A small gate opened, and gratefully he staggered into the relative shelter of a porch. Two men in thick furs and skins began questioning him, even as they took him inside, into the warmth. Where had he come from? What did he want here?

'I'm looking for someone. It's very important.'

In the gatehouse were more dark-skinned guards, who looked up in surprise. As Sam unwrapped his scarf and semi-collapsed by a flickering fire, the light of the flame revealed his distinctly European features. Immediately the questioning became more aggressive. With a lot of neglect to its history, Europe was not held in the highest esteem by Tibetans.

'How did you get here? What do you want?'

'I'm looking for someone,' he repeated. He directed the full force of his gaze on the nearest guard, who flinched. Yes, now that his face was illuminated, there was little doubt. In the firelight his eyes, which people readily saw as dark, dark brown, were nearly pitch black. *Or possibly it was the flame*, thought the man. *Yes, a trick of the light*. Everyone thought that.

'Someone who's been in contact with another European, probably travelling by the name of Freya Oldstock. Blonde hair, blue eyes. Tall. Very pretty. Came out of nowhere, I expect, like me.'

They looked uneasy. 'What's your business with the other European, if she has been here?' asked one.

'Has she been here?'

'She has.'

'Who did she see?'

'What do you want?'

'I'm her friend. She's dead.'

There was a shocked silence. 'Dead?' asked one. 'The lady's dead?' They, like everyone who'd met Freya, had been won over.

'I need to meet whoever it was she saw.'

'We don't know who. She always went to the monastery.'

'Then that is where I need to go.'

They were defensive again. 'Have you got your papers? Who are you?'

At this Sam seemed to lose his temper, rising and stretching up to his full height. *His eyes seem to burn into you, as if reading your mind*, thought the captain of the gate. *The lady had had eyes like those, but hers had been blue – and softer, kinder*.

'I am Luc Satise, I am Sam Linnfer. I am Sebastian Teufel. Now you tell the people at the monastery that I'm coming under one or all of those names, I don't mind which. Tell them that whoever of *my* family murdered

Freya may be after them too. Tell them that she was killed with a dragon-bone knife, which can destroy even an immortal. Tell them all that, and show me to the monastery!'

Something about Sam didn't allow for arguing. A boy ran ahead, while the captain trucked up with Sam in a rackety jeep that took five goes to start moving, and stalled on every street corner. The guards seemed very proud of it.

All the way the captain went on talking nervously in Tibetan. He had known Freya. 'She came out of the snow one day. Said she had to visit the monastery. She was kind, very kind indeed.'

'How often did she come?'

'Recently? Once a month, maybe twice. We never saw how she arrived, nor how she left. All she'd say was that she was trying to track down a long-lost cousin.' He laughed. 'That's like telling a child to keep his nose out of things he can't understand.

'Her visits started about six months ago. She already knew someone at the monastery.'

We always do. If you know where or how to look there's someone we know in every street of every village of every country.

The captain added, 'How do you know her?'

'I'm a long-lost relative too,' Sam replied mildly. 'Well, half-brother. Same father, different mothers.'

The streets were narrow and bumpy, not designed even for the rough tracks of the jeep. As they went people turned to stare, huddling in doorways from the snow but nonetheless following with wary eyes.

'Forgive them,' the captain said, as though embarrassed by his people's lack of European manners. 'Apart from the lady they have never seen another of your kind.'

Our kind? I suppose we are another species. 'Was she alone?'

'There was a man with her the first time. She left him at the monastery. As far as I know he's never left.'

Sam was bursting with questions, but the captain was there first. 'May I ask – where did you learn Tibetan?'

'I've spent time in a lot of places.'

'Forgive me,' the captain said again – apparently he felt obliged to apologise for everything – 'but how many languages do you speak?'

'Lots, many of them defunct.' It was the only answer Sam would give.

The monastery appeared out of the snow. At the gates a couple of monks, in orange robes, were ready to usher him inside. Hastened down freezing candlelit corridors, he glimpsed tapestries and golden Buddhas and heard the distant low chanting and rumbling horns of other monks at prayer. Without a word from his escorts he was barrelled into a small stone room in which a fire glowed. A man, in a robe dashed with the streak of red that marked him as abbot, turned, bowed slightly and said, 'You came.'

'Were you expecting me?' Sam asked, taking the seat offered him. It was the only one in the room, and it embarrassed him that the abbot had to stand. But the abbot insisted, and it was near the warmth of the fire.

'Before I tell you more, I require proof that you are Sebastian Teufel.'

'Ah.' Sam stood up, took off his outer clothing and unslung the package on his back. He drew out the long silver sword.

With a sigh of satisfaction and a dip of his head as though in the presence of a holy object, the abbot lowered his hand over the blade and let his eyes drift shut. 'Yes,' he whispered. 'I hear it. She said I would. I do not know much of your world, and believe less of what I hear, but it was the same with her. I could hear it around her belongings too; everything she touched seemed to hum.' He looked up sharply. 'You have more?'

Sam also produced the dagger and the circlet. This he held before him by the tips of his fingers as if his touch might profane it, even though it was his own.

It was on this that the abbot focused most of his attention. 'So. You were crowned too. As well as your brothers. Tell me, is it true that if anyone other than its real owner wears this, he will go mad?'

'I believe it is the case. Do you?'

The abbot smiled thinly. 'I believe that superstition has a lot of power, whether its claims are true or not. And I also believe that, somewhere, every myth is grounded in reality. If the lady was so afraid of wearing it, then it seems likely that her brother would be afraid too. Either you have no fear, or it is a lie that the crown is your own. I do not believe it to be a lie, though I am not sure whether I believe it to be entirely true. So you will not mind proving that it is truly yours?'

Sam hesitated. This caused the abbot to frown. 'Why so reluctant? It is a fair test, the one she told me to use. Make him wear his crown, she said. No other man dares.'

'I don't blame them,' murmured Sam, almost inaudibly. Carefully he placed the crown on his head and looked at the abbot. 'I am not mad,' he said. 'I am who I claim to be.'

Still the abbot wasn't satisfied. Leaning forward, inches from Sam's nose, he peered into his eyes.

Finally he said, 'Yes. It isn't just a trick of the light. You came, *you* came.'

Sam retrieved his dagger and put away the sword, ignoring the disbelief that lingered in the other's voice. 'You said you were expecting me.'

'Yes. There was a backup system.'

'Tell me. I mean, everything.'

'Now that is a lot to tell. And I fear I only know parts of it.'

Sam sat down again. 'Then tell me what you do know. That, for you at least, will be everything.'

'Ah.' The abbot smiled. 'You even speak like she said you would. I imagined your voice – it came very close.' Wrapping his robes around him and acquiring a serious tone, he assumed the storyteller's pose. The abbot, Sam decided, was one of those rare beings: a man who reported everything as received by his eyes and ears, not as his mind had interpreted it.

'Six months ago,' he began, 'your friend and her companion arrived at my monastery. He was younger, and where she was quiet he was loud, and where she was serene he was always on edge, striving to do something else. So when she requested that I take him into my order for a while, I was doubtful. But my librarian, whom she knew, spoke well of them. In the end I did not regret my decision to take her companion . . . Andrew' – he pronounced the word with difficulty – 'into my order. He was a meticulous worker, and when he wasn't with the librarian his time was spent helping my monks with their work. He often visited the sick and went with the monks into the lowlands to pick up supplies. He stayed here . . . oh, for two out of every four weeks, unless the weather prevented him from travelling. We just called him Andrew. He never gave any other name.'

An immediate clue, thought Sam. *Weather wouldn't have stopped one of us. We would have used the Portal.*

'He was always sending postcards – in Cantonese – to England, to France, but mostly to America. He seemed to be looking for something. Each time he returned from the lowlands he'd be carrying more books. Our library nearly doubled. One day I asked him, "Since you have to go down the mountain to buy all these books, why bother to come back up?" He only laughed. "Because up here I am safe. Down there other eyes are watching." And he was particular about security. No one outside the monastery was to see his face. In the city he would always go through at least four dealers to get one book that he could have got by direct means for half the price. He gave the impression of a man on the run. Except when here, working all hours with my librarian.'

'What changed?'

The abbot made a judicious noise. 'First, let me tell you of the backup to this security. He explained it fully to me, you see. "If I'm ever caught out at my own game, there's someone else. I am, after all, only mortal. Accidents do happen. But he – he will see this thing to its conclusion." He didn't have to do anything, he said, because you'd find your way here of your own accord. If something happened to him, Freya would contact you. If something happened to Freya, he was certain you would try to find out what. And once you got on to a scent, he said, you didn't stop hunting for anything. He seemed very confident that you'd come. I was to give you full cooperation, but to be utterly certain it was you.

He described you, your eyes, your crown, your weapons.'

'He seemed very trusting,' Sam murmured.

'He was playing a big game. That much I could tell.'

'What changed? What went wrong with security?'

'He made a discovery. I don't know what it was, but he seemed overjoyed. "I've found it," he said. "I've found out what the whole game is." A few weeks later and he announced that he was leaving. He was very scared. So was my librarian, for that matter. Both seemed terrified. "Tell the one who will come that it's worse than we thought. Tell him that at least one of the keys has already been found, and they are foolish enough to be going for the fourth."'

Sam said nothing. He'd acquired a stony expression and was sitting with his chin in his hands. His eyes were fixed on the flames as though he wasn't even listening. In fact Sam was a good listener; the best.

'They were to leave the same day. Andrew headed directly into the lowlands, and my librarian planned to follow a few hours later by a different route. I could not convince them to stay. Before my librarian could leave, a snowstorm began. It was so sudden I almost couldn't believe it – there was no reason why it should have started. At this my librarian became even more fearful. "They're coming," he said. "They know I'm still here." The next morning he was missing, and hasn't been found since. No caravans left in the night. No furs were taken, nor any animals.'

'Dead?'

'No one could survive without either,' he said calmly. 'Unless they were a brother to Freya, that is. Yet now you tell me she is dead?'

'Yes.'

'I am very sorry. Freya was special.'

There was a long silence. Sam seemed frozen to the chair, staring into the fire. The crown still rested on his head, lop-sidedly, as though he'd forgotten about it. Finally the abbot spoke again. 'What was Andrew looking for, that has already cost lives?'

'I don't know. I suspect, but I don't know.'

'The keys?'

'Yes. The Pandora keys.'

'Will you tell me about them?'

Sighing, Sam sat back. 'A legend, little more. Four keys to unlock four forbidden doors behind which are imprisoned four spirits or people. Hate, Suspicion, Greed are the spirits. Forbidden from Heaven and locked away for all time from that world at least, though their siblings thrive in Earth and Hell.'

'And the fourth door?'

'The big granddaddy of them all. Cronus.' Sam's eyes became slightly misty as he murmured, 'In the beginning was Cronus, and nothing changed. In the beginning was Cronus, and Cronus was the emptiness of life without death and time without seconds. Then came Time, who with his children imprisoned Cronus in a place of nothing for himself. But Cronus is hungry, and wants to add to his nothing the whole universe.'

Sam seemed to shudder, as though snapping out of a trance. 'The truth is, Cronus is a vastly powerful entity who no one really believes in, who's sworn to destroy Heaven, Hell, Earth and, most importantly of all, Time.' He gave a discomforted smile.

'It's like the big bang theory, but in reverse. The universe began when Time took over. You get your explosion, after which the universe will continue to move for ever because Time is giving it that nudge it needs, in the form of seconds, minutes, hours etc. But *before* the big bang, when everything was compressed down at a single point with no change, no movement, no *life* but still *existing* – that was Cronus. You have to be careful about defining him. He exists, sure. But I don't think you can say Cronus lives.'

'Locked away.'

'Yes.'

'How fortunate,' murmured the abbot. 'And what would happen if these spirits were freed?'

Sam smiled faintly. 'Oh, I'd guess we're talking minor apocalypse, fall of kings, death of princes. Whoever controlled the Pandora spirits, you see, would literally be able to destroy his or her enemies at a word.

'So, say I had Hate under my control. I could enter Heaven, march up to . . . oh, Nirvana, and say, "Hi pals, surrender or you die." And the guys in Nirvana would naturally answer, "Die, die, evil scum, die." At which point I would release Hate on to them. Brother would hate brother, sister would hate sister. A soldier preparing to charge my army would suddenly loathe the man standing next to him, and attack his own comrade. The commander would despise his generals and order their deaths, the generals would despise their commander and try to decapitate him. It would be a bloodbath – while I just sat watching with a smug grin.'

'A fate worth avoiding, then,' said the abbot. 'But why do you think Freya and Andrew were looking for the keys?'

Sam thought for a long time. 'I don't know. Freya would never use the Pandora spirits, of that I'm sure.

She was a Daughter of Love, so employing Hate would be against her nature, against her *blood*. Perhaps the keys are in danger from elsewhere – from somebody against whom she was trying to protect them, by finding them herself. And perhaps that someone got to her first.

'In which case Andrew is now very important. Not only might he know where the keys are, but it's fair to assume that if he's caught his captors will use his knowledge to their own advantage. Which wouldn't be at all nice.'

The abbot sighed, and folded his arms across his chest, the first sign of feeling the cold he'd shown. 'I do not understand the movements of your kind. I have read in books that you wander the Earth, and every legend at some point is grounded in fact. I have seen people emerge untouched out of a snowstorm with nothing on their backs and then disappear again without a word. I have seen Freya, Andrew and my librarian turn pale at the mention of keys and spirits. I have seen a man with black eyes who wears a silver crown and stares at the fire without moving, no matter what he hears. All this I can attest to. Believe it I do not.'

Sam smiled, the half smile of one who knows more than he'll say, and has seen sights no man will ever see again and who still doesn't think much of them. He turned towards the fire. 'Where did Andrew go?'

'I don't know.'

'How can I find him, then?'

'Freya knew where he would go. They had it all worked out. But . . .'

But Freya's dead.

'Have you got a picture, a description, even?'

The abbot fumbled in a desk and produced a small photo. It showed a freckled young man standing in front of the Kremlin and grinning at whoever had taken the picture. Sam pocketed the photo without a word, all his thoughts kept to himself. He asked, 'Who was the Historian?'

'Historian?'

'There was a message in Freya's diary – meeting with the Historian.'

'I heard of no Historian – though Andrew himself was very knowledgeable in that sense.'

'Or someone called Gail?'

'Andrew did mention Gail. He said Gail was the inside source, the one who gave him early warnings or vital little clues. But that was all he did say.'

'Have you any idea where Andrew might have gone?' Sam urged again. 'Anything? What languages did he speak, for instance?'

'He spoke a little French. Also he was fluent in Russian.'

That wouldn't help, in a country the size of Russia.

'What have you done with the books they were reading?'

'Locked them away. Very deep.'

'If someone comes, asking to see them . . .' Sam hesitated, then dug around in a pocket until he came upon his travel guide and a very old biro that worked after you licked the end. He ripped the back page off the guide and wrote on it a name and address: Adam Hartland, 12 Britannia Drive, London, E8. A house whose owners were fictitious, but whose mail never went ignored: Adam was a regular checker. 'Hartland' meant it was for or from Sam.

'Please, write to this address. Say nothing exact, and sign yourself only as the abbot.'

'How dangerous, exactly, was this game Andrew and Freya were playing?' asked the abbot.

'Everything with my family is dangerous,' Sam replied, rising to his feet. 'I pity you mortals who get caught up in it.' He slung his sword over his back, put on his thermal gear and turned to go.

Behind him the abbot called out, 'Why were you given a crown, being a bastard son?' His harsh words cut through the quiet of that place.

Sam Linnfer, alias Lucifer, alias the Bearer of Light – the terrible weapon that some said would destroy its very user – froze as though the question were a knife in his back. Without turning he replied in emotionless tones, 'I don't know. They say, because Time declared I was his necessary child.'

And left the room.

SIX

Bubble

Staggering once more through the Portal into the little dungeon, it was clear to Sam that someone had been there and recognised his bag, for the door was open and a fire burned on the floor in the centre of the cell, which was otherwise bitterly cold. Two heads stuck round the door at Sam's arrival. Each wore a tight-fitting iron helmet, possessed frost-silver eyes and had patches of blue scale across their pale skin. Thick white hair grew from the base of their necks, and coiled down their backs. They wore light chain mail beneath white furs and carried iron-tipped spears.

'Corenial, Setrezen,' said Sam politely.

'The Prince is expecting you, sir,' growled one. 'Your normal room has been prepared.'

'Thank you.' He had taken off his crown, and it now bumped around inside the box at his hip. The demons' eyes watched it every step of his way down the corridor. They hungered to wear it, he knew, but didn't dare.

It wasn't necessary to take off the thermal gear. Tibet and the part of Hell where Sam had arrived were one and the same when it came to winter temperatures. The only difference was that in Gehenna, at least, it was always winter. Seven eighths of Hell burned for sixteen months a year, and he, Time help him, had chosen to come to the one eighth that didn't.

Gehenna was a city with a lot of history. He knew that, because he was an integral part of that history. He'd built most of the place, after all. It rested in the far north of the planet, and for eleven months a year it saw sunlight for a maximum of five hours. The rest of the world, save for another small patch of ice on the southern pole, could claim the opposite. It hardly ever saw night.

In Sam's lifetime Gehenna had been a village, then a town, then a city with a castle, then a pile of rubble, then rebuilt, then once more reduced, then rebuilt with city walls and a standing army, and never defeated again, although people tried.

Oh, how they tried.

But he'd been careful. Not only did he now have a resident Prince and council, but a network of spies and messengers. He could hear of an attack months beforehand, and travel Earth until the day it was due, to return to Gehenna in time to lay waste the approaching army with all the fiery tricks of his specialised trade.

Once, he'd ruled full time as king. But in recent centuries he'd become less an administrator and more a part-time emergency worker, as Gehenna, after years of nurturing, had come to do without him except in times of great crisis. He trusted the Prince and the council to manage their own affairs, and reasoned that after thousands of years of Hellish cuisine, and washing in water with bits of ice in it, he'd earned the right to Earth, caviar and central heating. Not being needed any more made him very grateful.

In the cold corridor, more demons nodded at him as he passed, a mark of respect and little more. They were the perfect winter warriors, he reflected as he acknowledged them. Their hides were thick, their white hair and blue scale were good camouflage, and they could fight for hours, assuming they'd had a big meal beforehand. They excelled in the snow, their summer cousins thrived in the burning desert. With such an obvious line drawn by evolution, Sam couldn't understand why the demons were constantly warring. If frost demon couldn't live comfortably in sand demon's territory and vice versa, why so much war?

Because they are demons, he thought with disgust. *And, for all that I've done, they're still warring primitives who understand nothing outside their own armoury and ambitions. And Time help me, I gave them half the weapons they call their own. I taught them about walls and sieges and craft and cunning, thinking they wouldn't war any more. And look what happened. For all my services, I bet half of them would still be willing to stick a knife in my back.*

Climbing a flight of stairs he marched past stony walls hung with tapestries to keep the heat in, towards a wing of the huge Gehenna fortress where the fires always burnt. The tapestries depicted frost demons doing various things to their enemies that Sam didn't want to look at. He was familiar with them, and they still sickened him.

He came to a large wooden door guarded by two demons, strode up to it and hammered loudly. It opened immediately.

Of the two people in the room, one was very old, one quite young. The elder lounged in a padded chair by a fire, wearing a mild smile that never waned. He'd been playing cat's cradle, relentlessly patient, moving in and out of shapes with the concentration of a master crafts-man. His long blue robe was frayed around the hem, and he wore fluffy slippers over a pair of outrageously coloured socks.

Sam, as he entered, was fixed with old demon's unchanging smile, and the same ancient eyes that never showed emotion. This demon's voice never rose in anger. This demon had never desired the bloodlust of slaughter or killed his own wife for disobedience. This was the nec-essary demon, who filled the unsung post that the silent thinkers of the world – the children who never wanted to play the violent games in the playground or who invari-ably handed in their homework on time – always fill: civil servant. Court Vizier. Old Beelzebub. The power behind the throne.

No one knew he embodied such a power, but Sam knew. And Beelzebub knew. They could read the knowl-edge in each other, through each measured nod, and in each level word that revealed nothing save what it left unsaid.

The younger demon was in every way Beelzebub's opposite. He didn't even look up as Sam entered, but continued pacing round a map laid out on a table. Sam saw little wooden blocks with flags in them, and sighed inwardly. A child was playing with his toys again.

This younger demon wore long blue and white robes with trailing sleeves and lavish embroidery that, for all that they made him look regal, also gave the impression of a boy playing with his mother's wardrobe. Nevertheless, this was the same Prince who had intimidated many a baron into submission and had won his crown by slaying his brothers in duel after duel. He radiated energy as always, brow crinkled in a frown and fingers drumming up and down his sword.

And yes, he was a good Prince, thought Sam. The kind of Prince who knew when to bribe, or when to call in the services of his all-too-eager soldiers to drag a confession screaming out of some innocent's lips, which he could wield against a guilty man who'd become too big for his boots. A ruthless Prince. Therefore a good one, for all he wasn't a good man. The distinction had to be drawn somewhere between the two, and Sam had drawn it long ago. He admired the Prince. He disliked the man. He suspected that the feeling was mutual. *One day*, he thought sourly, *you're going to decide that I'm not necessary. And you're going to be so high on your own glory that you think you can succeed where countless others have failed. Poison me in the night, send assassins. Maybe even challenge me to a duel. But you don't know how to kill me. You don't even know there's any special way I must be put to rest. You think mere iron will do the job.*

'Ah,' said Prince Asmodeus. 'You're back. Had a nice time on Earth?'

'Mildly interesting.'

Beelzebub was watching, silent as always. 'Tell me,' demanded Asmodeus, 'do you think I ought to send a demand to Belial, ordering him to withdraw his forces from the Clawed Pass, or should I go for a surprise attack?'

Sam wandered to the table and looked down at the map. 'If you send a demand to Belial,' he replied evenly, 'he'll refuse it as an act of stubbornness.'

'A surprise attack, then?'

'I doubt if it'll be a surprise. Belial has been looking for the right opportunity to invade for years. I don't advise giving it to him.'

'Hum.' Asmodeus strode round to the other side of the map. 'The Clawed Pass protects one of the best slave routes. The desert beyond is relatively undefended after his damned fort – the slave raiders would have a wonderful time if they can only get there.'

'I won't help you take slaves.'

'No, you probably won't,' he said sourly. 'You don't seem to do anything, do you? You're never here.'

That's because I've given up on you, my boy. 'Would you rather I was here? Ruling as once I ruled? Wearing another crown?'

Asmodeus glanced to Beelzebub for help against this attack on his status. But the old demon had frozen over even more than usual and was staring into the flames. Though the Prince struggled to find a suitable answer, none came. Angry, with embarrassment making him more so, he strode towards the door, mumbling something about 'state business' as he went. As childish a tantrum as Sam had ever seen.

'Don't provoke Belial to more war,' warned Sam, but Asmodeus had already closed the door.

Sighing, Sam sank on to the fireside chair facing Beelzebub, folding his legs up so that his chin rested on his knees and he was no larger than a child. 'Why did we crown him?'

'Because demons acknowledge physical strength only. Because they want for Prince a man ruthless enough to kill his own brothers, and because we too want a man ruthless enough.' He was giving the answer Sam had heard many times before.

The old demon added, 'You're spending longer and longer on Earth. Are you finally giving up on us?'

'I don't know. But I'm sorry anyway.'

'No. I am the sorry one.'

They sat in silence a while longer.

'Bubble, there may be bigger trouble coming than we thought,' said Sam finally. Bubble was the name he always used, partly to infuriate his companion, partly out of fondness, partly because he'd worn so many names himself he'd got into the habit of applying different ones to others.

'Bigger than Asmodeus waging another futile war on Belial?'

'Much. My family is at war again.' Sam described the circumstances of Freya's death.

He added, 'I believe she was conducting investigations into the four keys.'

If Bubble's face ever showed anything, it showed surprise then. 'The four keys?' he echoed. 'The Pandora keys? They're lost.'

'That's what I've been told too. But Freya is dead. There is war in Heaven.'

There followed another silence, longer and more pained, in which their minds ran to certain obvious conclusions. Images of war and destruction played before their eyes, full of beings gloating at the future to be wrought.

Sam found himself yawning from exhaustion at his thoughts. Bubble asked, 'Are you staying here?'

'No. The humans have got it into their heads that I may be part of Freya's death. And there are people I must find – urgently.'

'What do you want me to do?'

'I need information on the keys. Clues as to where they're hidden, what it means if their powers are unleashed, everything. And do what you always do. Keep Asmodeus out of trouble. Forestall the inevitable war as long as possible.'

Beelzebub looked worried, a flicker across his otherwise serene face. But even a flicker was so unusual that Sam was immediately alarmed.

'What is it?'

'Oh – anxieties. I'm growing old, you know. Perhaps it's only me, but Asmodeus is becoming harder to control.'

'Do you control him?'

The demon gave a knowing smile, sharing in the secret that only they knew. So obvious was this secret, so blatant and so simple, that no one else had seen it. Sam had often said that the best place to hide was in the open.

'Of course not. I . . . *influence* his decisions.'

'And it's becoming harder?'

'Yes. Half of my influence stems from you, and you're not here.'

Sam felt a start of guilt at this simple statement. 'I will try. All I need is a little time to deal with whatever Freya wanted me to do.'

'At least,' said Beelzebub with a smile, 'doing what she wanted was never a problem for you.'

But you, old demon? thought Sam as he trudged the last few steps up to his flat. In twenty-four hours he'd been to Devon, Tibet and Hell. Returning to London had a sense of homecoming, and it was with relief that he unlocked the door. *Have you got time? Sometimes I forget how soon you people die.*

But he didn't forget now. As he lay down to sleep he remembered things he'd rather not. He'd been arrogant in misusing the years, when he was younger. He'd let everything move at a snail's pace, forgetting that by the time one flower bloomed, the other would have withered.

He didn't forget. Remembering Annette and others, he thought, *Mortal child, why did you have to grow so old?*

It had been one of those memorable cool spring evenings before the war in Heaven had finally spilled over to Earth. He'd been trying to have a cigarette, smoking being an almost universal trend in bustling Paris, but found himself unable to. Whenever he tried to inhale, his body's natural defences had kicked in, and the blood had thundered in his head as regenerative powers worked themselves up to action. So he'd given up trying to smoke, and was now leaning on a balcony watching the occasional car drive down the street, passing from pool to pool of light.

Behind him, a bright, crowded room and the uproarious laughter of his French hostess as another tasteless joke was delivered. The humour had been getting noisier all evening, the smoke thicker, the drink flowing faster. *People are nervous*, Sam thought. *They can feel the danger lurking in the future. Nineteen thirty-eight, the year that appeasement gains peace, and a German army wins its first little, disguised battle. But a battle nonetheless, albeit fought with papers and threats – and the memory of another war, still fresh in our minds. You're all nervous. You can feel what's going to happen, and you're declaring that you don't believe a word of it, because that's what you want to be true.*

He took a gulp from the glass in his hand. No –

however hard he tried, he found it difficult to get drunk. *Time, Time, Time!* he swore. *Why can't my body not work for once?* He'd already downed half a bottle of whisky. Yet there was no sign of its effects, but for the smell on his breath and the occasional turning of his stomach as his body broke down a thousand little toxins that might have half killed a human.

Someone staggered out next to him on to the balcony. A young woman, twentyish, giggling violently. She gasped down several gulps of air, clinging to the railing; then her head tipped forward as though it were a dead weight. Indeed, but for a small groan it seemed she might have died standing there.

'Shit,' she declared finally.

'Why?' he asked in French.

Rolling her head around a few times and hugging herself against the cold in her thin dress, she declared in a slurred voice, 'I'm drunk.'

'You are.'

'Shit.'

'It's not such a bad thing,' said Sam, wishing he could share her mindless condition, hangover and all.

She seemed only now to become aware of herself, and smiled prettily, as if just noticing his existence. 'Who are you, then?'

'Luc.'

'And what do you do?' she asked, almost crooning the words. She staggered, and he caught her automatically. Leaning against the railing, she began again to giggle.

'I'm the Devil in disguise,' he assured her. 'Are you okay?'

She laughed. 'My name's Annette. What's yours?'

'I said. Luc.'

But Annette just went on laughing.

Why did you have to be mortal? he thought wearily, rolling over on one side, struggling to find sleep, that like the effects of drugs, alcohol and cigarettes, seemed denied to him. *And since you are mortal, why can't you simply die and leave me to my memories? Why do you always have to be there?*

He woke to the thud of mail falling on the mat. The sun was already putting his threadbare curtains to shame, and a quick glance at the clock shamed him too. Was it already so late?

Sam managed to wash and dress in a little over ten minutes. He took his mail into the kitchen, reading it over a bowl of cereal and not caring that he might splash it with milk or coffee.

It was after he'd opened three items – a bill, an ad declaring that his house was perfect for a certain housing agency to represent, should he *ever* require their services, and another bill – that he came across a letter sealed in a brown envelope and addressed in Adam's hand to Luc – no, that was crossed out – Sam Linnfer. He wondered what Adam could have found out so swiftly.

There was a single note inside, on which a hurried hand had scrawled, 'The old hammer's found you. The valkyries took every address I know. Get out. Adam.' It had been delivered by hand.

He stared at it for a long while, reading and re-reading as though he couldn't quite believe it. Then he sprang into action, leaping round the flat in a flurry, digging out passports, keys, clothes, maps – everything he could fit into one small rucksack. He couldn't afford to be burdened.

As he hurried to and fro he struggled to remember how many addresses Adam knew. Three, maybe four? All but one in England. What else did Adam know? Contacts, emergency meeting-places, alternative names. *Assume Sam and Luc are known. How far does Thor's influence stretch — will he have eyes in passport control too? Or am I the only one who's bothered to set up proper networks? Will he just send the valkyries after me, or is that too blunt even for Thor's little mind?*

How many addresses could they have checked so far? Quite a few, he decided. Shouldering his luggage, he slammed the door behind him and galloped down the stairs. 'Mrs Dinken! If anyone asks to go into my flat for whatever reason, please don't let them. Oh — and have you got a pen?' it occurred to him to ask, going through his pockets as she stood in the hall before him, her head bobbing up and down in agreement to words not being said. She waddled back into a room, emerging an eternity later with pen and paper. Sam scrawled a hasty note, bounded back upstairs and stuck it to his door.

'I'm sorry, but Mr Sam Linnfer is currently away on business in Oxford. Please contact his assistant for a telephone number.' He had no assistant, but that wasn't the point.

In the street, every car held staring eyes and the sky felt full of ravens. He tried to use what he knew about finding pursuers. Check cars, look for interesting features that help you remember them. Look for faces in the cars. Look for pedestrians who spend too much time staring into the same shop windows as you. Remember what other contacts Adam had access to, what others he knew of.

Sam walked briskly down the road, ignoring bus

stops and passing endless shops offering half-price sales. This place, unlike Holcombe, had lost all personality. Teenagers pressed their noses against the window at Gap, and businessmen drank over-priced coffees, thinking of them instead as 'expresso grande' or 'special mocca'. The main street was one large chain store, divided by a river of cars and trucks aggressively seeking the end of their road. The man in the small red convertible had his stereo up full blast in an attempt to drown out the classical music of the family in the large green Volvo: one wife with flowery silk scarf, one father with tie, two tidily dressed children with sulky expressions who'd grow up to be lawyers, maybe High Court judges.

Thor thinks I killed Freya. Or maybe he doesn't; maybe he's just using it as an excuse to get even on past hatreds. Why? I never did anything to him.

There's no evidence against me, either. They can't prove anything.

The inevitable rejoinder piped up. *Thor doesn't want to prove anything. He just wants to beat a confession out of anything that moves, and I've been moving for too long already.*

He'd reached his first destination. A side street thronging with market stalls, erected in all their plastic and metal glory in front of fish and chip shops, DIY stores and florists selling authentic plastic blooms, one pound each. This litter-filled byway of noise and colour had personality, albeit of the watch-your-wallet variety. Twisted towards the shady side of the law, by dubious boxes of watches and videos in unorthodox covers that had somehow been released at the same time as the film itself.

Here Sam brought a cheap green anorak and a base-ball cap, reasoning that these were what he'd be least expected to wear. He did have *some* taste – enough at least not to dress as a trainspotter. *Hi, I'm the Prince of Darkness, is that really a Castles Class, 1923? Wow, let me write down the serial number.* Pushing his way back to the main road, he got on the first bus that came along. He had a definite destination in mind, but planned on taking a long time to get there.

The bus was bound for King's Cross down the Caledonian Road, with its dismal blocks of flats, run-down terraces, pet shops, municipal pool, and prison. Yet here too was life, of a sort. A few blocks to the east were green squares and private gardens and luxurious restored houses in which bankers, accountants and politicians neighboured one another in competitive bour-geois elegance. None of them said they lived near the Caledonian Road; they were from Islington. Their children had neat hair and played with clean new toys. The streets where they lived were tightly parked with sensi-ble cars for the school run. And this not half a mile from the seedy streets round Pentonville Gaol. It was as if God, in all his wisdom, had drawn a social boundary down the middle of a road over which the local pub glowered at the new wine bar and which none but the foolhardy crossed.

At King's Cross Sam changed buses. The station was a scruffy building, made shabbier beneath its huge wrought-iron roof by a plaza full of McDonald's and the like, and notices declaring that this train was also delayed. It was horribly dwarfed by St Pancras next door, with its fairy-tale towers and gothic majesty, even though the people going through King's Cross quite out-numbered those in the sister station.

Down the Euston Road in the next bus at walking speed, turning now towards Tavistock Square and an

area of hotels, offices and underground car parks. At
Russell Square there was the shade of great trees, and
university buildings whose offices had spilled over into
the tall Georgian terraces. Sam leapt off at a traffic light
and made his way towards Holborn, where a third bus
took him down to the river. Walking along the
Embankment he was careful to take his time. He was still
alert for pursuers, magical or mundane, however confident that he didn't have any.

Besides, he had to work out what he was going to say.
'Hi, you used to be a spy and had access to a network
that I need. Where is it?'

To which the obvious answer would be, 'But that was
sixty years ago and it was *you* who decided to close down
the Moondance network.'

Why had he done that? Had he convinced himself he
didn't need it, and could live a nice peaceful life without
its help? To say the least, a rash thought.

Not so rash, though, that he'd left every door closed.
*You left her a back way in, in case she ever needed Moondance
again. And because she has a back door, so do you. Maybe you
haven't been so naïve.*

The river was at high tide, and a tracery of sea breeze
blew away the fumes of the Embankment; it was even
possible to shut out the roar of traffic edging towards
Westminster. At a small park near one of the grand
hotels claiming much of this part of London as its own,
Sam cut inland and took a flight of stairs two at a time
between giant buildings full of civil servants. The steps
came out on a back street, empty of traffic except for a
postal van. Glancing back, he saw that no one had followed. He moved faster now, his destination in sight,
slipping through more small streets where sunlight rarely

peeped over the high buildings, until any traffic was a distant roar, a world away and little more than a minute from where he stood.

The building he was looking for had two brass plaques by the door. One declared that the bottom floor was the property of Noble and Transton, lawyers to the very rich and trivial, no tradesmen please. A much smaller one, weatherworn, and green around the edges, announced the residence of Mrs Annette Wilson.

He rang the bell, and a curt voice declared from the speakers in a slight French accent, 'Yes?'

'It's Luc.'

There was a long silence, in which he imagined what she was doing. Probably staring in shock at the speaker, trying to convince herself that her failing ears hadn't heard what she had, rubbing her withered little hands together and straining her bent back as she reached for the open button. Didn't she keep a nurse? he remembered. A watery-eyed girl who hardly spoke a word of English and looked after Annette as punishment for a sin from some other lifetime?

Finally the door buzzed, and he pushed. Inside, the hall was marbled and cold. He jogged up the stairs, trying to get a little warmth into his system after the chill of the February streets. A heavy panelled door opened and this same sinner peered down at him, and asked with a heavy accent, 'Mr Luc?'

He nodded, and without another word she showed him in.

The carpet was so thick Sam felt he'd be engulfed. He had forgotten what a taste for luxury Annette had. She was not by any means a poor woman – the French government had rewarded her well for her work in the

Resistance and she'd gone through a collection of rich husbands as a child consumes his favourite sweets. Sculptures, strange things of twisted wood, adorned the room's corners, and bent lights illuminated numerous paintings, some of them her own. As an artist Annette had been good. At least one shelf was full of books on her favourite occupation – weaving. *Poor Annette. Can your hands hold anything, these days?*

And there she was, bent over in a huge chair bursting with pillows. Even now her ancient, wrinkled face bore signs of how pretty she'd once been. Her eyes, still horribly, accusingly bright with intelligence, looked him up and down as she vaguely waved the sinner from the room. Finally she spoke.

'It's true. You don't age, do you? Why couldn't you have grown old, Luc? Why couldn't you have been like my husbands? As soon as I married them I forgot why, because they were old and lifeless suddenly. Why couldn't you be like that?'

'How are you?' he asked, squatting at her feet and taking her hand, her cold frail hand. She smiled with contentment at his touch.

'You never grow old,' she murmured wearily. 'How many hearts have you broken by refusing to die like the rest of us?'

'I need help. I need to get in contact with some old friends, very old. I know we closed the network down when the war was over, but now I need access again.'

'Which network?' she asked feebly. 'There were so many.' Annette had been parachuted behind enemy lines, then moved around a lot.

'Our network. The one nobody else knew about. The network that helped you, if you helped it. *Our* network.'

'Ah yes,' she said, as if just remembering. 'The Moondance network, founded nineteen forty-one, headed by Luc Satise. Purpose . . .' her voice trailed off again, as she tried to recall the unwritten files that no one had dared to record . . . 'to employ aid of a non-mundane nature against occupying forces. Magic. Can you still do your tricks, Luc? Can you still light a fire with a sigh and make the wind sing?'

'The Moondance network,' he repeated. 'You were a special operations executive behind enemy lines. I approached you, told you I could give you access to a group of untraceable saboteurs willing to help.'

'Moondance,' she said dreamily. 'You were our luck. Whenever the Resistance tried something that went wrong, but everyone got out alive, or whenever we were being chased and a fog fell, or whenever the charge didn't explode and we thought we'd failed, only to have it explode when we were miles away – we called it luck. But it wasn't, was it? All those extraordinary Moondance operators.' She frowned. 'But it was broken up. The world wasn't ready for magic, you said. And peace was the ultimate good luck.'

'Yes,' he said quickly. 'Moondance was broken up, it was no longer needed. But I kept on deploying some of the sources; for my own use, you understand. Remember Adamarus?'

'Ah yes. He was the one who heard what people said as a kind of song. If someone lied, he heard discord. Or was that the other one . . .?'

'Yes – Adamarus was the truthkeeper. I was the ring-leader. And you were our link with the "real" world; you told us what was wanted when and where. Remember Whisperer?'

'The one who called the fog. The emergency backup,' she murmured, her mind far away in another time, another place. 'The one I was supposed to call, if something went wrong.'

'Yes. Yes, that's him. What was the procedure he gave you for contact? How were you supposed to summon him?'

But she'd already lost hold. 'Are your family still warring?'

'Yes.'

'Hum. And you?'

'In a shit-load of trouble, thank you for asking. My prime contact is blown and I've got an angry relative trying to find me with intent pertaining to violence.'

'Ah.' This didn't seem to worry her in the slightest. 'You broke up the network when the Allies turned the tables. You said after four years fighting on the losing side, you couldn't break the habit and went to Berlin to dig out Germans from the rubble they'd brought collapsing on themselves. You danced between causes like a troublesome child between tired friends.'

'I fought for the French when they were dying. When they began killing I fought for the new sufferers. Any doctor would have done the same.'

'But if you change sides you merely prolong the agony.'

'If I don't help I will be what they want me to be,' he replied softly.

'You and your pride.' She sighed, tossing back her head as if posing for an unseen artist. 'And why do you want to find Whisperer?'

'Because even without the Moondance network officially functioning, they all hear something. I want to know what they've heard about who killed my sister.'

This still didn't arouse any interest. He might as well have said, 'I want to hear who put sugar on the table instead of salt.'

'Why don't you ever grow old, Luc?'

'What's the procedure?'

She began to hum. He held her hand tighter, willing her frail old mind to come up with the answer. She stopped singing and muttered, 'Tell the man in the bookshop you're looking for a first-edition copy of *The Whispering Game* and wait in the park.'

'Which bookshop?'

'River Bookshop,' she said in French. 'Paris. By the church.'

'Is it still there? The bookshop, same owner? Is it still functioning?'

'The owner was one of them,' she replied, switching back to English with such ease that Sam wondered if she'd even noticed the change in language. 'He'll never die. Never, ever, ever die.' She whispered the address.

He realised she was nearly in tears, so rose and wrapped an arm round her shoulders, letting her head droop against his side.

'Why don't you just die?' she whispered.

'I can't. Not yet.'

'I hate you, Luc. I hate you.'

'And I still love you too.'

She sniffed. 'Oh Luc. Why couldn't you have been someone else?'

'Because then I wouldn't be me.'

'Tell me again. When we die we all go to Heaven. Not to Hell. To Heaven. Tell me that, Luc.'

He stared down at her guiltily, feeling the horrible truth press against his tongue, demanding to be spoken.

No, he wanted to say. *This is your great chance. This is your life, and Heaven or Hell is merely what you've made of it. Real Heaven, the place on the other side of the Portal, is somewhere neither you nor I can go.*

'Everyone goes to Heaven,' he said softly, shamed at how easily the lie slid up his throat. 'Everyone.'

SEVEN

Moondance

The difficulty was getting to Paris. Fortunately he knew how rigorous Dover passport control would be on a freezing night when the rain came from all directions at once, and the white cliffs hurled the gale straight back at the ferry port below them.

Otherwise he would have been inclined to Waywalk again. But no. It would probably take no longer to catch the ferry, and thence the train to Paris. There'd been times when he'd had to walk miles across Paris, so low was the city's ratio of Portals. Unlike London, a lot of its Portals had been built over. Sometimes he wished Paris was dirtier, darker than it was. That way he could use a Portal without worrying about whether he'd come out in the middle of some well-kept public park or children's playground.

The bus from Dover Priory station swung towards the entrance to the ferry port, and Sam mentally began practising his German accent. If he was going out under

Sebastian Teufel, he'd better sound the part. The result made him resemble the villain in a James Bond movie, but it was the best he could manage. If anyone asked him to speak in German, that was another matter. Hopefully no one would demand what he carried slung across his back with the rucksack. 'Golf clubs,' he said in his German accent, experimentally rolling the words around.

'Uhuh. Have a good trip.'

'Thank you,' he told the woman in passport control, playing the polite German tourist to the full. She'd hardly glanced up to check his passport photo. His own senses were at full stretch, listening, feeling for any sign of Thor or his minions. *I'm the only one with the really good networks*, he thought fervently. *The others have been so busy in Heaven, the systems they've got down here are ramshackle, to say the least.*

Still, the valkyries.

The *Pride of Calais* was unusually full for an evening crossing. On a rough sea, and in such rain, everyone avoided going on deck, preferring to cower inside among arcade machines and shops. Impossibly, irrationally, as the ferry pulled away from the docks, and the lights of Dover were lost in foul weather, Sam realised he might just have made it. Thor was in England. The police were in England. He was going to find the Moondance network, undetected. They would know where Andrew had gone, and Andrew would explain everything. It seemed so simple.

He knew in his heart it couldn't be.

Sitting in one of the many bars, sipping a beer, Sam felt something, and knew it was in response to his

probes. He froze, looking around in sudden panic. A
slumbering lorry driver, a tired woman trying to read *The
Times*, a couple of businessmen talking. A lot of casually
dressed people failing to sleep as the ship heaved up and
down. Outside, on deck, it was dark.

'Where are you going, then?'

'Pardon?' he asked, remembering his German accent
just in time.

The barman, practically the only person on the boat
not upset by its constant motion, was polishing a
glass. 'Oh, you're German . . . Why are you going to
Calais?'

'I'm meeting my family. I've finished work, and now
we're going on holiday.' He gave a nervous smile, made
doubly so by the alarm now blazing across his sixth
sense. *Danger. Danger is near.* 'I love golf, you know.'

'Really? Those your clubs?' he asked, nodding at the
bundle across Sam's knees.

'Yes.'

'Oh . . . You got kids?'

'Two girls, little terrors,' he lied with the embarrassed
laugh of the fond father trying not to boast.

'Really? I've got a girl myself. Birthday next week.
Loves the Teletubbies, Lord help us.'

Sam gave another uneasy laugh, not sure if the
Germans had Teletubbies or if they'd been spared.
Something moved in the darkness outside, on the deck.
His head snapped round like a snake, but there was no
one there.

'Rough night, isn't it?' said the barman, indifferently.

'Oh, yes. I'm sorry, I've got to go and get a breath of
fresh air. It's a little hot, you know.'

'Hey, it's not nice out there.'

Sam ignored him. 'Would you see no one takes my bag, please?'

Sliding open the glass door that led on deck, Sam was hit in the face by the slicing rain. His stomach lurched violently. He heaved the door shut behind him and edged along the darkened deck, choosing his footing carefully. *I can feel you. I know you're here.*

Above him, something moved. He burst into a run, swinging round a corner with his feet nearly going out beneath him on the soaking deck. Slipping and scrambling up a flight of metal stairs, turning to clamber up another staircase and peering through the darkness.

It was the top deck, the most exposed. Rain tore at him from everywhere at once, and the huge funnels of the ferry rumbled loud. Looking wildly round, he felt the movement in the air behind him. A valkyrie, soaked from her climb on to the deck, sprang over a railing, spun and thrust at him. He saw the gleam of a blade and ducked, bringing his hands up and locking them round her arm, before swinging his body into hers.

Centuries of surviving had given Sam his own method of fighting, requiring perfect coordination and never-ending practice. No part of his body stopped moving; as his elbows thrust back against her, one foot locked around her ankle, pulling forward to topple her. She fell – and he was already away, stepping behind her and pulling her arms so taut it seemed every bone might break. The dagger clattered from her fingers. With a look of disgust he picked it up.

'Steel?' he yelled in her ear. His pin had her locked on the soaking deck, teeth gritted in pain. 'You *are* badly prepared!'

She tried to scream, not calling for help so much as in

defiance. But he'd already braced a knee against her back in order to lock his hand across her mouth. Shouting straight into her ear over the storm he said, 'Thor sent you, didn't he? Nod.'

She didn't.

'Look, lady, I'm darkness incarnate, the bastard Son of Time. And I'm perfectly prepared to break your arms if I don't get a good answer. I *know* Thor sent you, so just nod!'

She nodded, furious with herself. Struggling in his grasp, she strove to bite his hand.

'How did he know I would leave by Dover?' He removed his hand, and she began to scream. Immediately he covered her mouth again, and savagely twisted her arm. 'Tell me! Or I'll kill you!' He removed his hand again, gave a sharp flick of his wrist and the silver dagger was in his hand, the point dangerously near her eye.

'He knows you don't like using Portals! He called in the valkyries to watch ferry ports and hired mercenaries to watch the airports!'

'Mercenary humans, or spirits?'

'Both! Some natural wizards, mostly spirits.'

That stood to reason. Mercenaries, wild spirits, were mainly the ones against whom Sam had established his networks. They obeyed nothing but their desire for magic to feed on, or serving the strongest master.

He shook the valkyrie harder. 'Tell him I didn't kill Freya. Tell him to leave me alone!' he shouted, unmoved by her struggles. He laid his hand over her forehead. Her eyes flickered shut, and she slipped to the deck and lay there, face down in the water.

Sam re-sheathed his dagger, trembling with cold. For Thor to have his valkyries watch every port was to stretch them thin indeed. *He must really be angry.*

Returning to the warmth of the inner decks he collected his bag without a word to the astonished barman, and hurried down to a cubicle in the men's lavatories. He took off his wet black coat and replaced it with the green anorak. In the shop he purchased a different rucksack, describing him as a 'world trekker', and piled his belongings into that. He'd put on the baseball cap, but ruled out buying a pair of sunglasses, in gloomy February.

Holidaymakers are often disappointed by their arrival in Calais. After leaving Dover, which for the most part was bombed flat and poorly rebuilt, they usually want to arrive in a gleaming port where, for preference, a man wearing a silly hat is selling wine and garlic. Not so with Calais. From the port it's straight on to a motorway which commands views over railyards and industrial estates. The bus to the centre of town goes past advertisement hoardings, and giant steel sheds in which foothills of builder's cement are stacked for some unhappy day when the world finds itself needing that much of the stuff. The first indication of being in another land is the red-brick town hall, make-believe Flemish medieval, with a colossal clock tower. As the more cynical tourists point out, it surely isn't Dover Castle. But it is different.

The bus's final destination was the town's two stations, one international, the other regional. Sam bought a ticket and ran on to the Paris platform, catching the last train seconds before the whistle went. But surely not too soon. When would his trance on the valkyrie have worn off? Was it known even now that he'd got off the ferry in Calais?

Did he dare sleep? he thought as the train clunked out of the station. Or were there more enemies out there,

waiting for him? Because of a crime he hadn't commit-
ted? Or for some truth whose discovery had got Freya
killed?

Sam resolved to stay awake.

It had been on another train journey, Paris to Orleans,
when he'd first decided, all those years ago, to intervene.
He'd done so reluctantly, knowing how dangerous inter-
ference was in mortal affairs.

His travelling companions were a woman in a hat and
a neat suit, sitting up straight, her face empty. Either a
spy or an informer, he decided in a flight of fancy. A man
wearing rough, greasy clothes, with uncombed hair and
dirt on his hands and face. A pair of giggling young children, pressing their noses against the window and trying
to see the darkened landscape rush by. Another woman,
in a shabbier suit, sat with her husband. An indelible
little frown was etched on her brow.

Sam had known he would intervene sooner or later.
He'd seen the cratered homes in London, heard whispers
about concentration camps, witnessed the Warsaw
ghetto. In his heart he knew the only thing holding him
back was fear. Even now, he feared mortals.

'Papers.' A German soldier, speaking heavily accented
French, entered the carriage. Sam's Luc Satise ID was
briefly examined, and given back. The papers of the
frowning woman and her husband were inspected,
however, and not returned. Outside the closed compartment door the soldier engaged in a half-heard
conversation with his commander.

'There's a notice about them, sir . . .'

'Are they the ones?'

Sam glanced at the couple, their faces now empty,

hands locked in each other's. *Resistance workers. They've been betrayed, the soldiers can identify them.*

The compartment door opened again, and the soldier gestured with a pistol. 'You two. Out.'

They rose without a word, the fear evident in their eyes. Sam looked at their faces, at the darkness outside, and back again. Even the children had fallen silent.

The man and woman were led away towards the front of the train, their heads already bowed in the submissive emptiness of prisoners. Sam turned to his neighbour and spoke in a low voice. 'How far to Orleans?'

'We're nearly there.'

'They're going to be shot, aren't they?'

'Interrogated first.' The man seemed indifferent.

Sam rose to his feet. Clinging to the handrail in the narrow corridor, he staggered to the end of the carriage, and flung open a window. Luckily the wind was carrying the smoke to the other side of the train. Sticking his head out, he looked towards the engine. His eyes flickered shut briefly, as his mind detached itself. There was a scream of brakes, and he was thrown to one side. The train groaned under the pressure of sudden deceleration. As it juddered to a halt, Sam slipped a door open and jumped down into the night.

He ran through the darkness, keeping close to the train. Suddenly a German soldier sprang out ahead and began yelling at the driver. Sam dived underneath a carriage, crawled to the other side and continued running, keeping his head low, before climbing back up. Now there were two soldiers shouting at the train crew, who were standing in confusion by the engine, trying to understand why its oiled and efficient parts should have locked so violently in place.

Outside the first-class compartments Sam risked peering round the edge of the window. Two bored German soldiers were staring over their rifles at the silent French couple, now handcuffed, with the man already showing signs of a large bruise across his mouth.

Again Sam intervened, hating himself for a blind fool even as he did so. All four heads snapped around as he tapped on the glass. He knocked gently once more, then moved quickly back against the side of the train. The door opened, and a German soldier stuck his head out. Sam leapt up, catching him round the neck and pulling him into the darkness, digging through his mind as he went. Mortal mind, unprepared – besides, humans had never understood how to defend themselves against another's thoughts. There was a cry from his comrade, who sprang from the carriage, gun raised. But Sam was ready to catch him in magic. As the man jumped, his leap carried him down on to the far bank, where he sprawled, one leg at an odd angle. There were more shouts.

'Come on!' yelled Sam. The man and woman needed no prompting and clambered from the train as hurriedly as their handcuffs allowed.

'Quickly!' They broke into a run, rushing blindly into the thorn-filled embankment below. There was a rattle of gunfire, and Sam felt something strike his back, spin him around and throw him to the ground. The man and woman stopped, but in a breathless, anguish-filled voice he yelled, 'Keep running!' They hesitated, then fled into the darkness.

Snarling with pain, Sam crawled on hands and knees through thorns and bracken, not caring as his clothes and hands were torn, and collapsed behind a tree, gasping for breath. Already he could feel his body initiating the trance that would heal the wound, but he wouldn't let it. The automatic trance was a leftover from the days when most weapons didn't lodge in you; bullets were different. Gritting his teeth, he set his mind to what he had to do, and kept on concentrating. Agony tore through his back, when at last the bullet was pulled free as though by a surgeon impatient of others' suffering.

This is what comes of interfering, he thought sourly, before pitching forward on his face.

He'd woken in a place that stank of death, and knew he wasn't out of trouble yet. His back was searing him, and his heart was only just picking up its normal beat. His body had broken from its former state merely because the trance had been snapped by his warning wards. Danger had woken him, danger which needed him to be conscious.

He was face down in a muddy pit, wearing the same clothes as before, soaked with his own blood. As he wondered who he was and what he was doing there, a splash of wet mud fell across his legs. Then another. With the return of awareness, he heard the sound of a shovel, and felt more mud fall. Someone was burying him, without a coffin, in an unmarked grave.

Though every nerve screamed against it, he sat up. There was a single Frenchman burying him. In his shock the man let the shovel fall thudding to the ground.

'Hi,' said Sam. He could feel mud fall in showers from his face as he tried to work his parched mouth.

The man ran. *Oh come on, I'm not in such a state as all that*, he thought, before losing consciousness again.

❊

The train pulled up in Paris in the small hours, and Sam was reminded how hard it was to find a hotel that stayed open late. Eventually he found a place in a side street where the girl on the desk, who was from somewhere in Eastern Europe, was nearly falling over with fatigue. He took a grungy single room under the name of Michel Lesson, choosing it at random and hoping no one would ask for proof of identity.

As the city's clocks tolled two, he slipped into yet another strange bed in a musty room with a black and white TV and a window that overlooked concrete rooftops, and drifted asleep without even bothering to set his customary wards. He was simply too tired.

As he dreamed, his mind was full of images: of snowstorms in the Tibetan mountains, Historians, Andrews, Gails, and Freya's blood on a brother's hands. Though he was under several blankets, he woke shaking with cold.

The River Bookshop was next to a small church that, were it not for the sign declaring it a house of God, Sam would probably have missed. It was one of those modern churches built in the belief that all that mattered was praying, not where you did it. As such it was little more than a small office with polished floors and a few pretty pictures on the walls. But what the church lacked in personality the River Bookshop, established in the first year of the twentieth century of Our Lord, made up for ten times over.

Sam pushed open the door hung with fifty-year-old posters and heard the dull tone of the old cowbell. He looked round a shop that was evidently managed by a Collector, capital C. There were a multitude of signed

copies, several first editions, a whole shelf of old
manuscripts and even an original copy of *Pride and
Prejudice*, to be sold for thousands of euros to some
prodigiously rich connoisseur. A ginger cat was curled
up on one shelf, sleeping peacefully. In the corner a pile
of cushions marked where children sat when stories were
read to them. A tray of leaflets suggested that yes, this
was a 'community' bookshop.

The cash desk was unmanned. Sam made a point of
browsing round before wandering up and ringing the
little bell that stood on it.

'Coming, coming!'

A wizened little creature, more dwarf than man,
entered the room. He had half-moon spectacles on the
end of his nose and, though he had long grey hair and
bulged around the waist, he moved as lightly on his feet
as a child. To Sam he was unmistakable – a certain
shadow followed him, perceptible only out of the corner
of the eye. This man, like Adamarus, like Whisperer, was
one of the Fey.

'Run this shop long?' Sam asked quietly.

The little man looked at him, and nearly yelped, dropping his spectacles as he realised exactly *what* it was that
stood inside his door. 'A fair while, sir,' he mumbled, jug-
gling with his glasses as though they were wet soap.
'How can I help you?'

'I'm looking for a first-edition copy of *The Whispering
Game*, please.'

The man jumped even more at this, his old ears prick-
ing at a code which he hadn't heard for many a year. 'I
don't suppose you know the author?' he asked in a
breathless voice.

Annette hadn't mentioned anything about authors.

'No. I know the publisher, though. It was brought out in nineteen forty-one by a company called Moondance.'

'What's your interest in this book, please?'

'I was commissioning editor.'

The man gave a nervous little laugh, even more on edge now that he knew not just what, but who, was making this coded request for a meeting. 'I'll try and order it, sir.'

'I'll be waiting.'

With a fiendish smile, Sam left the store. There was a small park a few blocks away, which he knew from Annette was the right one. He walked down to it, found a bench and sat down. Even in Paris, February was a miserable month and it wasn't long before he was blowing into his hands and rubbing his arms in an attempt to keep warm. How long would it take to get a message to Whisperer? Would he come at all?

After a while he was on his feet and hopping around to keep warm, attracting strange looks from passers by. In his green anorak and baseball cap he wasn't surprised. Fashionable Paris probably regarded him as little better than a street beggar. Finally he sat down again and shivered unobtrusively, meeting no one's eyes and trying to give the impression of another lost stranger waiting for a friend who hasn't come.

There was movement behind, then next to him.

'You're dangerous,' said a voice in his ear like the sighing of the wind.

'I'm always dangerous.' He turned to get a better look at Whisperer. 'Thanks for getting here so fast.'

'I thought you might come here; it seemed the logical thing to do. I've heard rumours. A Waywalker is dead. The faerie whisper that it was Freya who died, and that you are being watched.'

Whisperer was an old, old spirit, like Adamarus. But where Adamarus could easily get by as a normal human being, Whisperer was pale as snow, with fingers so long, and frame so thin it seemed if you even breathed on him too hard he would shatter into a thousand shards. He wore blue jeans and a blotched shirt underneath a blue coat, which hung on him as though from the neck downwards he was a skeleton. Which, Sam reflected, he might well be.

In Whisperer's face there was none of the boyishness that lightened Sam's looks, and no stranger, on spying Whisperer pass by, would call him anything but ancient. There was wisdom and knowledge and time written in his unwavering pale eyes and faintly smiling lips, which, like Beelzebub's, never seemed to alter their expression. But where Beelzebub's features were worn with care, Whisperer's were eroded by a look of apprehension.

Of me? Or of what the world has become around us?

'I know spirits keep in touch at all times. There are things I need to find out.'

'Of course. In our own way we all loved Freya. And I still remember the old days. The Moondance network.' Whisperer sighed, with a sound like the breeze off a slumbering river on a summer's day. 'We were the only ones who actually did anything, you know? The others were too scared of the mortals. Or hated them, for what humankind has done. Driven us from our homes, destroyed our shrines, denied our memories. But we did make a difference.'

'Have you any idea how many Thor's mustered after me? I need to know how serious it is.'

'Thor?' echoed Whisperer with disbelief. 'From what I'm hearing, Thor is the least of your troubles. A mindless thug whom you can beat in any game. No, what you need to worry about is the younger school.'

Sam gaped. 'The youngsters? Why are *they* after me?'

'I don't know that they're specifically after you,' Whisperer admitted, 'but valkyries and angels have been seen. I also know certain mercenary spirits have been employed to report your location.' Whenever Whisperer spoke the word 'mercenary' he did so with a passion. Mercenaries, to him, were dangerous adversary spirits who hated mankind and all its works. 'Those with connections have also engaged the services of mortal wizards.'

'What connections?'

'Those who spent more time on Earth. They say Jehovah was close to Freya before she died. They say that Odin has been spending less and less time in Valhalla, that he disappears to Earth for months at a stretch. That's not common, in Waywalkers – Earth is just a resource to them, not a world. Some even say that Odin has gone to Hell, a kingdom shunned by all Waywalkers. Well, nearly all.'

Sam nodded, though his heart was pounding. If any of his brothers were visiting Hell . . . 'Why there? Are they recruiting?'

'Possibly. Hell does a good line in Oni and Balors. There are rumours of a few Titans in certain areas too. And Waywalkers, as you know, are revered in Hell. The arrival of a Son of Time wearing a large sword and a wise expression would be enough to get up a considerable following.'

'They wouldn't recruit in Hell unless they were serious about getting their numbers together. Traditionally it's where you go to look for whole armies.'

'I know.' Whisperer's tone, even by his standards, was unsettling. Sam looked up sharply.

'What is it?'

'Firedancers have also been seen.'

Sam's attention redoubled. 'How many?'

'Two were sighted in Rome. Two have been seen in St Petersburg, two in New York. We're sure there are others.'

'Where,' Sam began carefully, 'is Andrew?' He told Whisperer what little he knew, all the while aware of Andrew as the unknown factor, to be handled like a bomb.

'We don't even know who Andrew is.'

Sam took out the photograph given him by the abbot. 'This man.'

Whisperer thought, searching his memory. 'The man who fled the monastery? Yes . . . a historian.'

'You're sure of that? . . . So where did the Historian – Andrew – go?'

'We don't know. There's at least one Firedancer after him. Possibly a valkyrie too. They're masking his path. Judging by the trail of darkness on him, anywhere east of Poland is possible. Certainly our sources are now finding it hard to track anything in Russia. We think – but it's only rumour . . .'

'Since when have we ignored rumour?'

Whisperer looked uncomfortable. 'There are said to be things happening in Tibet. Someone has been gathering specific books together. Rare books. The Illthoran, the Arrenisi Codex, the Ashen'ian Journals, the texts related entirely to—'

'Cronus and the keys,' said Sam quietly. 'The Historian has been seeking out books to do with the Pandora keys.'

Whispered nodded. 'The keys are lost, though. You need all three of them to free the Pandora spirits. It would only take one key to free Cronus, but that is lost – they are all lost.'

'So's the crew of the *Marie Celeste*, but that didn't stop them Feywalking home.' Sam lowered his voice. 'Has the Historian found them? Does he know where the keys are?'

Whisperer shrugged.

'At least give me odds.'

Whisperer didn't meet his eyes. 'No one has ever tried looking for the keys before. They're too feared, too dangerous, hidden by Time himself. But if it *is* just a question of looking, then – yes – there's a chance he does know where they are. Not even Time can cover up every trace. Then there's the amount of research he's done, his sudden flight, and the resources deployed in seeking him. The death of Freya. Surely, to warrant all this he must know something of immense value.'

'The keys? He knows where they are?'

'Probably. Two to one in favour.'

Sam cracked his knuckles. The sound made Whisperer wince.

'Tell me,' Sam said, in a voice loaded with purpose, 'where's the nearest travel agent?'

EIGHT

The Historian

He was in the war again, playing the spy.

Which war? He'd been in so many.

Any war. The rules are the same for them all.

He had to find Andrew. Andrew would explain everything – why Freya died, what pursuers were after Sam himself. Or, if he didn't, he'd provide a link to Gail, whoever she was.

In his hotel room Sam finished a letter, sealed it up and handed it to Whisperer. 'I want you to get this to Thor, by whatever means.'

'What does it say?'

'Why, you should know!' said Sam with a smile. 'Someone in your network is supposed to have written it, after all. Someone willing to betray my location, and wanting to meet Thor in person. Only whoever that someone is won't be there.'

'You want to meet Thor? Will he fall for it?'

'Thor will believe it because he wants to. He'll come.'

Whisperer frowned, uncomfortable. 'Why are you risking this subterfuge to speak to him?'

'I suspect there's a lot he can tell me. I also think if he knows it's me he won't come.'

'Why Thor? Why not Odin?'

'Because, unlike Thor, Odin is brighter than he looks. Thor is less wary.'

'Especially if you contact him as a spirit would do? Without magic?'

'Precisely. And contact every Russian source we have. If they refuse to cooperate, tell them they'll wake up with heavy curses on their backs.' He sighed and stretched. *I can't do anything more until Thor responds and we find the Historian. Nothing save what I always do – stick my nose into dusty books and hope some clue from the past will tell me what's in the future.*

'Where will you go?' asked Whisperer.

'To Hell.'

Bubble took one look at what Sam wore and burst out laughing.

'Stuff it,' snapped Sam. 'I was forced into this.' Self-consciously he stripped off the green anorak and threw it in a corner. Bubble ignored him, returning to a long list of notes he was arranging.

'I did some research on the keys, while you were gone,' said the old demon, as Sam struggled into a warm black jumper and folded himself into the opposite chair.

'How nice,' he said, still annoyed by Bubble's laughter. 'Anything interesting?'

'Depends what you know.'

'About the Pandora keys? Just legends. That's all they told us servants.'

Beelzebub ignored the bitterness and anger in Sam's voice – to him such emotions were an everyday part of demon life. He ran a long finger down his notes. Seen from a certain angle it gave the impression more of claw than nail. 'Did you know the Princes of Heaven once tried to destroy the keys, and the spirits that they trapped?'

'I know they failed, too.'

'Did you know that Time once tried?'

That aroused Sam's interest. 'My father? What did he do?'

'Tried to smash up every door, to destroy the spirits behind each one with a single blow. But he couldn't. Earth shadows Heaven, Hell shadows Earth. The Pandora spirits drew power from the hate, suspicion and greed of Earth, renewing themselves as fast as Time could destroy them.'

'When did this happen?'

'The year before you were born. If that signifies anything.'

'I didn't know.'

'Well, it's a pretty major event – Time being incapable of destroying something. People must have been more than a little scared by this proof of the spirits' power. Cronus's power, too.'

Sam pulled a face. 'Cronus. I bet he wasn't even scratched.'

'I believe not . . . I've also had a rummage through some of Hell's own records. You know Belial is a third-generation offspring of Fire and Chaos?'

'I had heard.'

'Belial was once questioned on his parentage. When he talked about Chaos being a Queen of Time, he is known to have said, "Time never fully trusted her. She was one of many whom he didn't tell how the Pandora spirits could be destroyed."'

Sam, for all he was in Hell and therefore as far from Heaven as could magically be, responded like a perfect Son of Time. 'Impossible. If Time couldn't destroy the spirits himself, then no one can.'

'Logically speaking, Time is the least likely to destroy them,' Bubble mildly conceded. 'Hate, Greed and Suspicion, yes – he might be able to annihilate those. But not Cronus. Cronus is everything Time isn't. Once those two had engaged face to face, there'd be nothing left for either to rule.'

'Oh, come *on*. Belial was just showing off! He was trying to prove that, even though he doesn't have Time's blood and can't Waywalk, he knew what lay beyond the Portals. Well, here's news, Bubble. He doesn't. He can't imagine what shadows spawned Hell's miserable little world – he can't begin to guess at the things which mortals and immortals alike have made or dreamed of.'

'I'm merely reporting what I found, as you asked. Whether the source is authentic or not, I cannot tell.'

Sam immediately felt guilty. *And I'm supposed to be the Heavenly one.* 'I'm sorry.' For a few moments he became an empty-eyed statue, but for his fingers drumming on the arm of the chair.

Beelzebub patiently allowed him his silence, not bothering to wonder what other, unrevealed facts Sam was drawing on from his long past.

'All right,' Sam said finally. 'What became of the keys?'

'Scattered.'

'By who?'

'By whom,' Bubble corrected without thinking. 'By Wisdom, Time's most trusted Queen.'

'And no one knows where?'

'No.'

'Hum.' Silence again, this time for long enough to make even Bubble uncomfortable. 'Is there anything else?'

'Nothing you don't already know.'

Sam thanked him and got to his feet. Unusually, given his great age, Bubble rose with him. 'Actually – there is one more thing.'

'What?' It came out terser than Sam had meant – he was already impatient to go, bursting with new theories and schemes.

'Asmodeus. You really ought to talk to him.'

'I can't. Not now.'

'Well. Whenever you get an opportunity.' Bubble looked crestfallen.

Sam sighed, and patted the old demon on his scaly back. 'I'm sorry. But if things get out of control on Earth then you know what'll happen in Hell. Every world mirrors the other, well-known fact.'

'I do know. But please don't forget.'

Sam laughed. 'Me? Forget? With my memory?'

'I'm worried that it's getting a little full.'

'Oh, please. The brain is bigger than some people might make you think.'

'Do you want to know why you ought to talk to Asmodeus?'

'I thought you'd just explained it.'

'No.'

Sam folded his arms and said calmly, 'All right. You've saved the worst for last, I can tell.'

'You're absolutely right.'

'Hit.'

'The Gehenna Portal opened.'

'And? What demon waltzed through, and did it bring chocolates?'

'A Waywalker . . . "waltzed" . . . through.'

'You astound me. Was it someone I know, or just any old Waywalker?'

'Seth.'

Sam's look of complacency was blown away in an instant. *Seth? What's Seth got to do with anything? Why Seth, why the Son of Night?* 'Seth?' he echoed, for want of something better to say. 'Why?'

'I don't know.'

'How long did he stay?'

'A few hours. I always watch the Gehenna Portal.'

'Where did he go?'

'I don't know.'

'You watch the Portal, but on those rare occasions when someone other than the Prince of Darkness comes through you decide not to follow?'

'He *is* a Son of Night. In this kingdom, it's hard to follow a man born to darkness.'

'The way you put it . . .' murmured Sam. 'You must see *Dracula* one day. Great film. You'd crack up in hysterics.'

'I don't understand,' Bubble said mildly, 'and you know it.'

Sam frowned. 'I'm sorry,' he heard himself murmur distantly. But his voice and his thoughts were miles apart. *It can't be coincidence. Seth . . . here?*

He'd heard the rumours, of course, about how Seth was behind the attempted killing of more than one of his own brothers. He'd also observed with interest how the suave

Son of Night, in his elegant robes, had bowed, flattered and charmed his way along. The smoothest talker in the whole of Heaven. The one who lies as easily as he ties his shoelaces, who flatters even the most reluctant listener and who can smile a smile on which all the stars above have bestowed their favour.

It was in that long-forgotten age – deliberately forgotten by Sam – when his father, Time himself, had spoken of him to his other offspring. This child is necessary for my grand design. Do not harm him. Sam had woken in a strange bed, to find a dozen strange faces staring down at him. You are illegitimate, their expressions had screamed. We do not associate with you, save that our father has forced us to. And though we smile and smile and call you friend, there will be whispers behind you always and we will never, ever think of you as one of us. We will drive you out with things unsaid, until you are deafened by them.

Jehovah had cut him out of his life completely. Not a word, friendly or aggressive, polite or sour, had passed between the two of them since the revelation of Sam's true birth. But Sam had heard the rumours spread by the Son of Belief, and known they were honed by one who wielded faith like a sword. It was when the Children of Time had wondered what necessity prompted the honouring of an illegitimate child in Heaven, uncertain whether he was enemy or friend, or of the extent of his powers.

Seth had come in search of him in a grove by a river where Sam liked to sit. There were other people about, but they all avoided his eye. Not Seth.

'Lucifer, isn't it?'

Sam had glanced up questioningly, and automatically risen to his feet on seeing another Son of Time, albeit of dubious reputation. Seth laughed and gestured to him not to stand, sitting down next to him like his oldest friend, at ease in Sam's company already.

'Don't bother with formalities. I'm the lowest villain of Heaven and it's not right that the Son of Magic should honour me.'

'In that case I'm pleased to meet you, villain,' replied Sam. 'What may I do for you?'

'Oh, I'm just up to my usual games. Plotting, scheming.' He waved the words airily away. 'I'm afraid you'll think I am rather abrupt, but I'm only being true to my nature. Tell me, Lucifer – if I may call you that – what are the extent of your powers? I mean, really?'

Sam had hesitated. 'I don't know how to define them,' he'd said finally. A lot of people had been asking him what he could do, whether in quest of an alliance or to know his strength as an enemy. He had grown immediately protective of his magic. It was the only secret still remaining to him.

'Come now, you can tell a villain like me,' said Seth. 'Actually, I'm probably the last person you should tell. I must warn you – all my friends end up hating me very soon.'

'I'll keep that in mind.'

'Come now.' He was wearing a charming, sparkling smile and nudged Sam when he spoke. 'I know you trust me as about as far as you can throw lightning. But that's the point, isn't it? Because you might well be able to throw lightning, for all we know.'

'I fear I really can't help.'

Seth looked ready to urge the point, but instead his smile widened and he threw up his hands in defeat. 'Well, I can understand your position. But if I may ask one more question – don't feel you have to answer if you don't want to – but what is it? The . . . thing inside you that was released when you first put on the crown?'

'I don't know.'

'The plain and honest truth?'

'That's it. Our father told me to put on the crown, and I obeyed. What secret is inside it, what Time's purpose was in giving it to me, I don't know. I assume it's some kind of punishment.'

'Do you? But he described you as the necessary one.'

Sam said nothing, his eyes fixed on some distant point. He had a look of almost serene aloofness. Seth was silent too: a brotherly silence of shared pain or whatever it was he thought Sam might be feeling at that moment.

Finally Seth spoke in his quietest, calmest voice. 'Look. I want to help you – we are brothers, after all. There have been rumours. Whispers. I feel I ought to tell you, that's all.'

Sam turned, his face unreadable. 'Tell me.'

In his most conspiratorial tone, Seth murmured, 'They've been doing research. In the libraries, asking the powers, the elements. There've been a lot of ideas, but the one currently in favour is that this . . . light is a kind of weapon. At the least it will blind or stun a victim if unleashed. No one's sure how it works, but they think the basic principle is that the Light, when released . . . pulls all thoughts, all consciousness, every emotion into itself. To discharge the weapon only requires an exact target, some kind of image superimposed over the spell.'

'Go on.'

'Just imagine it. Every aggressive thought ever, every evil, every sin condensed into one blast of light. Think what would happen to the target. Instant breakdown. Their head would explode.'

Sam said nothing. He was staring into the distance again, listening to another thing left unsaid. At length Seth realised he'd get nothing out of his brother.

He rose to his feet. 'It's only a theory. But there are people out there who believe it – are scared of it, even. The ultimate in destructive power, that's what they're calling it. They're frightened of you. I thought you ought to know.'

He turned in a flurry of well-cut silk and headed away, but Sam's voice made him stop and turn back.

'You haven't mentioned the rest,' said Sam. His voice seemed to be trying to follow his mind, so detached was he. 'The thoughts and emotions of everything the Light could touch, channelled against a single target, would not only destroy the target, but the person who directed it. Used on a grand scale, that is. If a discharge only picked up the thoughts of ten or twenty minds, it would be no problem. The bearer could probably cope with the noise of those minds, even while provoking them to terror or hatred or love.

'But on a grand scale, channelling a million, a billion, *ten* billion minds?' He shook his head. 'The bearer would be adrift in a sea of minds, lose his own identity. If the shock didn't kill him, he'd probably go mad. *I'd* go mad, if I discharged in any other than a small, local way. A thousand minds fighting for space inside my head would be enough to destroy me. I know you know this. Don't pretend otherwise, brother.'

Seth said nothing, but there was sympathy on his face. Whether real or no, Sam couldn't tell. It was a long time before he spoke to his brother again.

NINE

Light and Fire

'Is he coming?'

Whisperer had been waiting in a battered old Toyota, chin resting desolately in his hands. Sam pulled open the passenger door, threw his bag on to the back seat and sat down in a rush, breathless after running up the hill from the local bus. Even so close to Paris, the ride had taken forty minutes, past a seeming eternity of new apartment blocks and huge building sites, out to the surrounding countryside. Whisperer was parked on a wooded hillside with glimpses of a distant river.

'He arrived at a Portal near here half an hour ago.'

The meeting Sam, in the guise of a Moondance traitor, had offered Thor wasn't due for another half an hour. But already he was on edge. 'Is everyone in place?'

'Yes.' Whisperer looked uncomfortable. 'You do realise that if he attacks, we won't be able to help?' As a Prince of Heaven, Thor, like Sam himself, would have total power over those of the Fey.

'Just make sure you don't endanger yourselves. You know where to meet if something goes wrong?' Whisperer nodded.

'Right.' Sam shook Whisperer's ice-cold, insubstantial hand, keeping his grip deliberately light, and scrambled out of the car. He started walking, up a muddy path half overgrown with bracken.

In the cold dimness that follows a winter sunset, a large stone barn lurked amid growing shadows. It had been abandoned for years by everything but invading ivy, and rats. Sam had chosen it for the surrounding woods, which kept it out of the way of most mortals. He could feel the eyes of the Moondance network on his back, a prickle on his neck and the gentle hum of his senses.

Pushing open the old, cracked barn door he stepped into musty gloom, picking his way over floorboards that creaked as if about to collapse. He checked the windows. Most were broken, and brambles or elder had thrust their way in. Yes. It would do.

As he unsheathed his sword, from far off there was the sound of a car engine. He turned, sword raised, hearing the distant thunk of a heavy door, followed soon after by footsteps. Sam retreated deeper into the shadows of the barn. They were early – but wasn't every good contact, to see that the way was clear?

A valkyrie entered first, long sword held lightly in one hand. With a start Sam recognised the same figure of dread he'd encountered on the boat. Following her, with his rune-inscribed axe already out, came a larger, darker figure. Helmet pulled down over his face, obscuring the ruddy features. Long green cloak, soft reindeer boots. Head movements like a pigeon waiting for a cat.

And, to make things worse, the wrong man.

Odin saw Sam, and smiled. 'Hello, little boy. No spirits after all?'

'Where's Thor?'

'He's not the important one, little Lucifer. Little Light and little Fire.'

More figures entered the barn. Valkyries, swords drawn, death in their eyes. Sam began to back away. 'What are you doing?' he asked quietly. 'Why are you chasing after me?'

Odin simply went on smiling. 'You've made a strategic error, Lucifer. You should have thought it out more carefully.'

'You'd kill me, rather than find the man who murdered your sister?'

'You went to Tibet, little Lucifer. You spoke to the abbot. You've been asking questions.'

Sam continued to back away. There were now at least a dozen valkyries in the barn. And Odin was a Son of War. *This is so unfair.*

'How do you know I went to Tibet?' *Something scared the librarian . . . he was found out. By people watching, watching the library, watching the Historian.* 'What are you doing this for?'

Odin shook his head as if in jest. His hands hung at his sides, the huge axe clasped in one as if it were a feather. Sam felt his back touch a wall. Very quietly, in the depths of his mind, he thought, *Shit, this is really not good.*

'I am trying to help!' he exclaimed. 'To find out who killed your sister!'

'But Lucifer, doesn't it occur even to thick-headed you that we might not want you to? Freya died of an overdose of knowledge. You, I fear, will die pathetically ignorant.'

'You don't care,' breathed Sam. 'You're working with whoever killed her! Your sister!'

To his credit, Sam had a good sense of timing. When you're cornered, nowhere left to run, the last thing anyone expects is for you to charge as if the armies of Hell were marching at your back. So, in that moment of bitter revelation, Sam attacked. He went straight for Odin. And as he went, he changed.

He'd been told, long ago, of a race of spirits who treated shadows as real objects, and who could walk as shadows, *become* shadows. This effect he'd learned to copy, crudely, with magic – but making it a dozen times more deadly. By the time he'd taken a pace, his shadow had grown thicker, then begun to cast a shadow of its own. By the time he'd taken a second pace his shadow's shadow had become real. A third pace and there were four Sams, all charging towards the line of valkyries, silver swords raised and murder in their eyes. By the time Sam's sword came up and round to strike Odin, the barn was full of him.

The illusions meant nothing to Odin, who would see through them in a second. But to the valkyries, with eyes less attuned to the otherworldly, they were as real as day. So it was that the valkyries attacked every Sam except the real one. And Sam, plain, quiet little Sam, little light and little fire with his boyish smile too rarely seen in recent times, brought his sword crashing down hard on Odin's upraised axe.

In that second of impact, when Odin's arms seemed to move in a blur to parry Sam's reckless swing for his head, Sam knew he didn't stand a chance. Odin had gone from static to straining in the blink of an eye, a

reaction that Sam, with all his years of hard practice and
cold showers, could never replicate. Against a Son of
War, and in the terms of battle, Sam could not win.
Around him swords were cutting through illusion like
the air and mist they were, and by a process of elimina-
tion the valkyries were turning towards their one real
adversary.

Sword and axe locked, Sam found himself staring
straight into Odin's wide grin. 'What are you doing?'
hissed Sam.

'Pathetically ignorant,' repeated Odin.

Sam gave an inward shrug. 'Then I guess I'll die ignorant. And dishonourable.'

Odin, for all his supremacy as a fighter, had not
expected to be kneed in the groin with such savagery. As
he staggered, Sam broke loose. He ducked a sword
aimed for his head, brought his own blade down and
across to draw a line of blood across a valkyrie's thigh,
drew his sword back to parry a blow – and in that instant
let go with his left hand, to bring it sweeping up.

The air moved. The valkyries staggered in unison, like
an unrehearsed ballet. Sam was already running for the
door. He cleared the valkyries in his path with a graceful
flick of the hand. In response to his gesture the straw in
the barn ignited as if soaked in petrol, scattering them in
panic. Sam himself wasn't worried about the oddly
coloured flames. A well-placed silver axe in the back
would kill him. But not fire.

Just inside the doorway something caught his arm,
spun him around. He looked into Odin's eyes. By firelight they looked more crazed and terrifying than ever.
Sam almost cried aloud as the butt end of Odin's axe
struck his wrist and the pain, then numbness, swept

through his arm. He heard the clatter of his dropped sword, saw Odin's axe sweep towards his face, staggered back and fell. The fire was all around. Its heat was incredible. The pain in his arm was extraordinary too: a dull throb that was somehow worst in his shoulder, while almost impossible to feel where the axe had struck.

Odin loomed. Better than most, Sam decided. If ever he'd been asked to award a sinister-gleam-in-the-eye prize, Odin would have been right there on his shortlist. He wondered what spells he had that Odin couldn't shake off. He felt fire stir inside him. Cold, white, blinding fire. He saw the great axe rise. The thought came . . . *Ah, what the hell. It's only torture.*

He let the fire rise, and burn, and build. Closed his eyes. Opened his hands.

He'd never really understood the nature of the Light. No one had felt obliged to tell him; it was as if, by possessing the thing, he'd immediately understood what it was and how to use it. But he knew that it shaped itself to his thoughts, for as long as they stayed coherent, and that when it reached out to feed on more thoughts it seized, not the hearts of men, but their minds.

So, fallen down in a burning barn, a lone figure with black hair opened his hands, and let out the Light. It expanded around in him a blinding circle of energy, making onlookers shield their eyes in pain. It erupted through walls as if they weren't there, passed through the mind of Whisperer and leaped onwards across the Parisian countryside in an ever widening circle of power.

And where the Light touched minds, they responded to Sam's own fear. Thus it whispered to them of dark corners and unseen snakes and the empty street late at night and the figure half-perceived in the lamplight who was gone when you looked again. It took the fear, fed on it, became powerful on thought.

Sam could feel his control slipping as the Light encompassed so many other minds. He tried to rein back his mind, but it was hard to remember that he was Sam, not Jean-Paul nor Jeanette nor Julien, hard to remember that he was afraid of being consumed by the Light, rather than of the spiders in the garden and the rats in the sewers and the figure who was gone when you looked again, and the corners and the darkness and the minds and the fire . . .

He caught hold of something inside his own mind that felt as if it were hot to the touch. Mentally he closed his fist around it and thought of the pain in his shoulder. *His* shoulder, something to centre on, his heart, his mind, his desires.

Somewhere in the distance, the running white line of light slowed, paused, and began to contract in on itself, racing back towards the centre, growing brighter as it did. It struck Sam, who lurched as if physically hit. For a second all was darkness. Odin was reeling, blinking away tears. The valkyries dared to look in Sam's direction again . . . What next?

Sam's eyes opened. The black irises were pure white, and the thoughts that before had given such life to his face were lost. There were simply too many other minds competing for room.

There was a brief silence. Then, with the distant smile of a madman, Sam raised his hands and opened them. A beam of white light shot towards Odin, struck, spun him around like a puppet. The full force of a thousand people's fears passed through Sam and out again, filled the barn with the chitter of insects coming to kill, the howl of wolves in the forest, the buzz of the broken lamp on the darkened street that for a second showed the half-perceived figure in the gloom . . .

Odin had rarely been heard to scream. When he did, it wasn't a particularly impressive sound, caught as it was between a gurgle and a gasp. Now, however, for a second he was rooted to the spot. Then he turned, stared at the fire as if he'd seen death in it, and ran. The valkyries fled too, charging into each other in their haste to escape whatever unseen demon pursued them.

Somehow, Sam moved. He got to his hands and knees, tried to rise and half fell again. His face contorted as he squeezed his eyes shut and put his hands over his ears against the roar of all those minds.

Strangely, though he could clearly perceive Odin's mind, there were no words. Just images. On the one hand the terror of the unknown, the clattering of claws on stone stairs, the feeling of being watched but not seeing who was there . . . Yet, on the other, he sensed the determination that this enemy – he, Lucifer – should fall, and heard Odin's thought that truly this was a weak Bearer of Light.

Seen the faces.

The face of the man in the picture he'd been given in Tibet. Andrew. Odin had seen Andrew. More faces. Freya, as beautiful in death as in life. Jehovah, handsome enough as seen now through Odin's eyes, images of the two shaking hands, memories of voices. *Your house is falling, Odin*, whispered the memory of Jehovah that Sam had never had until this moment, plucked from Odin's mind. *My house has always been isolated, alone. Together, we can be strong.* Memories that weren't his, flashing across his mind too fast to see. Others too, familiar faces that suddenly, for the first time, Sam found he didn't understand. Thor, Seth, Michael, Uriel.

Who, out of these last, might be just a tool? And who Odin's accomplice?

Then there was the terror of the Light's discharge. And Odin's thought. *He does know how to use it! He knows how it can kill . . .*

The door was thrust open and Whisperer erupted in, shaken to the core. He too had felt the repercussions.

'Light have mercy,' Whisperer exclaimed as he helped Sam stagger to his feet. 'You released it?'

'Blindfold,' whispered white-eyed Sam, pleading for an act of mercy.

Whisperer reached into a pocket and produced a spotted scarf, with which he deftly bound Sam's eyes. Then he picked up the sword and, like a nurse leading a frail old patient from the operation room, he helped Sam stagger to the Toyota, and away.

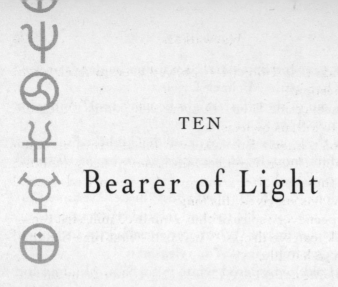

TEN

Bearer of Light

S am was aware that they were driving to the airport, or so he'd been told by Whisperer. But he was sure of nothing else in his ringing, burning world made only slightly more bearable by the darkness of the blindfold.

'Why did you do it?' demanded Whisperer.

'Odin was one of them. He's in it as deep as anybody.'

'Who else?'

'There lies the problem. There were so many others, once I got a sight of his mind. I did see Jehovah – he was one who stood out. But as to what it means . . .'

Whisperer fell silent. He drove like all spirits, carefully, and exactly on the speed limit. Like all spirits, he disliked cars, and motorways especially. To his mind, every car was a monster trying to catch him, and it was only grim necessity that forced him into the driving seat. He held the steering wheel with the very ends of his fingers, as if disgusted to be touching it.

'What would you have done if it got out of control?'

'It didn't, so I don't feel obliged even to think about that question.'

Silence again. Then, 'Do you really think Odin conspired to kill his own sister?'

'I don't know. But whoever killed Freya is being incredibly clever. I think Odin is out to keep me busy, while they go after Andrew. I'm surprised mortal Andrew has survived this long.'

'I expect every spirit within a hundred miles felt the—'

'Look, can we drop it?' It was the first time Sam had spoken so harshly.

This time not even Whisperer dared break the silence.

Sam shifted uneasily. 'Can we have the radio on?' he asked, in a tone made contrite by his outburst. Usually he didn't like most radio, French or otherwise. Much of it seemed a mad dash for the end of the story, or a brash ditty summing up the mindless haste of mortal life.

Whisperer pressed a button on the dashboard.

'Your voices too loud?'

'They're fading.'

'How are your eyes?'

'Don't know.' Sam raised the blindfold, blinking fast as though a flash had just gone off in his face. 'Ouch.'

Whisperer glanced at him. 'They've gone grey. Nearly there, then.'

With a sigh and a shudder, Sam replaced the blindfold and sat back again.

'Don't worry, you've got plenty of time.' Whisperer pressed more buttons on the radio until he found some soothing music. After a release, Sam's mind was full of things he could only guess at. 'Go straight to the hotel, assuming you can see straight. I've arranged for one of our jinn to meet you there. I'll be following by the Way

of Fey, and Adamarus will join us as soon as he's sure
he's not watched.'

As so often when leaving for another country, Sam
was faced with an instant change of nationality. This time
to prepare himself he began reciting in Russian. 'Three
times three is nine,' he chanted. 'I am the devil incarnate,
what do you do? There are some languages where you
need a bad cold for perfect pronunciation. I haven't been
to Russia for years. How's my accent?'

'Fine,' replied Whisperer, in the same guttural language. 'How do you intend to find the mortal, with such
tight security around him?'

'The nasty way. I'll find someone in Odin's employ-
ment and beat the living daylights out of him or her until
they tell me where to go.'

At the airport Sam walked unsteadily across the car
park, passing from one orange pool of light to another
while overhead the planes pointed their noses to the sky
and blasted upward.

'You up to this?' asked Whisperer.

'You suggest I Waywalk in this condition?' Sam
asked, attempting a counterfeit humour. He'd taken off
the blindfold, but Whisperer was concerned to see how
his usually boyish smile was pained and how his eyes still
burnt light grey. *Were I human, this would be a friend*, he
thought with a sense of shock. *Were I human, what I feel
now would be loyalty. What an interesting concept.*

'Oh hell, the German accent,' Sam exclaimed, fumbling in a pocket for his Sebastian Teufel passport. 'And
we'd better get the other passports out of the bag and
into my pocket. At least I won't be searched.'

'I'll be interested to see how you get that through

customs.' Whisperer indicated the sword slung once again over Sam's back. 'What if they want to put that through the machine?'

'You just watch a master do his work.'

They walked to the Air France desk, where Sam attempted to speak French with a German accent as he handed over his passport for inspection, before claiming his single ticket to Moscow. *If you have to start searching for Andrew anywhere, let it be the centre.* Sam was still blinking painfully and his voice was laden with fatigue. Observing his condition Whisperer said, 'Try humming. That'll shut out the sounds in your head.'

Sam began humming 'Swing Low Sweet Chariot', out of tune and with no real conviction, but the frown uncreased slightly between his brows, and his grey eyes continued to darken.

At the boarding gate he took Whisperer's hand. 'Thank you for everything you've done.'

'See you in Moscow,' replied Whisperer. 'Just as soon as I find a Fey Portal.'

Only spirits used Fey Portals. Whether it was the same principle as Waywalking, Sam couldn't tell.

He said, 'Watch your back.'

'I always do. Aren't I the one who gets lost in the fog?'

'Of course. I hope Adamarus is as good as you at losing followers, being the blown end of the network.'

'It's hard to track through a Feywalk.'

The queue moved a little further towards the metal detector and customs, and Sam touched a finger to his lips, a little of his old humour returning. 'Now why don't you watch Satan weave his magic? You may be able to use it yourself.'

Whisperer laughed. 'Mortal minds are no one's domain but yours.'

He knew as soon as the words were out how misjudged they were, considering the torrent of voices Sam was still receiving in his fragile state. Sam however made nothing of them beyond a gesture of acknowledgement. He turned and walked towards the gate, his face assuming the empty look of every commuter catching a late flight.

'If you wouldn't mind putting your bags through the machine, sir. And if you could remove all metal objects.'

Sam unslung his luggage and laid it on the machine. He emptied some loose change from his pocket, and without a qualm he stepped through the metal detector. The dagger failed completely to alert the machine.

A security officer was staring intently at the screen as Sam's bag, containing both sword and crown, began to pass through the machine. Indeed, thought Whisperer, watching from a distance, he was staring so intently it was a wonder his eyes didn't pop out.

Suddenly the man sneezed, then sneezed again, huge explosions that shook his whole body. Tears sprang to his eyes and he groped blindly for a packet of tissues before blowing his nose with the sound of a volcano in full eruption. In the meantime Sam's bags had passed through the system without provoking a peep. He retrieved them without glancing back at Whisperer, the magician who has carried off a perfect trick. The only clue that he was even slightly different from the other travellers was a smug gleam in the corner of his still-darkening eyes.

He was like that, thought Whisperer. You brace yourself for a huge performance involving fireworks, and the minds of mortals being re-written in bursts of concentrated magic, and all Sam does is tickle the man's nose.

Sam Linnfer, Luc Satise, Sebastian Teufel, Lucifer, Satan, the evil one – whatever you wished to call him, as he himself would say – stepped on to international territory towards an uncertain truth locked in the mind of a mortal.

No one disturbed him on the plane. He appeared to be asleep, with the blindfold over his eyes and his headphones playing whatever in-flight music channel he'd first found. Apart from the occasional yowl of a child, the whole plane was silenced by sleep. It was the kind of silence in which the hum of the engines became more pronounced, along with the odd shudder whenever they encountered turbulence.

But Sam wasn't sleeping. How could he, when his eyes burned so and the whispers of numberless other minds still filled his head? Which was why he was listening to the in-flight entertainment – endless songs about the trauma of breaking up, played, probably, by people with the same hairstyles. At least it shut out some of the voices.

He'd nearly lost control; that was what shocked him most. He'd come so close to losing what little power he held over . . . *it*. That buried curse, written into blood and bone in lines of fire and left to haunt him for the rest of his days. And he'd nearly let it loose.

'When you release it, does it hurt?'

Annette speaking. He glanced up from his study of the map, surprised by her question. In this deep, cold cellar full of old wine bottles and spider's webs, they'd been discussing the local Resistance's plan for sabotaging a military plant. Her query had come from nowhere. At twenty-six, Annette was a woman made wise by war. From a spring evening in pre-war Paris this bourgeoise, who'd thought the whole world was made up of cocktail parties, had lost a husband, had learnt to parachute and kill with her bare hands, and, in her own quaint way, had sold her soul to Satan.

But, as Sam often said, she hadn't made him an offer. She'd just thrust her soul upon him.

'Does what hurt?' he asked, annoyed at being taken out of his train of thought.

'The Light. When you release it. Does it hurt?'

He went on looking at the map, but no longer seeing it clearly. 'Sometimes more than others. It depends how far it goes. Usually the after-effects hurt more than the actual release.'

'It seems strange.'

'What does?'

'Well . . .' she gestured vaguely. 'You're the Devil. Surely you should release pure darkness or something?'

'Define "pure darkness".'

'Oh, come on!'

'No, seriously. What effect would pure darkness have on the world, were it released?'

She looked uncomfortable. 'I don't know. Kill everything, I guess.'

'And what's the effect of the so-called "Light" in me?'

She didn't answer his question. "Lucifer . . . Luc . . .'

'It burns. It blinds. It consumes its vessel and opens the souls of men, removes every stitch of human privacy and bares the darkest, deepest thoughts of mortal minds, makes them sing their lies and their selfish plans to him who hears. It only makes the lies and the hatred sing, though. It opens none of the goodness in the heart. Subjected thus, is it really so surprising that the Devil should possess it?'

'I guess not,' she'd replied. Sam, for a few brief seconds, had been his age, twice his age, when talking of the Light within. It always unsettled her, to be reminded that she would grow old and die, but that this man before her would stay as he was now. The Bearer of Light. The eternal shadow that haunts sinners. Her Luc Satise. Yet no one's Luc.

Annette had also asked him once, 'Why are you Sam?'

He'd been surprised – it had taken her until 1969 to put this question. Perhaps she'd only now mustered the recklessness to delve into something she'd vowed to keep out of in 1941.

Already there was a streak of premature grey in her hair, though he'd been too polite to mention it.

'I know it, you know. You think I'm getting old.'

He opened his mouth to say something along the line of, 'No, of course not' – and saw her expression. 'Oh.'

'"Oh?" What does "oh?" mean?'

'Just "oh?" As in . . . no matter what I really think, I've never once won an argument against you.'

'Do you still drink coffee?'

'My tastes are liable to all sorts of change. Two thousand years ago I ate dormice with the rest of Rome.'

'I never believed they ate those.'

'You wouldn't believe a lot of the things they got up to in Rome. Civilisation leads to boredom, and boredom leads to anarchism, but in a very *civilised* way.'

'And I imagined *you'd* remind me of my youth. You sound older than I look.'

'There might be a reason for that,' he pointed out mildly.

She smiled faintly, turning her head to one side. 'You've met my husband?'

'The man outside weeding the garden?'

'Yes. This is his house. That's his grandfather on the wall, that's his sofa, that's his whisky cabinet.'

'Ah.' The man Sam had seen outside looked like a character out of Charles Dickens – complete with fob watch, whiskers and quite possibly a top hat in some wardrobe upstairs in the grand mansion that Annette was currently calling her home. The 1960s seemed to have passed by this rural English village without anyone being aware of what they were missing. Except Annette, of course.

'He was in the war.'

'Ah. What did he do?'

'A navy captain.'

'Wow. I'd never have thought that . . .'

'Stationed in the Caribbean.'

'Oh. Well, I mean . . .'

'Luc, stop stuttering.' She stared at him. Then she burst out laughing.

'What?'

'I can't believe I'm chiding a man thousands of years older than I am, in my motherly voice.'

'I'm used to it. "Do you know how old I am, young man?" – "Who, me? I'm just walking down the street here." – "Yes, you! When I was young, men were different! What's your name? . . . Sam? What kind of name is that?"'

'Well? What kind of name is it?'

'Sam. Derivative of Satan.'

'And Luc derives from Lucifer?'

'Which one do you prefer?'

He shrugged. 'Lucifer is the name I was given at birth. Satan is what they dubbed me, when they found out what my real name meant. Bearer of Light is hardly a friendly way to describe the soul of darkness, evil incarnate, the great deceiver.' He spoke bitterly, his mind cast back to things he'd tried to forget.

'But what do you prefer, of your human names?'

'None. They're necessary, that's all. Luc reminds me of what I truly am. Sam reminds me of the disdain of my own brothers and sisters – who threw me out of Heaven for being what I am. The bastard son. The necessary one, where all of them were clearly not necessary. And though Time passed bitter judgement on me, still he gave me a crown. Still they think he favoured me.'

'And of course, you tempted Adam from the Garden of Eden.'

At this he openly laughed, making Annette blush. Whenever Sam laughed for no reason she felt a pang of insufficiency. *Who knows what he's seen in his life? I am a child in his hands.*

'Do you really believe that?' he demanded. 'Surely you of all people don't believe in the Garden?'

'Well, what was it you were banished for?'

'I was banished for following my conscience, and you people should all damn well thank me for it!'

'Why?'

'I *saved* Adam. Not that his name was Adam. There was a host of them, anyway. Ready to die for their various interesting deities, so that a group of self-important Waywalkers could fulfil their misguided dream and step to the place above Heaven. It was a pathetic, brutal, stupid experiment and I' – he gave a mock bow – 'was Castro to their Baptista.'

'Above Heaven?'

'Eden,' he explained softly. 'The realm of the greatest, warmest Powers. Powers that make Time look rather vulgar. Eden.'

'And you stopped them? Why?'

'Because,' he explained, still smiling, 'if my mad brothers had gone through with their scheme to get into Eden, not only would your precious Adam and Eve have perished, but humankind wouldn't have lasted long enough to invent the wheel.'

But it wasn't just following your conscience, was it? thought Sam sourly of himself. *I was trying to prove something. I was trying to free myself of something, and I thought that by doing what I did it would be enough. What a fool I was.*

'This is your captain speaking. We will be arriving in Moscow in one hour's time.'

'Tell me about your father.'

Again, later. When the 1960s were well and truly over and the 1980s were trying to pretend they weren't as systems-built as they seemed.

'What's there to tell?'

Annette had shrugged. 'How can Time be King of Heaven?'

'How can he not be? Time conquers all, Time is the inescapable fate, everywhere, everywhen. Time knows how the universe will end, sees his own demise. Yours. Mine. And does nothing, save keep the clocks ticking.'

In Heaven, the Room of Clocks. A room that roars with

ticking. The walls, the ceiling, the huge floor are covered with clocks, sundials, hourglasses, candles of every kind ... When these clocks stop, Time will be dead. When they begin to run anticlockwise —

'What would happen, if your father ever died?'

'Ah. Now you're talking about Cronus.'

When they begin to run anticlockwise, Cronus will be king. And when they stop altogether, it's because we've all been compressed down to a single point of existence. Not alive, not dead, just there. *Inside Cronus. For ever.*

He reached across and took her hand in his, something she'd demanded increasingly during the rough period after divorcing her third husband; her hair was now entirely grey. 'Feel my pulse?' he asked, gently pressing her fingers against his wrist.

'Yes.'

'That's a sign of life. With every heartbeat I drain the existence of Time a little further, stealing a few more seconds off his life. But everyone does that, and Time's life is a thousand, million, billion times greater than the universe. But if Cronus usurped Time, there would be no pulse. Where we feed on Time's life, where my pulse keeps perfect rhythm with my father's, Cronus feeds on *our* life. He will let us be reduced to the tiniest thought, but he will keep us there, taking our thoughts and our souls, which will still produce the smallest spark, until the universe is just one factory for his desires. Cronus is the only creature in the universe who doesn't feed on Time, but on that part of the universe that's timeless. He is not-life, not-death, he is a very, very simplistic way of existence, compressed down to a single point and going nowhere, never changing.' He shrugged. 'Timeless.'

'Like what? What is there that is timeless?' she asked

scornfully. 'You're always going on about how Time controls everything.'

'Not everything. There are things that are frozen outside Time's reach. Concepts are timeless. Human hate a thousand years ago is the same as human hate today. The same applies to love. The same to compassion. The same to envy. Memories are timeless – you either have them, or you don't. Cronus feeds on those memories, until their owners are reduced to nothing. Cronus feeds on those concepts, until all that remains is the bare bones of anyone who feels those things. Where Time gives life and the future, Cronus takes souls and the past, freezing everything in place, *inside himself*. There would be no death, under Cronus. But there would be no life either.'

She sat still for a long time, feeling his pulse in her hand. 'You say Time is everywhere, in the future, in the past. It's all the same to him.'

'Yes.'

'Then he saw that war would come?'

'Yes. He's seen every war, and every man who dies in it.'

'Why doesn't he stop it?'

'What? Time freeze the world and say, "No, this shall not be"? And what then, when these armies are frozen in place? How would that be better than Cronus, keeping armies suspended in living death? Time didn't set evolution in process, you know. He doesn't control the minds of humans. All he does is maintain them.'

'Yet you say he deliberately made sure Magic conceived you. Why?'

'To use me. Just because Time doesn't affect human lives, he's not above letting humans affect humans, or even immortals. He created me so that I could make some piece of history happen in a certain way. Why, I don't know. What, I don't know. But I'm sure that, when that history is supposed to be made, I'll spot it. Time is not an entity who'd create a pawn and let it waste its life – his life – on a worthless cause.'

'He doesn't directly interfere?'

'Good grief, no. Too dangerous. There are hundreds of Powers out there, hundreds of Incarnates. Not many Greater Powers, it has to be said, but the odds are that there's always a bigger fish. And they've all got their invested interests and schemes. For Time to say directly to one Power, "This shall be so, because I command it" or, "I rule here, you shall go elsewhere" is to risk upsetting a system that is already . . . unstable, shall we say?'

'How unstable?'

'Well, the last time the Greater Powers had a really impressive argument, the dinosaurs got wiped out. So now Time always works through mortals. So he can just sit back and go, "Nah, I didn't do nothing."'

'You're afraid,' she said softly.

'What makes you say that?'

'Even speaking of it, your pulse is faster.' She smiled faintly. 'I was trained to spot these things, you know.'

Self-consciously he extracted his wrist from her grasp and sat back, not meeting her eyes. 'I'm afraid,' he agreed. 'Time conquers all, but sometimes he has lessons to teach. I'm afraid he's going to use me to teach that lesson for him.'

'What do you mean?'

He rolled his head back on his shoulders wearily, as if beset by old aches and pains. 'Think about it. You've read the New Testament, were brought up a good

Christian. Lessons in it are taught by a man who died on the cross at Roman hands, or so the legend goes.' She opened her mouth to ask a question, but he was already there. 'Many people died on the cross, Annette. I know, I was there. But my point is, the symbolism of this death has sent shivers through history and rewritten the whole course of the world. Now Time sees, as well as the past, present and future, the pasts and presents which could be. So you see why I'm afraid. I'm afraid that to make a certain future happen instead of another, he is willing to let my death "repercuss" through the ages. Without consultation first, I might add.'

'Why? For what possible purpose would he sacrifice you?'

'I don't know. This is all hypothetical, you understand. I can't see the future. I can only study the past, and wonder if my father is going to let us go round and round in circles for ever, or if he is already teaching those lessons to shape those worlds, and I haven't noticed.'

'Time conquers all,' she murmured. 'Except Cronus.'

'Except Cronus,' Sam agreed. 'It's almost reassuring to know there's something my father can't cope with.'

His eyes had returned to black, the voices were all but gone. *Is my fate inescapable? Father, I know you can hear me, because every thought I give takes Time, takes some of you. Have you seen my entire future, and don't care? Are you going to let me die so that some reality comes to pass instead of another? And what possible interest could you have in fixing realities, unless you were afraid of things that lurked in other futures? What are you so afraid of, Father, that you would let my eyes burn so and fill my mind with the thoughts of mortals? Or don't you care?*

There was, as ever, no answer.

Sam remembered when the Moondance network had been founded.

Adamarus had been astonished. 'Intervene? You? *Us?*'

'Yes.'

'Where? Why? How?'

'Everywhere, in every way possible. Because what the mortals are doing is not only in violation of every human morality, but should even strike a few chords with the Fey. It takes a lot of evil to do that, so when chords are struck it's only . . . moral' – he savoured the word – 'that we do something.'

'You're lecturing me on morals? *You?*'

'You shouldn't believe everything you read in the Bible, Torah or Koran, you know. I'm really a nice guy.'

It was Jehovah. At least Sam felt comforted by the blessing of blame. *Jehovah did this to me, made my name a curse. Jehovah was the one who first coined the term 'Satan'. Son of Belief, what did you do to me?*

The music in his headphones was fading again – the inflight entertainments were more trouble than they were worth. But now his head was almost free of the voices, and he could focus the full force of his resentment against Jehovah. *Not hate*, he reminded himself. *To hate is to be what they want me to be, and I'll never do that.*

ELEVEN

Could-Be City

Moscow is one of those could-be cities. It could be one of the greatest in the world, with its imperial architecture, and its strange old buildings mingling east and west. It could be beautiful, it could be regarded as the centre of the world, were it not for the burden of a crushing past, and a climate so harsh that much of Russia might as well have been wiped from the map. So many could-bes were buried here, in dark suburbs and litter-filled streets which, after resisting for so long, had yielded to the omnipresent American chain stores.

At night, when the streets around Sam's suburban hotel were deserted, and a bitter wind tore at the icicles hanging from the lips of buildings and disturbed little giddies of dirty snow, the darker, haunted Moscow came to life. He could almost hear its whispers of a bitter past, and thought of all those people – Napoleon, the Bolsheviks, the invading Germans, banned and angry ethnic minorities – who'd wanted to tear this ghost apart.

My life consists of one inescapable, seedy hotel, Sam thought as he staggered out of the ancient, unlicensed taxi that had been all he could get at the airport. The hotel was a run-down building lodged between an old café and a large grey housing estate.

'Sebastian Teufel,' he told the woman on reception. 'I've booked.'

He was greeted with the usual Russian warmness, and wondered whether it sprung from genuine delight at seeing a foreigner, or at seeing a foreigner's wallet. He'd barely remembered to exchange his euros at the airport; what would she have done if he'd tried paying in foreign currency? *Probably accepted it with a smile*.

The room seemed no different from the one in Paris he'd left only that morning, save that there was mould in one corner and the wallpaper was peeling even more freely. Somehow he managed to draw a ward on the door and window, and collapsed on the bed, not bothering to take off his boots.

How long Sam slept, he didn't know. But by the time he heard a respectful knock on his door, full daylight was stealing through the thin curtain. From outside there came the crash of ice falling in the sunshine.

Groaning and feeling dirty, Sam struggled out of bed, taking half the sheets with him, and opened the door. 'Yes?' he snapped.

A slight creature stood there, wearing a large fur hat above tufts of hair so red they must surely be dyed. Seeing Sam he bowed respectfully low. The word that came first to Sam's mind was 'skateboarder'. He had the build of an athlete, but the wild red hair and intelligent eyes whispered of a different life entirely. After discarding skateboarder as a description, Sam found himself reminded of textbook pictures showing spiky-haired Celtic warriors charging to kill or, as was more often the case, be killed.

He waited for the man's first words, curious to hear his diagnosis either proven or denied.

'Your honour.'

'What?' Sam was taken aback. 'Your honour' was neither the language of a skateboarder nor a Celtic warrior.

'Your honour, I have been sent by Whisperer.'

Invited in, the man seemed to walk on nothing, and when Sam passed too near him in the cluttered room, there was an improbable sensation of heat radiating off his padded body. Heat, and the smell of . . . leaves? By the time Sam had turned on the tap, hit it until water began to flow, and stuck his head in the sink, realisation was dawning. The shock of the ice-cold water on his skin jerked everything into focus. That and the fact that all the time he was washing himself the man had just stood next to the bed, not even sitting down. Now Sam knew why.

'You're the jinn, right?'

The creature bowed again. 'Indeed, your honour.'

'Cut the honour crap. Right now I'm Sebastian, and would like to stay that way.'

The jinn seemed astonished at this informality. It had clearly expected someone, or something, more . . . Satanic. Sam, being as he was strong-willed and proud, quickly found himself annoyed at the diffidence shown by the jinn. At the same time he recognised, in the stiff way the creature bore itself, that here was a spirit that had probably had its own share of fights. Certainly it looked like a warrior – but a warlike Celt who'd decided against screaming defiance in favour of the temperament expected from the treasurer of a cricket club. The result was an unsettling combination which made Sam feel that behind this external conflict of warrior and clerk lurked the worst aspects of both.

'What's your name?'

'I use the human name of Peter Zhukov, your — sir.'

'Sir' was an improvement on 'your honour', but Sam was in no mood for tolerance, especially towards a creature as confusing as the jinn. In Sam's fatigued state, being confused made his annoyance even harder to suppress.

'Have you anything to tell me?'

'About the mortal you seek? Yes, sir.'

'Well? And please, sit down.'

The jinn sat nervously on the edge of the bed as though it were some holy object. He was clutching a large bag, which he opened as though only just thinking of it. From it he produced a black overcoat of the long thick kind favoured by Russians. 'I brought this for you, sir. It's colder here than in Paris.'

Sam took the gift gratefully, feeling some of his animosity fade away. 'How, uh, foresightful. Thank you . . . The mortal?'

'He is here, sir.'

'Here?' Such unexpected news caught Sam off guard.

'Yes, sir. In Moscow itself.'

'How do you know?'

'His pursuers are here, and have been for several days. Two valkyries have been recorded, one angel and two Firedancers. All of them are searching through the city.'

Sam raised a hand. 'Do you mind if I'm sceptical?' Ignoring Peter's astonishment at such a query, he added, 'If the valkyries, angel and Firedancers are working together, rather than trying to kill each other, why haven't they found him?'

'They're not working together, sir. Yesterday there was an open confrontation between the Firedancers and the angel, and at least once the valkyries have almost come to blows with all of them. And there's more, sir.'

'There's a surprise.'

'Someone is shielding the mortal. We can't see or find them, but we know they're there.'

'How?'

'A few of us tried scrying the mortal in anticipation of your arrival. We ran up hard against a blank, sir.'

So. Andrew has friends as well as enemies. 'Who else is watching for Andrew, besides archangels and the like?'

'A small witches' coven, some mercenary spirits of our own.'

'Witches? What kind? There are so many.'

'They won't know anything, sir. No one ever tells mortals why they're watching, just who to watch for.'

Sam was silent a long while, digesting the jinn's words. The creature waited, sitting upright on the edge of the bed and radiating alertness and duty.

Sam said, 'Whisperer told me many of our sources are being blocked. How is that?'

'There have been raids on the mortal cover offices of local spirits known to be loyal to the Moondance network. Those who do not use cover have been openly attacked. Never hurt, just repulsed from the area round Moscow. There is a tight cordon of mercenaries about. The mercenaries are here to keep us out, while the

Heavenly scouts look for the Historian. In the meantime someone is shielding him from harm.'

Sam looked thoughtful. 'In Tibet the abbot told me Andrew had known I was coming. And that he'd advised the abbot to help me.'

'Sir?'

'I'm wondering about the nature of this shield. Whether it might let me pass, for friendship's sake.'

'It seemed a very good shield, sir.'

'I'm a very good magician,' Sam replied. Not correcting, but stating the truth.

Someone knows I'm not just trying to find Andrew. They know I'm on the trail and getting closer – in the right city, even.

'What will you do, sir?'

'Right now? Have a shower and a very big breakfast.'

This whole business is a walled city, with the answer somewhere inside. Through Freya's death, Odin's enmity, Andrew's flight and the abbot's revelation I can see clearly the size and shape of the walls. But until I find the Historian all gates are barred to me.

Breakfast consisted of 'authentic European cuisine' – greasy eggs and bacon on a plate where two red stains marked what had once been grilled tomatoes. Looking at it, Sam reflected that he hadn't come to Russia to eat what he could get in any of his European homes.

As he ate he considered the pressing question of Freya's security methods. How had they failed? They must have been tight, judging by how she'd so secluded Andrew, her prime researcher. Even Sam, on Earth so much longer than the other Princes, had failed to recognise that she, one of his sisters, must be on to something.

All those backup systems. How long had Freya known she'd turn to Sam for help, if necessary? How long had Sam been the unwitting accomplice, the one relied on to find the answers and go to the right places? *Is everyone, my father, my sister, fated to use me as their unwitting pawn? Even Jehovah used me to his advantage, with his half-mortal youth, and I naïvely helped him on his way.*

Sitting opposite him Peter watched without a word while Sam breakfasted. All the jinn had was a cup of coffee. If Sam correctly remembered the feeding habits of most jinn, they had more . . . unusual tastes than human catering could supply.

Perhaps it was the confident way Sam pushed back his plate and stretched his fingers to their furthest extent. Whatever it was that prompted Peter, the jinn suddenly looked up and said, 'You've decided what to do, sir?' It wasn't really a question.

'I have. If Freya's plan was tight enough to wheel me in so effectively, then I'll bet she's still reaching from the grave to clear my way. I'm going to scry for him."

Sam had to confess that Peter was a good worker. There was many a sly glance out of the corner of the jinn's eye as he scrutinised Sam's face. And whenever Sam turned quickly enough to catch his look, or appeared even slightly annoyed, Peter would immediately bow as though the fault were his.

His competence spoke volumes as they returned to Sam's room. Without a word Peter went to the washbasin, put in the plug and turned on the tap. Here was someone, diffident or not, who understood scrying. Briskly he filled the basin with ice-cold water, pulling the threadbare curtains shut and hanging his coat over them so that the room was lit only by the single yellow bulb in the centre of the ceiling.

For his part, the jinn looked on respectfully as Sam set to work, turning off the light so that the room was plunged into near-darkness behind the makeshift black-out, and going to the sink with the casualness of a master about an everyday task. Outside, the roar of traffic seemed suddenly louder. In the street a couple were fighting noisily. A pair of cats hissed at each other in backyard rivalry. A baby was yowling. By night a half-asleep child might fashion any kind of story from such neighbourhood music.

Sam heard none of it as he lowered his hands, palms down, a few inches above the surface of the water. How squalid, Peter thought, to be performing such magic in these conditions. A Prince of Heaven should be casting his spells over marble pools, in temples brilliant with candlelight. Everything here seemed an insult to the greatness of a Waywalker: the improvised blind wedged over the sagging curtain rail, the pink plastic basin, the plywood wardrobe. Peter wanted to exclaim that, no, they could do better than this – anywhere but this sad, noisy little room.

But Sam was already in the spell, indifferent to the grimy sink and its matching cracked mirror. Peter found his own indignation converting to self-reproach. Who was he to care about such details, when they meant nothing to a being who could walk between worlds and summon all-destroying magic? He kept his peace, and watched the magic do its work.

A scry, Sam had once announced, is just like a magical television. This had failed to arouse the expected reaction

from his audience of spirits, who'd wanted to hear that a
scry was the greatest magical advancement ever devised,
and that its manipulation of images defied understanding.

No, Sam had said flatly. It is, like a TV, a particle
accelerator, and the mind is your remote control. We
press a certain button to tell the TV what it is we want to
see, a signal is sent to the TV, and the TV switches to the
correct channel and receives an image. This image is then
projected against the screen by hurling particles towards
it at a very high speed. So it is with a scry. The only difference is that with a scry the TV takes its power directly
from the one who presses the remote control, and if you
take your finger off the button the signal will die.

Oh yes. And it may be necessary to hit your TV now
and again, to make it work.

Light glowed beneath Sam's fingers, a misty whiteness
that, as in his imaginary TV, filled the surface of the
water, from an unseen thought. Sam thought of Andrew,
of the picture he'd been given of that freckled smiling
youth. He pressed down on the image and made it the
focus of his command, telling the scry to find *this* signal
and this one only.

It was slow in coming, but at last it was there. The
same freckled face – but the eyes were now tired, heavy
from not sleeping. Andrew wore a filthy old coat and his
hair was a mess. He hadn't shaved for days; already a full
beard was starting to grow from stubble, though Sam
wasn't sure if this was meant as a disguise. There were
lines across his brow and around his eyes and mouth that
hadn't been there in the picture.

Then, abruptly – as soon as the image was there – it
was gone, and what remained was just a pulsing white
mistiness beneath Sam's fingers. He pressed for the

image once more, but it was as if a solid wall resisted him. Taking a deep breath, half unaware that he did so, Sam fell to studying this obstacle that so repulsed him.

He was the only Son of Magic and Time. If he couldn't get past a mere shield . . .

Yes, he saw its weaknesses – typical flaws in typical spots. The slight failures where spells had been tied, tiny imperfections in its otherwise immaculate casting. This wasn't the work of a human or even of an ordinary spirit. Truly Andrew's friend was someone powerful.

Just in time, he decided against tearing it down. The process would have been laborious – one of many hard classroom tasks his mother had used to set, testing his endurance, back before he'd even known the other side of his parentage. And, once it was down, others would find themselves able to scry. That was something to avoid at any cost. If Andrew was going to be found, he had to be the first one there.

He began skirting the surface of the shield, probing for receptor spells, which, like a human body, could read the antigens on the surface of an attacker and detect how best to repulse it. Usually it was something he never did – to be declared to an enemy was to lose your best weapon. But he did it now, relying on Freya's foresight for the shield to let him in.

And there it was. A receptor spell grafted hastily to the surface of the shield itself, exactly where he would have put it. Judging by the way other powers still clung to it in their various different shades of magic, more than one person had also run into this spell and been classified enemy.

But Sam opened himself wide to the spell and let it roll over him, felt it clawing through the depths of his magic to his deepest soul in search of proof as to who he was and what were his intents. And behind the spell, a conscious mind. Weary, battered by too many attacks – the same mind that had and was sustaining this cursed shield. He opened himself to it fully, whispering through the spell, *I am a friend. You know who I am and what I want. You know I want to help.*

He felt the other consciousness stir. An old, old mind, fatigued from battle, yet radiating such determination, and such pain. Sam found himself wanting to be one with it, to comfort whoever it might be that felt such things. His sudden urge to murmur, like a kindly parent, 'There, there,' shocked every part of him that had ever claimed the name of Devil.

<You came.> A whisper of thought, so relieved that he felt his heart lighten in sympathy. <Time be praised, you came.> Suddenly the voice deepened, darkened. <Help me.>

<What would you have me do?>

<I can't sustain the shield much longer. Help me!>

<Where's Andrew? I can get him to safety.>

Images flooded his mind. A square, a little café just visible behind the crowds of men and women trudging by. The crash of ice as it fell from the eaves on to the pavement below. Feeding his own strength into the other mind, Sam twisted the image in search of something, anything, that might suggest where this place was. At length he recognised a building near the café – large and bold as many Moscow buildings were.

The Museum of . . . of—

<Keep the shield a little longer,> he urged. Under the stress of sustained contact the other mind was weakening.

Now he could see a sign. The Museum of Natural History.

<I can be there in half an hour. Don't let Andrew move.>

<Hurry.>

Sam was already breaking free of the spell. The darkness in the little room became complete as the light faded beneath his fingers. Hardly had Peter risen to his feet, full of questions, than Sam was at the door, having switched on the light and snatched up his coat.

'What's the fastest way to the Museum of Natural History?'

'Taxi, sir. The subway and trams take much longer.'

'Run downstairs, order one. Tell him we're going to the Science Museum.'

'But sir, the Science Museum is—'

'I don't want to be followed.'

Downstairs in the hotel's entrance, Sam listened. Now he gave the sounds of the neighbourhood his full attention, sending his thoughts through the streets to hear if there was something, however small, that was out of place.

'It'll be here in ten minutes, sir,' Peter told him, emerging on to the icy front steps.

Sam frowned. 'How many people do we have stationed around here?'

'Four in Moscow, sir. A further seven are watching the Portals within a radius of twenty miles.'

'And roughly how many against?'

'About twelve in Moscow, and twenty in a ten-mile radius beyond, most of whom moved in this morning.'

'There aren't twenty Portals, though.'

'They're watching airports and roads, sir.'

'Did they see me arrive?'

'We don't think so. There are more moving in every hour, and they're getting more aggressive as their numbers increase.'

Sam bit his lip. 'Order everyone we have to pull out,' he said finally.

'Sir!'

'Tell them to make no secret of the fact that they're withdrawing. And ask someone to book two tickets under the name of Luc Satise to London, earliest flight possible.'

'Sir?' Peter knew, as did Sam, that Luc Satise was probably the last name under which he should travel.

'Just do it, please. Also we may need a fall-back plan, in case we get separated. I want Adamarus to get Andrew to London; but we must assume anything can go wrong. If it does, as many of us as are able must meet outside Kaluga railway station at seven tonight.' *I'm beginning to understand the enemy, whoever they are. Always one step ahead; their forces are forever moving a little faster than I can, and for every move I make a counter-move is already being played. So now we confound the enemy, make them think I've somehow managed to overtake them.*

But will they fall for it?

The taxi was a cramped little vehicle driven by a grinning Estonian. It had arrived in just under the promised ten minutes, which was a warning in itself; Sam knew that taxis were always late.

'Not the Science Museum,' he told the driver as they screeched away from the kerbside. 'The Natural History Museum.'

'It'll cost more!'

'I'm loaded.'

'Why are you taking your hockey stick?'

'Because I'm a vandal who's decided to smash up every treasure in the museum.'

'Right!'

The taxi climbed the kerb in a U-turn, and a gaggle of pigeons shot skyward. Sam was soon reconsidering exactly what it was that could kill him. If any mortal might claim the distinction of terminating an immortal life, it would be this man. Peter, too, was giving the back of the driver's neck some nasty looks. Two furry dice bounced against each other beneath the mirror, and a sticker on the rear windscreen declared that the driver was a fan of one of St Petersburg's football teams.

'It's the fucking traffic,' declared the driver cheerily as they raced through a red light. 'Ten times worse than it was.'

'Really?' asked Sam weakly. At the next set of lights a lorry had to swerve to avoid calamity. Peter had gone pale – jinns, if Sam remembered, were easier to kill than immortals. The driver must once have been a kid who played too many motor-racing games – the kind where it doubled your score if you ran over the nuns. *Still*, he thought desperately, *any follower will be hard pressed to keep up*.

He kept watching the mirror even so, and extending his senses skywards.

'I used to play hockey. Ice-hockey, I mean. I was counted very good.'

'Really.'

'What position do you play?'

'Right back.'

'You any good?'

'I'm probably better at fencing. My brother teaches it. Fighting. Various martial arts.'

'You got many brothers?'

'Lots.'

'Which one teaches?'

'"Teaches" may be an over-statement. I get occasional crash courses. Usually without warning. Some of my brothers are temperamental.'

'You fight them for real? . . . Bastard!' This last was yelled at the driver of a red Saab, a businessman with slicked-back hair and a whiff of gangster about him, who'd swerved out of a side street and just missed them. 'Lucky for him he didn't fucking well hit us!'

As they approached the museum and the café nearby, Sam's heart swelled with expectation. How many, many questions Andrew could answer.

He felt something. A tendril of thought brushing against his senses. He forced it back, feeling his stomach turn. Some enemy had sensed the passage of a spirit, and investigated. Who was it? Firedancer? Angel? Valkyrie?

'They're very near,' he said softly.

'What?' demanded the driver.

'You're sure, sir?' asked Peter, to whom, in Sam's presence, any 'demand' was an unthinkable sin.

'Yes. Very near indeed.'

But so were they. Swinging round a corner Sam could see the museum, then the café itself. As the taxi slewed to a halt he could distinguish Andrew sitting in the window, nursing a cup of coffee and looking as much tired as afraid.

Sam stuffed cash at random into the driver's hand. 'Keep the change.' He sprang into the street, sword slung

over his back, and ran towards the café. Behind him
Peter struggled to keep up.

Outside the door Sam stopped. Even at a moment like
this he knew to affect a leisurely stroll. Andrew looked
up as he approached. His eyes widened. 'You came,' he
said in a voice hoarse with not enough to eat and no
sleep.

'I came,' replied Sam, sitting down. Andrew's hands
were clamped tightly around the coffee cup, his knuckles
white. Around him Sam could see a faint shimmer of
protective magic of the same kind drawn by whoever
had written the shield.

'So did they,' he replied weakly. With a jerk of his
head he indicated a couple of dark-skinned Asians
staring unashamedly from a nearby table. They wore
red. Red jeans, tasteless red shirts, dark hair, scarred
faces probably made less so by a touch of magic. If they'd
planned on staying anonymous, Sam didn't rate their
current efforts. Above them a speaker blasted out harsh
electronic music. Beneath their coats, each doubtless
carried a curved sword, short but deadly.

'When did they get here?'

'Ten minutes ago.'

'How did they find you?'

'I was a fool. I booked into a hotel a few nights ago
and left my toothbrush there. Freya had warned me they
could track you through a single item, like sniffer dogs.'

'Shit.'

'It's worse,' said Andrew. 'I can't move from the neck
down.'

The level way in which he tried to speak was marred
by a shrillness bordering on hysteria. 'I . . . I can't move,'
he repeated. 'I took a sip of the coffee – I was a bloody

idiot!' There was none of the smiling young man in the picture; all that remained was terror.

'It's all right,' murmured Sam, thinking of a thousand ways in which the Firedancers might have poisoned their unfortunate victim, and finding only a handful of possible solutions to this new problem.

Standing back like a dutiful servant, Peter finally spoke. 'If Firedancers are here, others will be coming. The shield can't protect against them.'

'Who's he?' asked Andrew in a frightened voice.

'A friend. Peter, I need a wheelchair here as fast as possible.'

'A wheelchair?' repeated Peter. 'How can I get one of those, sir?'

'Call an ambulance to the street corner, and when it arrives steal one. I leave the manner of the theft entirely to you.'

With some reluctance, Peter made his way out through the traffic to a nearby phone box, a warrior sent to do a criminal's task.

Sam turned his attention back to Andrew. He had begun to sob quietly. The Firedancers wouldn't attack in such a public space – no further than they had.

'You *shall* be fine,' he insisted as Andrew's tears flowed faster. 'There's nothing the Firedancers can do that a Son of Time cannot undo.'

'Damn Freya,' whispered Andrew, unable to wipe his own eyes. 'This is all her fault.'

Sam was tempted to agree, as apprehension jostled his lingering grief at Freya's death. He said, 'Where's your stuff?'

Andrew managed to nod in the direction of his feet, where under the table a small bag held his possessions.

'You got a passport?'

'Yes.'

'Under what name?'

'My own.'

'Ah. What nationality?'

'American.'

'Where will you be safe?'

'Nowhere.'

'You're a great one for optimism.'

Somehow Andrew forced a grin. 'Strange thing,' he said, 'but optimism is really easy to feel right now.'

'A side-effect of my presence, no doubt.'

'Oh, sure.' But he looked slightly happier.

Across the road in the telephone box Peter was standing, head tilted to one side as he made his call. Then Sam's gaze moved past the jinn, to where a pair of blonde women were striding down the street.

'Shit!'

'What?' exclaimed Andrew.

'Valkyries,' Sam whispered.

Peter turned in the same moment, and his eyes widened as he too saw them. In one movement he slammed down the phone and ran from the box towards the café.

He burst breathlessly through the door. 'The ambulance won't be here for at least five minutes! What do we do?'

The valkyries were crossing the road, heading purposefully towards them.

'All right,' said Sam. 'Peter, will you kindly take Andrew under the arm? Andrew, we're going for a stroll.'

The jinn hefted Andrew up like a puppet. With Sam

on his other side the American's arms hung down uselessly and his toes trailed along the ground. Andrew
found it hard even to stop his head from lolling.
Evidently the Firedancers' poison was still spreading
through him, threatening him with unconsciousness. All
eyes in the café were on the trio as they advanced to the
door, two strangers supporting a limp doll. There was a
scrape of chairs as the Firedancers rose to their feet.

Outside the door the two valkyries had stopped,
waiting for them.

'Peter,' said Sam in a low voice, 'help Andrew to the
street corner and wait for the ambulance. Don't get in it
until I arrive.'

'Sir?'

'Just do it. I won't be long.'

He turned to go, but Andrew croaked something. Sam
turned, trying to show sympathy despite his racing
heart. 'Gabriel,' breathed Andrew. 'If I don't . . . then
Gabriel. They're on to her anyway, I might as well tell
you.'

'Why are they after you?' asked Sam quietly.

Andrew gave a bitter laugh. 'I found the location of
the keys. They're going to free Pandora – God!' His face
twisted in pain and Sam instinctively took a step towards
him, even as his eyes involuntarily rose to the closing
forces around.

Andrew looked very small and fragile and somehow
not strong enough to support the knowledge he possessed. 'There's more, you're in danger . . .'

Sam gave his shoulder what he hoped was a reassuring squeeze. 'You've time to tell me later,' he urged.
'When we're out of here.'

On the street the door thudded shut as the

Firedancers moved in behind them. The valkyries came forward with careful menace, intent on stopping their departure.

Sam turned so that he could see both enemy parties while keeping himself between them and Andrew. 'Ladies, gentlemen,' he said, politely bowing to each. 'Can I help you?'

'Give him to us,' said one Firedancer softly.

'Ah. We have a problem there,' said Sam, backing up slowly to keep near Peter and Andrew as they moved down the street. 'You see, I'm a very suspicious person. And I suspect you might not be the people to care for my invalid friend.'

In the hand of one of the Firedancers something gleamed. A small blade, fashioned from what might well be dragon bone.

'Give him to us,' repeated the Firedancer.

'No.'

People were staring, unsure what this strange confrontation signified, or how to interpret the dangling figure of Andrew.

A car braked suddenly at the kerbside, and the window was wound down. Out of the corner of his eye Sam saw Whisperer, reaching behind him to open the passenger door.

'Peter! Put Andrew into the car!' he snapped. 'Whisperer! Get Andrew out of here by whatever means!'

Peter began lugging Andrew towards the car, and a valkyrie made her move. Sam was already there, raising one hand with his palm thrust towards her chin like a martial arts fighter. Even though he didn't connect she staggered back as if struck. One Firedancer sprang forward. A knife flashed, and watching mortals scattered in panic. Sam got his dagger free, and used it to stab through one knife-wielding hand. The other he caught in a fist of magic, twisting both down simultaneously.

'Come on!' screamed Whisperer.

'Go!' he yelled. 'I'll find you!'

The second Firedancer lunged for the car. Sam leaped after him, catching him round the middle and dragging him away from the door as it slammed shut. He heard someone yell in rage, and kicked the nearest shin, before leaping away and yelling in Russian, 'Help me! They're mad!'

The crowd hardly blinked. Too much TV had clearly inoculated them against such sights as a lone man being attacked by a group of strangers. They could have been waiting for Sam to scream a ninja challenge and disable his enemies with a double-backwards somersault. Typical mortals.

The trouble about being noble, thought Sam as the car pulled away, *was that you rarely get away with it*. He couldn't hide from himself the realisation that, single-handed against four of Heaven's maddened servants, he stood utterly no chance of winning. Taking a risk, he passed his left hand in front of him with a sweeping gesture. In the trail of his upraised palm his attackers staggered back – and Sam turned and ran. Sprinting down the centre of the busy road, he was counting on being able to regenerate physically in ways that the others couldn't. Cars swerved and screeched around him, but he kept on blindly running. He saw a tram stop and headed towards it, eyes fixed on a tram advancing in the distance. The sounds of pursuit were close on his heels. Turning frantically he saw that in some measure his mad dash through the traffic had thwarted his adversaries. A Firedancer was nearest, then a valkyrie; the other two, following in dense traffic, wore the fear of all things mechanical inscribed on their faces.

But even as he reached the stop, Sam knew the tram wouldn't arrive in time. He was going to have to run for it all the way. He felt his heart beat faster and his skin pale as chemicals, similar to adrenalin in all but a few subtle ways, began coursing through him. He wondered again how well Firedancers could run. Not faster nor farther than he could, surely!

So he ran, hardly aware of where he went, and all the while unconsciously pouring magic into his feet. Pedestrians scattered, and cars hooted as he rushed unseeing into their path. He caught sight of a signpost, and turned sharply on seeing what it said: station.

His pursuers were fast, but he was faster, and that bit sharper. And against his flight was fear – fear that he'd abandoned Whisperer to his fate; Peter and Andrew too.

Follow me, he thought desperately. *Forget about Andrew. I am your target, not them.*

The next street he turned into was crowded enough to give more protection. Slinging his sword from off his back and cradling it, he began to focus less on just running. Against him pressed flowing masses of people like the current in a stream. By chance he found himself shoved by one passer-by into the doorway of a shop. He was choking for breath – in his mad flight he hadn't noticed how far he'd run. Behind him in the crowd he could see four ripples where each figure was pushing towards him. But there were now so many people between them and him that he felt just about safe enough to try . . .

*

The beggar was watching the stranger with interest. Did that coat, and the hockey stick he grasped so tightly, suggest a man of wealth and leisure? Might that boyish face, flushed from running, be graced with a smile of generosity once his breath no longer came in rushing gasps?

So intent was the beggar on this potential client, as he liked to call them, that he was the only person on the street who noticed when . . . it . . . happened. The man's skin grew darker, his clothes lighter; the coat grew a dense fur, the face a beard to match. The hockey stick became a violin case, slung over the man's now wider, taller back. The eyes drew further apart and lightened, the hair turned a mousy brown and stuck out in jagged spikes from underneath the hat. And as the stranger moved from the doorway into the crowd with the air of a local doing the daily shop, the beggar had already convinced himself that this was what the man had been all along. By the time this altered figure was lost in the crowd, the beggar was chiding himself for being an old fool.

And Sam's illusion was complete.

TWELVE

The Faceless Man

There must be a religion somewhere that classifies me as the faceless man. I wish they understood how hard it is to be faceless.

Already Sam was tiring under the strain of sustaining the illusion. Thinking about other things was so hard that, when asked at the station by the elderly booking clerk where he wanted to go, he almost went for his passport.

'You all right, sir?'

Even his Russian threatened to break down under the effort of concentration. He bought a ticket to Minsk, unsure why but knowing only that he wanted to get away as fast as possible. Peter had his bag with its passports in it – that probably meant a Waywalk had to follow.

But they won't have been able to get Andrew out of the country, will they? He's a mortal, he can't Feywalk. And his passport is blown. It's down to Moondance.

Sam pictured the workings of the Moondance network as its considerable powers were put into play. After driving for a few hours in a random direction, the car carrying Andrew would pull into a garage, where another vehicle was waiting, also with three people. Two would get out from each car and either go to the toilet or buy a sandwich or some such. On returning, each pair would casually get into the 'wrong' car, and drive off. This ploy would then be repeated elsewhere, possibly confusing any pursuit by using cars of the same make and with the same registration number.

But though the Moondance network moved fast, this was still enemy territory. If spirits were pouring in hour by hour to watch the roads and the airports, would they be watching stations too? Or had they fallen for his bluff and gone chasing after the airline booking for Luc Satise and his second, unidentified passenger?

Assume the worst. That way you can be pleasantly surprised if anything else happens. Meanwhile the effort he made to restore his illusion only confirmed that he didn't trust himself to sustain it.

He settled for a compromise. From a stand on the platform he purchased a broadsheet newspaper. Only on board the train, once it was clattering out of the station, and his senses hadn't stirred at any sign of danger, did he adjust the paper to obscure his face while the illusion faded. One passenger gave him a sharp, questioning look, but quickly convinced himself that the clean-shaven, dark-haired man sitting nearby had been there all along, and that he was remembering a bearded gentleman from another journey to another place.

It felt good to have his own face back. The scarred

Russian landscape tore by, making Devon seem quaint and neat notwithstanding Sam's disgust at the degradation of the English landscape. Russia, for all that parts of it had great beauty, was large enough for mankind to have no inhibition in disfiguring vast tracts. And at this season, when the ice was melting and the snow lay muddied and lumped into ugly mounds from a long winter, the land seemed battered to the point of desolation.

He got off a long way before Minsk, having re-erected his illusion, and fell to a study of the Russian rail network, so that a series of changes could bring him to Kaluga, and his meeting with Whisperer, after a whole day on the move. The final complicated route became a long routine of boarding trains, lowering an illusion to recover mental breath, waiting for a change, raising a new illusion, catching a different train, lowering another illusion . . . And at no time did he cease to wonder what his pursuers might be doing. Though he had the sensation of eyes watching him, he knew better than to trust his feelings. His mind was running haywire: if he had but thought of spiders he'd have felt them crawl, or if he'd dreamt of seagulls he would have heard their cry and thought it real.

'Why isn't anyone interested in taking over Earth?'

Sam had been surprised at Annette's question. 'You'd rather they did?'

It was in those twilight years when her hair was beginning to turn white, but before she'd started to wish for his death. That would come soon; but for now he padded around her small flat, bringing her tea and trying to ignore how old and tired she'd become.

'Why not?'

He'd thought before giving an answer, trying to find a way of phrasing his response without putting down her own world. 'It's . . . like the Olympics,' he said finally. 'Why rule Hell when you can rule Earth? Why rule Earth when you can rule Heaven? Everyone wants to be on the top podium.'

It hadn't been the best answer. But he didn't think he could explain about Heaven, how the stars themselves danced and every tree was laden with fruit and you could sleep anywhere in safety. Partly he felt bad about making *her* life and pleasures seem less; also he feared his description might now be wrong. He remembered Heaven as a place where dragons played in the sky with the angels, but that was before the war.

'Jehovah was interested in Earth, wasn't he?'

'Jehovah was a fool,' Sam had said, with more passion than he'd expected. Deep inside, a lot more was waiting to burst out than he liked to admit.

'Jehovah thought,' he'd said angrily, 'that Earth was the future – that one day the battle for Heaven would encompass mortals. He believed he could prepare mortals for that battle, in body and soul. He thought he could purge away their mortal vices and create another Heaven – *his* Heaven – on Earth. I told him his ideals would grow out of all proportion. I warned him it wouldn't work.'

Every word was spat as a snake hisses poison. But he knew that somewhere inside a childish part of him was gloating, 'I told you so!' – even as the self that claimed maturity was sickened at it.

He'd almost missed his station. In a rush he got off the

train, hardly aware of it having pulled up, illusion rising around him in a flurry of distorted features. Sam cursed himself for a fool, wondering what nearby watcher might have spotted his lapse. Swearing softly, he lurked in a corner of the cold, wet station, and waited, full of dread, for his next train.

<Tell no one,> he'd been urged. <Archangels are honoured. Their parents are powerful angels; but even powerful, powerful angels cannot do as you can.>
    <Yes, Mother.>
He was wearing the white robes of a newly knighted archangel, assigned to serve without question the Child of Belief. Assigned to lay down his life, if that's what Jehovah required. He was incredibly proud of himself, and had already met several other newly appointed archangels, with whom he'd struck up a booming friendship. Uriel, Gabriel, Michael, Rafael – they were all excited about serving their new master.
    'I hear he's got plans,' Uriel had whispered. 'I hear he's going to take us down to Earth.'
    This had extracted several gasps, with the exception of Michael. He was the easy-going one, on whom you could always rely for practical advice and a map. Sam liked Michael already – that friendly, foppish grin, the casual way he talked, and the relaxed manner in which he sent other angels about their duty.
    'Waywalking?' one had exclaimed. 'Us? Can we do it?'
    'Not alone,' Michael had replied, always with an answer – and frequently the right one. 'But if he takes us, leads the way, then yes, we can make it.'
    <Tell no one,> his mother had whispered in Sam's

mind. <You are not like the others. They will be furious if they discover what you are.>

Sam had obeyed, hiding his huge talent with magic, kneeling to Jehovah with the rest, playing the servant and feeling happy with his role. Back then, he hadn't known who his father was. Only his mother – his mother, the ever-present warmth inside his mind, the circle of fire that blessed him when cold, the dome of magic that protected him from the rain, the rush of power that caught him when he fell. His mother was Magic, and he told no one.

<Mother?>
  <Yes?>
  <Why must I be ashamed of what I am?>
He'd felt her amusement. It was one of those few peaceful times when he was alone with his own devices, not playing servant to Jehovah nor studying Earth for his trip. He was lounging on a balcony carved out of a marble cliff face, looking down at the pink scudding clouds of Heaven and unobserved by all. Few lived this high up – they didn't like the cold and the thin air. But Sam loved it. Up here, he was alone to do as he pleased. And what he pleased to do was learn about his hidden birthright.

  <Not ashamed. Never ashamed. But there is dissent in Heaven. Houses against Houses, Princes against sister Princesses. Jehovah is to some degree caught up in it, and therefore you also, as his servant. But if they knew what you are, you would be involved in it to a greater degree – possibly even in danger.>

He was playing a game with fire while they communed together, weaving it through his fingers like a cat's cradle, shaping patterns in the air. <Why? Didn't Chaos and Fire mate in Hell?

<Isn't Love a disloyal queen and aren't her illegitimate offspring everywhere?

<Isn't Magic honoured and granted a place in Heaven, albeit not in the Court of Time? But still in Heaven and untouchable as one of the great Incarnates?>

<All this is true. But though I am honoured, and you would therefore be honoured too, as my son, it would not be long before people asked who your father is.>

<And? Who is my father?>

Magic didn't reply. She never did.

He'd been travelling now for five hours. In an attempt to dull the fatigue of the journey, he'd purchased a puzzle book which he filled in, on the longer stretches between stations, with the mindless efficiency of a man often bored and with nothing to do. When the questions became too easy, and he could spot ten differences between pictures *a* and *b* in the blink of an eye, he delved back into memory. To that bitter day when Jehovah had taken the hands of his angels, and Sam had learnt his father's true identity.

It had been months in coming. Jehovah had given each archangel a huge list of tasks, ranging from the smallest tweaking of some tribesman's thoughts to the setting of a fire in a well-guarded palace. We are going to make mortals pure, he'd said. We're going to make them ours.

No one had really understood the plan. Jehovah was using his skills in manipulating belief; that was all they could agree. Somehow he was going to reform the belief of every mortal on Earth. No one doubted he'd do it, and no one questioned him.

Except Sam. He'd wondered, his mind racing ahead to the many, many possible outcomes of this toil. It had been named the Eden Initiative.

His mother had been uneasy too, when he told her of it. <Your master has big ideas. The bigger for being righteous.> Those who followed Magic's way of life had often suffered at the hands of people with righteous ideas.

So they'd stood before the Way of Earth, Jehovah looking proud and imposing at the gateway. 'We are about to change a world, my loyal servants.'

Sam had kept his face fixed in a suitable expression of awe as one by one the archangels linked hands, forming a chain.

He was at the very back.

'Don't let go,' Jehovah had warned. 'Follow me. If you let go you will lose your way. For you the Waywalk will seem dark and silent. For me it is full of light and noises. Try not to distract me. If you let go of each other, you will also lose me, and when we Waywalk I am all that keeps you from an unpleasant end.'

They'd finished linking hands, Sam behind Michael. Then Jehovah had led the way and they, silent and faithful, had followed.

Sam had immediately known something was wrong. Not with Jehovah, nor with the other archangels, but with *him*. He wasn't seeing the promised darkness, nor hearing the promised nothing. He saw a white mist, in which shadows lurked and leered, heard whispered pleas from lost spirits, sensing just on the edge of feeling a fading world behind and a growing world ahead. With their breathing harsh and shallow, the other archangels seemed unaware of the light and noise around them. Sam gasped as something lashed at his ankle, but passed straight through like a shadow. That gasp left his lungs burning and head swimming, there was so little air.

'Lucifer,' wheedled a voice in his ear. 'Please come to us, Lucifer . . .'

Ahead he could see a white doorway, towards which Jehovah was leading them. His palm was soaked with sweat – so was Michael's. Images filled his mind as he looked at that door – images of the darkened oasis where they were going to emerge. And others – of the shadows, of being lost in this endless white mist, of suffocating, of walking on a bed of death and breathing in pestilence as they went.

Only the Sons of Time could Waywalk, everyone else was blind.

But he wasn't blind.

'Lucifer.'

He turned slightly, and felt his hand slip from Michael's. Immediately he was being tugged back, ghostly claws curling round his shoulders and waist, trying to pull him down. He staggered free, running through the mist towards the white door, the image of the destination burning in his mind.

There was no air left to breathe. Jehovah had vanished through the door, and the others were disappearing with him. Sam rushed forward, closing his ears to the pleading voices, and caught Michael's hand again, holding with a grip of death. Through the mist Sam glimpsed a white, scared face turning this way and that, blind. He'd never seen Michael so frightened.

Abruptly they were through, the Portal closing behind them and the archangels gasping down huge breaths as Jehovah briskly counted them to see that they were all there.

'Horrible,' moaned Gabriel. 'Never so dark, never so quiet.'

'I think you'd find that what I see is worse,' replied Jehovah mildly.

Michael was staring at the gasping Lucifer where he'd fallen on the sand and was now heaving in great gulps of air, more shaken than the rest. 'I . . . thought I felt your hand slip from mine,' he said.

For a long while Sam was quiet. Mistakenly, Michael took this merely for the shock of the Waywalk.

'Must have imagined it,' said Sam.

He was on the last lap now, the train due in at Kaluga at six fifty-two. As he travelled he prayed to whatever gods he knew didn't exist that even if his illusions had been seen through, they would not realise Kaluga was the final destination. Then another prayer, this time more fervent than ever before, that Whisperer had made it too. Praying, although he knew there was nothing to pray to, was all he could do.

<Mother?>

<Yes?> She was always there when he called – in this place at least, this hidden place in the clouds.

<Who is my father?>

<A dear, sweet being.>

<We Waywalked today. I have spent a month on Earth, and today we Waywalked back. Who is my father?>

\<How did you like Earth?\>
\<Mother!\>
She was silent before answering. \<Why do you ask me this?\> she said finally. \<You have always known the answer.\>

On the train, Sam lovingly fingered his sword. Even through the cover and the layers of leather he could hear it singing its deadly song. It was his father's gift to him, just as the others, the legitimate ones, had all received gifts. It was the final proof.

He'd known that only Sons of Time were allowed in the Room of Clocks. He'd known also that only one son was allowed there at any time. Finally he'd known that it was guarded always, by angels loyal to Time and his Queens alone.

But his long hours spent learning spells and tricks hadn't been wasted. As the sun set over the clouds of Heaven and the stars came out in all their brilliance, Sam had pulled on his white archangel's robes, beneath which he'd concealed a roll of rope tied around his waist, and slipped from his home in the sky towards the gold and white marble palace that stood on a cliff of diamond.

During the day a staircase of sunlight wound up to it, during the night one of starlight. There was no other way up, and it was guarded. Lucifer dealt with this as only he could have. If it had been Thor trying to sneak into the palace like a thief, there would have been bloodshed and murders. Had it been Jehovah, the angels on guard would have found themselves believing that by letting him past they did the right thing. But Sam was neither of these. Moreover the angels were not expecting a Son of

Magic to be in Heaven, let alone trying to enter the palace.

Sam knew Jehovah was on Earth, and would be for a few more days. He knew also that only those highly gifted in magic could see through an illusion. He knew finally, as his mother had told him, that he was her only son not to possess mortal blood, and certainly her only child in Heaven. So at the base of the silvery staircase of starlight, he buried his head in his hands, and when he looked up again, it was not Sam who stood there, but Jehovah.

Confident now, he began to climb. An angel questioned him as he went, and he spoke in the same mild, serene tones that Jehovah always used. At the top of the staircase he wasn't even out of breath and his very gait was that of Jehovah – a kind of drifting along the ground, floating almost – so complete was the illusion.

'I am going to the Room of Clocks,' he told another angel.

There was a hectic moment when, outside the Room and waiting to enter, he saw a different door open, and Athena appeared. She gave Sam a nasty look, old school to young school, and swept by him. Yet just as she passed, she seemed to think better of doing so, and turned. 'You are visiting the Room?'

He nodded, remembering quickly how little Jehovah spoke.

'Why?'

'Because I desire it, sister.'

She frowned slightly, and for a moment he thought she'd seen through his illusion. But then she shook her head and went on, leaving him soaked with sweat and his hands shaking. He clasped them tightly together until the knuckles turned white, in an effort to subdue his trembling, and almost jumped when a soft-voiced angel announced that he could enter.

Bowing his thanks, respectful Saviour to the last, he pushed open the large golden door which at another time he would have denounced as vulgar, and entered a room that roared with ticking. Or, more to the point, one large tick. The walls, the ceiling, the huge floor were covered with clocks, sundials, hourglasses, candles of every kind. At each second the smallest hand moved on every clock, each with a precise click that, heard together, filled the room. Sure of being alone, Sam lowered his illusion and turned slowly, watching as every clock ticked its way towards infinity.

When these clocks stopped, he knew, Time was dead. When they began to run anticlockwise, Cronus was king.

Turning slowly, a tiny, tiny figure in the vast room, he suddenly wondered what he was doing there. Had he expected a sign? Time never gave any. You never saw Time, just as he'd never actually seen his mother, merely a shadowy projection of her. Greater Powers were beyond physical form, which made it hard to keep up eye contact of any kind. But you could ask boons of Time. How did He show He was listening?

Because he's always listening, because we're part of him, an extension of his will.

'Father,' he called softly, and immediately felt silly. What reaction did he expect? 'You know, better than I do, why I'm here. If there is a reason, that is.'

No answer. Slowly he knelt, staring everywhere at once.

'What am I?' he asked. 'Your bastard son? Another

bastard son out of so many? But you send your bastard sons away, and they're rarely by a great Incarnate. Children by the Elements, yes. Even children by mortals, where you think that child will serve your purpose. But what is my purpose, in your scheme of things? I have watched your children, and every one has a purpose whether they see it or not. Every one is acting out some scheme of your devising. Time conquers all, but I cannot see what there is for you to conquer.

'What are you so afraid of that you should keep a compromising child such as me close to you? For the children of Magic are hunted down and reviled. Their power is chaotic, unreliable. It is one of the few things that deny common sense – the miracle makers are all children of Magic, and miracles are not part of your great scheme.

'So why do you keep me here, yet ignorant of what I am? What future will you use me for, like Jehovah uses humans?'

No answer. But his ears detected a different kind of reply.

Somewhere, a clock was striking out of tune. There was the huge clamour of a thousand clocks hitting the second together – and then, between that second and the next, there fell another click.

So faint; just one clock out of place among them all.

Sam rose, scouring the room for it, searching it out. Refusing to hear any other sound but that dysfunctional tick, he wandered through the room. Halfway round he stopped, pressing his ear to a clock. Then to another. Then another, now staying within a small area and listening hard.

He found it. One clock, about the same size as his

face, plain, the numbers in some flowing script he couldn't recognise, was beating half a second out from all the rest. Sam ran his hands around it, noting the strange shape – distorted, as though a mad smith had started to melt it down and then thought better of it. His fingers, questing round the edge, found a little inlay – and at his touch the whole thing sprang open. He leapt back with a startled cry.

But nothing emerged. Heart pounding in his ears, knowing as he'd never known anything in his life that this was the closest he'd get to talking with Time, he advanced on the dark space behind the clock and reached in. His hand closed round something hard and cool. He felt a jolt on touching it, like electricity.

Withdrawing the object, he found a long, light, silver sword, sheathed in a plain leather case. Nervous, he drew it, and felt it sing in his ears and blood as it sliced the air. He made a few practice passes and knew he'd never felt anything like it. Sheathing it, embarrassed by the huge space around him and the loneliness of his sword games, he laid it carefully at his feet and reached in again.

His fingers closed round a small silver key, dangling by its chain and swinging tantalisingly before his face. As he touched it, images flooded his mind. Images of a silver door, beyond which lay a Portal to another place. A door which only his key, held in his hand, would open. Each Child of Time had one.

But there was more. A silver dagger that looked tailor-made to his stealthy nature. And at the back, unadorned, plain, a silver band. He didn't dare put it on, not knowing to whom these goods belonged – even though some part of him cried out that this crown sang to him only. Common sense decreed he should not risk the wrath of its owner, in case that owner was not him after all.

And at the very back, a slip of parchment, so old he feared it might crumble to dust in his hands. He unrolled it, and read the strange script slowly and carefully, wondering what language it was in and why he could translate it with no training.

I, Chancellor of the Room of Clocks – he'd never heard of this rank before – *do decree that the items enclosed herein be granted only under such situations as follow:*

1) When a Prince or Princess of Time is in dire need of such weapons and his or her cause is decreed just.

2) When a champion of Heaven is in danger of not completing his function and needs aid through magic.

3) When the Bearer of Light is chosen.

In this third instance let the reader be warned that the Bearer of Light is to be feared and respected, for he is forever cursed and blessed. His function is necessary, but he will be the target of the enemy when that necessity dictates action. Therefore let the Bearer of Light be made of curses, for he will better use the blessings that befall him. Here ends my warning.

Sam rolled the parchment up, wondering what it meant. He had a disagreeable feeling that the word 'necessary' was a reference to him. He returned the parchment to its dark cranny, reasoning that any items that went with such a firm warning were not for him. Reaching out for the other goods, he heard the faint footfall behind him.

Before knowing what he did, he turned, finding the

silver dagger in his hand as if flown there in response to his alarm, and was ready to pounce.

Jehovah stared down at him. Immediately he thought how impossible this was: Jehovah was on Earth and not due back yet. Besides, the guards would never have let more than one person into the Room.

Which left two alternatives. Either he'd been found out and Jehovah had come to evict him, or this being was not who it seemed. Yet as he probed he could find no illusion around the figure. Nor could he sense the power of Belief in Jehovah that distinguished him from a Son of War or a Son of Love. His probes came up against a blank.

'Put on the crown, Lucifer,' said Jehovah.

Sam said nothing. He bent down and drew the sword slowly, giving Jehovah time to run or call for help. Inwardly Sam prayed this was what he'd do, thus giving him some certainty of what was going on.

But Jehovah didn't move as Sam rose to his feet, dagger and sword both drawn and ready.

'Who are you?' Sam asked.

'I am you.'

He spun, to stare at himself, standing off to one side and leaning casually against the wall, wearing his own boyish smile.

<I am your mother,> whispered a voice in his mind.

'I am everything that lives.'

He turned again, seeing Michael, this time, moving next to Jehovah's side.

'I am everything that dies.' Jehovah again.

'You could have told me straight out. I wouldn't think any the less of you,' he muttered. 'Father.'

'Put the crown on,' whispered Jehovah.

'Why?'

'Put it on, it is yours!' said Michael.

<Put it on.>

Kneeling down and placing his weapons on the ground again, Sam reached out nervously. He took the band in both hands, holding it as though it were a fragile thing.

'If I put this on,' he said finally, 'it will weigh down not only on me, but on those who look at me. If I put this on, I cease to be friendly, smiling Lucifer.

'But I don't become something different. People who called me friend will see this and they will see a king. Yet I will see them and see a friend.'

'Put it on.'

'No. I am happy as I am.'

<Then why did you come?>

'To find out what I am.'

'Put it on!' roared Jehovah.

Sam raised the crown, not above his head, but towards Jehovah. 'You put it on! You who can control men's lives and decree when they live and when they die – you wear it! You have no need of me!'

Jehovah was gone. Sam was kneeling before the vacant air, crown held up imploringly to nothing. As empty and significant as a dream.

'Would you deny your father?'

He didn't turn his head, dreading what vision he would see this time. The voice had been kindly, compassionate. The voice he'd always imagined his father would have. He'd wanted his father to be some kindly old scholar, who'd play games together with him when he was young, and when he was older would listen to his woes with a wise smile on his face and laughter in his eyes. And he knew that if he turned his head now, he would see that father, the one he'd wanted, formed from his own imagination the better to manipulate him.

'Tell me what it is you want, what you're planning. Tell me why you kept me so close, and at the same time so far.'

'You are necessary,' was the simple answer. Sam closed his eyes as his father moved into his line of sight, refusing to look on his dream, knowing the power it would have over him if he did look. He felt warm old hands brush his cheek, then tilt his head up so that his father – *no, not his father, an illusion created by his father of someone his real father had never been* – could survey his not-son's features. He felt the warm old hands curl around his own and gently steal the crown from his grasp. He opened his eyes, staring up into his father's face as he raised the crown above Sam's head.

'Why?' he asked, ever so softly.

'Because I am afraid,' whispered his father, lowering the crown on Sam's head.

Alone, in the now empty hall, silver crown on his black hair, the clocks ticking in perfect unison again, Sam screamed. The silver crown turned white; that whiteness burnt through him and surrounded him with an aura of white fire. His eyes turned white, his fingers curled into claws as desperately he scratched at the crown, trying to get it off his head.

His head was thrust back with a crack like a gunshot as the fire poured out of the crown, into him, and out of him into the world. It filled the room, the palace, it blinded everyone who looked on it, filled Heaven itself, slunk into the Portals and filled the Way of Earth with fire, burning away the mists. It spread out through the

Portals into Earth, tore across the primeval landscape, found out more Portals, filled every nook and every crevice of every world until it was as thin as shadow, then thinner, then fading, then gone.

In the Room of Clocks, alone, his eyes white beneath their shut lids, the Bearer of Light crumpled like a doll.

THIRTEEN

Back-up

The sun had set by the time the train pulled into Kaluga station. Sam was ten minutes early. Under the cover of illusion he bought himself a foul instant coffee and perched, plastic cup in hand, on a bicycle rail outside the station's main entrance. He was too tired to notice the passage of people through the car park, the burning of neon lights or the crackling announcements from the station. It was a wonder his illusion didn't fail him then and there, his mind lost on paths too complicated for the body to follow. He'd finished the coffee, but unconsciously he raised the cup to his mouth again. Somewhere a clock struck seven. He waited.

Clouds were gathering overhead, and he felt a cold wetness as snow began to fall – mushy snow that melted on contact with the pavement. Holding out his hands he watched the little crystals settle on them, wither and turn to water, as promptly as if nature were on fast forward.

Quarter past. A kindly station porter, recognising a

foreigner, asked if he was all right. He replied that he was; but the question had jarred something in him to a state of alertness.

Where is Whisperer?

By now he felt every second crawl by. In his imagination every car that sped past the station held three figures, but none of them turned towards him. Simultaneously he blamed himself for this latest disaster – and strove to figure a way out of it.

The wet snow was falling faster. His clothes were growing sodden. The neon lights were starting to look blurred not only by damp, but by his own fatigue. Sam shook his head, trying to clear it, and realised that his illusionary beard had been thinning without him noticing. He willed it back, willed his skin to stay dark and his eyes light, in the front of his mind forcing the image of what he *should* look like over his true appearance.

A fog was descending. A strange fog, for Kaluga was not accustomed to such a thing, not at this time of year, not with this weather. It rose from all around within a few seconds, became thick, and suffocated even the snow. It pushed away the smell of car fumes leaving a faint tracery of – dead leaves? Soon it was dense enough so that the street lamps were merely glowing patches of orange suspended in the sky. Sam lowered his illusion, relying on the fog to give him cover. *Where are you, Whisperer? Why have you called on your power?*

A drunk was complaining loudly about the weather, staggering up the steps to the station, bottle in hand, in quest of a little warmth and shelter. A passing couple told each other how sudden this change had been. A hobbling old woman assured her aged companion that 'this is not natural weather'.

A car stopped hastily – but instead of Peter yelling his name a young couple rushed out, late for their train. Behind it, a truck blew its horn; with an ill grace the car's driver moved on.

The squeal of brakes marked out a small white Ford, looking ready to fall apart and turning into the car park too fast. Hardly the anxious driving of Whisperer. It stopped nonetheless in front of Sam, and a window was wound down. A pale face, one Sam didn't recognise, shouted at him, 'Get in!'

'Who are you?'

'Peter sent me! They're in trouble!'

Surprise me. Keeping his hands ready for a fight or trick, Sam edged towards the car. None of his warning wards went off, so he climbed into the passenger seat and sat back as the car accelerated away. 'Who are you?' he demanded again.

'I'm called Maria.'

He recognised a jinniyah, smelt the sea and observed her dyed blonde hair. Underneath the dye, the colour was probably blue. She had a small worried face, intent on driving.

'Where are Peter and Whisperer?'

'Somewhere that's safe. For the moment.'

'And the mortal?'

'Is nearer to Hell than you are.'

Sam's tired face worked, before his mind translated the words. 'Dying? Is he hurt?'

'The Firedancer's poison is stealing his life. He's in a coma, may not wake. He and the others are together.'

'Where, though?'

'Near,' she promised. 'But so are the enemy.'

They'd turned off a main road and were weaving through empty side streets. A housing estate loomed in

the fog, grey, concrete and forbidding. There was
smashed glass, and cars that hadn't moved for years. But
in one or two windows Sam saw that at least someone
had felt enough pride in where they lived to fill an ugly
plastic vase with flowers. When it was all you knew,
home could seem a marvellous place.

Maria pulled up outside one of the tallest blocks.
'They're in there. Third floor. Don't bother with the lift –
it's broken.'

'Aren't you coming?'

'I'm not involved with this. I'm not crazy.'

Some sixth sense twanged at this. *Oh, but you are. Deeply
involved.*

She too was bristling with suspicion as Sam moved to
get out. Her eyes followed every movement, or tried to.
'What are you doing?'

'Getting my things.'

Did she sense the lie behind his words? If so, he
trusted there was nothing she could do in response . . .

At the entrance to the flats he found the door was
inexplicably open, where someone had used an old telephone directory wedged between it and the frame.
Behind him the car screeched as it pulled away, even
faster than before.

He crept into the hall, hearing the drip of leaky pipes
and the crank of a lift stuck between floors. He smelt
urine and saw graffiti, and wondered again at
Whisperer's choice of hideout. Under the single electric
light in the hall he unsheathed his sword, then pulled the
dagger free from his sleeve and used the string from his
sword to tie it with loose, easy knots round his ankle. His
nerves were screaming danger, but from what or where
he couldn't say.

Sword ready in his hands, Sam padded up the concrete stairs, counting the steps for no reason, extending his senses simultaneously ahead and behind, and keeping his shoulder pressed into the wall. It was cold enough inside the building for his breath to condense.

He turned the corner from the stairs on to the third floor, and what happened next was as unsurprising to him as it was sudden.

They'd been hiding just round the corner. His senses had overlooked them, for they were human and he'd not been expecting a mundane threat. They leapt at him all at once, and he quickly discovered how hard it was to use a sword when three large men were pressing down on you. Hands grabbed his sword arm, and wrenched. An arm went across his throat, almost snapping his neck. Something hard jabbed the small of his back. He closed his eyes to gather magic and throw them off, and heard the click of a gun. And someone yelling, 'It's silver, Lucifer! Don't make me use it!'

Sam opened his eyes again, and felt the oily muzzle brush against his neck, knew that the bullet was silver, knew he would die. He gave up all resistance – which seemed to confound his attackers even more, so that it was several blows later before his dazed ears heard the words, 'For Time's sake, bring him in!'

It was the defeat Sam had been unconsciously preparing for all day. The final reckoning he'd known might happen. *You can only trust yourself*, he thought, *but if you do that, then there's no one else to tell you what you're doing wrong.*

He was aware that someone had taken his sword, and that others were dragging him into a small flat, sparsely furnished, where yellow lights shone beneath large lampshades and an old lady served tea. A witch, he noticed with only mild interest. There were more about than most people suspected. Old witches, especially, had the best form of magic. They understood that most of it was just sending your mind out while sitting around all afternoon with your friends.

Someone was searching him, but they weren't being very thorough. They'd clearly been told where to look, for they focused mainly on his arms and wrists.

Another hand felt round his throat. 'It's not there.'

Unprofessional indeed, thought Sam.

He was deposited, with little grace, on the centre of the carpet. Masking tape was the best they could find for his hands and feet; meanwhile he heard the old lady ask in a concerned voice, 'What about his eyes? Won't he do magic?'

Again, the touch of a muzzle against his neck. 'Not with that there he won't. You're too sensible, aren't you, Lucifer?'

Some part of his mind that had run for cover when the fighting started now crept forward and apprised him of several interesting facts. Firstly, Whisperer and Peter, also bound hand and foot, and blindfolded and silent, were slumped against a far wall, beneath a window. Next to them stood another spirit, who to Sam's magical eyes glowed with the same light as Whisperer possessed. Another fog-summoner, then. Secondly, sprawled in an undignified heap across a sofa was Andrew, unconscious, pale and soaked in sweat, his breathing shallow. Thirdly, and to Sam the most important factor, a pair of black, well-kept boots were a few inches from his nose and the voice which had spoken sounded . . . familiar.

'Michael? What are you doing here?' he asked weakly, face still pressed into the carpet.

'Seeing you don't get hurt, old thing.'

'Very kind of you, I'm sure. I assume Jehovah sent you? What's he doing messed up in all this?'

The boots disappeared, a pair of knees came into view, then a hand. Squatting down, Michael rolled Sam over far enough so that they could look into each other's eyes.

He was just as Sam remembered. The efficient one with all the answers.

'I would like to put a theory to you, Lucifer.'

'Fire ahead.' He grimaced at his own words, aware again of the gun. 'Maybe that was a misjudged phrase. But please, do tell.'

'I suggest you're caught up in matters which don't concern you.'

'Ah. Since nothing is meant to concern me save my own banishment, I find it hard to narrow down the range of what these "matters" might be.'

'Lucifer, I've been sent.'

'Really? How nice for you.'

'I'm returning a favour. Jehovah understands that I'm bound to do that. You once let me live. Now I'm doing the same for you.'

'Why don't you try getting rid of the life-threatening device, then? I might be better inclined to believe you.'

Michael ignored him and went on pointing the gun.

'Why are you telling me this?'

'To warn you. With this mortal as her accomplice, Freya was trying to find the keys to unlock the Pandora spirits. She knew that, if she was discovered, you could be relied on to complete her work. To find the keys and give them to her accomplice, who could conclude her plans. You've been a pawn in her game, Lucifer. A necessary part of the puzzle, nothing more.'

Sam was silent. Did Michael, loyal idiot, really believe
his own story? Finally he shook his head. 'No. No! I
don't know who told you to think all this' – he stared at
Michael, searching the other's face, but met only a look
of righteous obstinacy – 'but Freya was the Daughter of
Love. She would never release the spirits.'

'Take it or leave it, Lucifer. This is a debt repaid. There
won't be any more warnings.'

On the floor Sam snorted his disdain. Michael rose
again, gesturing at someone unseen. A couple of humans
moved towards Andrew, took him by the arms and legs
and hauled him up. Peter and Whisperer were also
forced to their feet. 'What will you do now?' called Sam.
'Leave me here?'

'No.'

He raised his eyes, straining his neck to see what
Michael was doing. While a human held the gun with the
silver bullet, Michael's weapon was loaded with an ordinary, human bullet. He aimed it calmly down at Sam's
back. 'Sorry about this. But we can't have you following
us.'

To his credit, Sam thought about Peter and Whisperer
more than the gun. Guns he could cope with. Guns were
physical weapons, and he cared little what further injury
was done to his body after thousands of years on the run.
'What about Peter and Whisperer? What will you do
with them?'

'If you come after us, they will die.'

Sam squeezed his eyes shut an instant before the noise
of the gun, and his head pitched forward on to the
carpet.

FOURTEEN

A Debt Repaid

He'd remembered Michael as an honourable soul. They'd been good friends, but Michael had always put duty before all things. If he'd been ordered by Jehovah to kill his own mother, he would have done it.

But it was also true that in some sense he owed Sam his life, a debt that had been repaid in Kaluga after almost five hundred years of neglect.

In the year of Our Lord 1582 Sam Linnfer had been pressing his weary way through an endless, dense forest complete with wolves and bandits. Stopping in his tracks, he found himself staring at the avenging angel ahead.

Sam was wearing a black woollen cloak, and old boots that were in constant battle with his feet as to how fast blisters could be caused, and leading a horse that if anything looked worse than he did. He was fouled and covered with dirt, and his face and exposed hands were flushed bright red. And no matter how good his regenerative abilities, they hadn't worked fast enough to banish the extensive bruising down one side of his haggard features. His clothes too were torn, as though slashed by the claws of a bear, and when he took his hands from the horse's bridle, they trembled.

'They tried to burn me,' he called. It was neither an accusation, nor a plea for help. It was a statement, warning the other away from him. The implication behind it was clear. If they couldn't burn me, don't think you can.

'I've been sent,' Michael said. He was wearing his archangel's white.

'I can tell.' He was still shaken, and Michael could see it. Even Sam struggled when fanatic mortals tried to burn him at the stake. 'Are the others nearby? They'd have to be, if you intend to wear that daft white robe everywhere.'

Michael had begun walking closer, his sword already drawn, the edge gleaming with fire. 'I was sent to find a witch. You'll do.'

Sam watched him approach, his hands not once moving towards his sword. 'They tried to burn me,' he repeated. 'Don't you find that ironic? They say I live in boiling pits of fire, and yet they think they can burn me.'

Michael took up the guard position a few feet from Sam, sword ready.

Sam didn't move. 'Why do you have to fight me? I know Jehovah can't bear my name, because I was right and he was wrong, and his grand Messiah plan failed. But why do you, *you*, have to fight me?'

'I've been sent.'

Sam sighed, and gently slapped his horse on the rump. Obediently it trotted away. He turned his full attention to Michael. 'Tell you what,' he said, 'you put the sword down and stop being an idiot, and I won't tell your master. How does that sound?'

Michael was lost in his own world – or one of Jehovah's making? 'You. A Son of Time, a Prince of Heaven, a Waywalker. I worshipped Waywalkers, thought they were almost . . . godly. And I trusted you, called you my friend. Do you know how I argued with Jehovah when he demanded your death? How I begged him to reconsider – even though he is my master, and not you. He no longer trusts me, you know, because I argued for you. I was cast out of his favour, all because you were my friend. *He's* the Son of Time, the Prince of Heaven. *You're* just the exile that I thought I knew. I would have given anything to be a Waywalker. And yet you . . . *you* . . .'

His sword whirled, but Sam was already there. His hands moved in a blur, and the silver blade was up as he ducked below Michael's blow. Expertly he swivelled, swinging his blade up and across as he exclaimed, 'These many years on Earth and you learn how to survive, old friend.' A thrust, a parry, an easy spin in which he stuck out an ankle to trip his opponent, who fell, then rolled clumsily out of the way of a tauntingly leisured down-stroke.

'I studied survival in China, in Africa, in France and now here and, you know, I feel really confident with myself,' Sam went on as Michael got to his feet. 'Did I tell you about the latest developments in Hell? I've actually managed to convince them of the wonders of plumbing. The fact that the temperature is always below freezing is a minor difficulty, but, as we say, Time conquers all.'

He ducked another thrust, danced nimbly away from a counter-stroke and in the riposte brought his sword swinging round and down in an elegant arc that pinned Michael's sword to the ground and locked them each inches from the other's face.

'You don't want to be a Son of Time, Michael,' he warned softly. 'It's not worth it.'

Michael broke free, jabbing with his knee at Sam's gut. But Sam was already spinning away, and used Michael's off-balance to deliver a ringing sideways blow with the flat of his blade.

'Archangels have it so much easier,' explained Sam in a louder voice as they whirled and thrust across the path and between the trees. 'Being created to serve somehow gives purpose to your life. When I was created to serve, things were so much easier. There was none of this self-doubt, none of this agonising over what it's all about. It's so simple to have your loyalties, faith, belief and hope grounded in one fairly safe bet. But we still gamble with our souls – every day, Michael. And for every day we lose, a little more of our soul is stolen from us. After a few thousand years of gambling, that's a lot of debts to pay.'

Sam had only one hand on his sword now. Too late Michael tried to scramble for cover while, palm out, Sam's free hand came across and up. As it rose, so Michael rose until he was pinned, helpless and motion-less in air, his wild eyes and fast breathing the only proof that he was alive.

Below, supporting his involuntary flight, Sam wasn't smiling at all now.

'They tried to burn me,' he murmured again. 'Do not seek to be a Son of Time. Do not seek to see everything you hold dear pass away, to be replaced by new hope that, again, passes away. Do not seek to see as clearly as Time makes his Children see. If you had seen the things that I have seen, or the things that I must see before I die . . . well, no more of that. You see what you want to see and, while it lasts, that is a marvellous blessing. If we saw what was really there, who would be able to face Time with a steady eye?'

He released Michael from the spell, and the archangel fell to the ground with a heavy thump. Sam brought his free hand slicing through the air, and the effect was like a iron fist to Michael's face, who slumped, hands opening around his blade and voice giving no cry.

'They tried to burn me,' Sam whispered.

It was the squeaking of rats that woke him, or possibly the sound of claws scrabbling on plastic bags. The sun was high in the sky, but his only way of telling this was by the stifling heat and the glimmer of light that shone through a small window at the far end of the room.

He was lying in a basement, unbound, on a pile of garbage bags heaped into a large plastic container beneath a rubbish chute. There was no bullet in his back, but there was also no sign of his sword, nor of Andrew, Peter, or Whisperer. He wondered where the bullet had gone, then as he rolled over he felt his stomach churn. *Oh, hell . . .*

Falling hard out of the container of rubbish, he managed to crawl several feet before he stopped and emptied the contents of his stomach. Tears sprang to his eyes, and he retched and went on retching. There was a warm wetness around his nose and when he wiped a hand across his face a clear liquid came off on it, tainted slightly with blood.

Now he knew what had happened to the bullet. His

body had broken it down, dissolved it into the blood-
stream. He wondered how long he'd been in the cellar.
For his body to have metabolised lead, probably days.

He managed to stand upright, and watched blearily as
the world rocked back and forth. The dagger against his
ankle was gone, but a gleam of silver among the rubbish
marked where it had broken free of its strings, rather
than been taken. He raised one hand and it flew into his
grasp, as fouled and smelly as he was.

Sam staggered towards the single metal door. His
hand blindly found its way to the handle, but the door
was locked. He started hammering, tears streaking his
face and the trickle from his nose turning into proper
blood. Metabolising lead was something he hadn't done
in a long time. He went on hammering, yelling futile
imprecations. No one answered.

Falling back and wiping his eyes with his filthy sleeve,
Sam finally gave an animal snarl of rage and levelled
both hands at the door. It exploded outwards with the
force of his anger and he rushed through it, howling like
a wounded creature. Hearing him, a janitor appeared,
gaping in surprise. Sam rushed straight up to him, a
madman with a knife, and shouted into his face, 'What's
the date? How long was I down there?'

'March the third!' stammered the man. 'March the
third!'

A week! Sam snarled at him, 'Have you got a car?'

The janitor took in Sam's wild appearance and the
furious way he waved the knife, and quickly said yes.

'Then you're going to drive me!'

The man was utterly mad. But he was a madman with a
knife. Having waved his blade at Ivan the janitor, sent on

his weekly round to empty the rubbish bins, the madman had growled, 'Get the car!'

And now he was sitting in Ivan's front passenger seat, one hand flung across the car so that the knife could rest near the janitor's belly, a blanket pulled up to his chin, tears mingling with blood all down his face, and muttering. And smelling. That was what Ivan noticed above all.

'Turn left,' the man snapped.

'Where are we going?'

'The Portal. I was beaten.'

'What Portal?'

'Just drive!'

The man fell silent again. He kept writhing about, pressing his back into the seat and then recoiling as though stung from touching his back to anything. Finally he found a position that seemed bearable and regarded Ivan with strangely sane eyes. 'What's your name?' he asked finally.

'Ivan.'

'Married?'

'Yes.'

'Children?'

'Yes.'

'Then rest assured I'll do my best not to cut your throat.' The madman gave a faint sigh. 'I thought I'd out-witted them, but I was wrong. Still, they won't be able to destroy the sword or the crown.'

Ivan took what to his mind was a terrible risk. 'Look,' he said, as kindly as possible, 'you need help, that's fine! I'll take you to the hospital; they'll look after you.'

'I don't need help! At least, not that kind.'

'What do you do?' asked Ivan nervously. *Be friends with him. Maybe then he won't kill you.*

'Me? I get caught up in other people's stupid, stupid wars and think I can out-manoeuvre them, that's what.' *But I did tag her.*

Ivan thought better of asking anything more. He drove. The man gave strange directions. His lefts and rights and keep goings didn't seem to have any knowledge behind them, and he gave his orders as though compensating for the shape of the land itself. A right here because we couldn't turn where I wanted. A left here because we have no choice. It was as if he had an internal radar and was trying to reach the centre of an unseen positioning system.

Abruptly, the madman told Ivan to stop. They had long left Kaluga and were in the middle of an empty road in a rural nowhere. Ivan stopped, not bothering to pull over. Perhaps someone would notice his plight.

The man was staring fixedly at a small copse of trees in a field. He wrenched the door open and half climbed, half fell from the car. Ivan felt his stomach turn through three hundred and sixty degrees and his heart clamber into his throat. The man's back was soaked with blood, along with a black substance he couldn't begin to guess at. Sam heard the car roar away into the distance, and fancied he heard Ivan's relieved and terrified exclamations fading with the engine. Warm wetness trickled down his spine, and he knew that his body was still trying to discharge the poisonous lead. He began to stagger across the field towards the Way of Hell. It would be a dangerous Waywalk, in his condition. But he was resolved. As he never had been before, he was determined now. Now things were different. Now he was alone. And alone, there was no one save him to make mistakes. Alone, he could weave his spells and be sure that nothing endangered them save his own foolery. Was he not master of magics? Time's necessary Child?

The message that came to Beelzebub was confused, to say the least. He was in his room, stretched across the bed and staring at the ceiling with wide, sleepless eyes. Sleep was a luxury that had long ago been denied him, but demon pride dictated that he didn't complain. So it was fortunate that he would lose none tonight, when the guards hammered on his door.

'Sir! Lucifer!'

'Sir' and 'Lucifer'? he thought. *What have these two to do with each other?*

But he got up, pulling on a warm robe and following the incoherent guards to Lucifer's room. He knocked warily on the door, wondering what it was that could have brought Sam back – and in a state desperate enough to have the usually level-headed guards go frantic.

'It's open!'

Stepping inside, he closed the door to the rest of the world and stared, dumbfounded. Sam was standing before the fire pulling on a large shirt – pale as a sheet, his hair wet from a bath, no sword or crown to be seen, and a bandage wound round him several times to catch the black discharge from an unseen wound in his back.

He grinned weakly on seeing Beelzebub, but though there was effort in his smile, there was little joy.

'I lost.'

It took Sam half an hour to tell his story. He described everything, through the quest to find who, in addition to Odin and Jehovah, might want the Pandora keys, right up to his defeat in Kaluga.

'What will you do now?' asked Bubble.

He shrugged. 'It's not as bad as it seems; I will regenerate. Then there are several things I can do. Firstly I'm going to get back my sword and crown. They can't destroy them, and they know that I can find them anywhere. So if they're clever they'll have thrown them away. But I *will* have them back.'

'And then?'

Again, a wan smile. 'They made a mistake. To convince me of my own safety they summoned fog, as Whisperer would have done. Then they sent a jinniyah to pick me up, with some story about trouble. I tagged the jinniyah's car, and before I left Earth I probed for it. The tag is still there.'

'So. You will continue in this battle, even though you are outnumbered and outgunned.'

'Yes,' he said firmly. 'For Freya, for Whisperer and for my own small-minded little pride, I will go on.'

'When will you return to Earth?'

'As soon as my back stops hurting.'

'When is that?'

'A few days? Regeneration is almost complete, and I've been using a few spells. Most of the work was done in trance.' He wrinkled his nose in disgust. 'A week in a rubbish tip.'

Beelzebub was silent again. Finally he stood up. 'Can you walk?'

'I got here, didn't I?'

'Can you walk comfortably?' he demanded, exasperation only slightly tainting his voice.

Mostly there was concern, and Sam was duly flattered. 'Yes.'

'I'd like to show you something.'

Sam wrapped himself in a warm cloak, attempting to stand tall despite the twinges that shot through his back.

Bubble was unreadable, but the firelight revealed the weariness in his eyes, and at the door his groping hand failed several times to catch the handle.

Sam caught his arm and opened the door. 'You're not well,' he said.

'I am old. It's something you wouldn't understand, Lucifer. Not physically, at least. Come. This is important.'

Sam followed Bubble up the corridor. His mind was already wheeling with possibilities as to what this 'important' sight might be. And with concern for his oldest demon friend. It hadn't occurred to him until that minute to consider exactly how old Bubble was. *When Bubble dies, then demonkind really is nothing more than a collection of savages.*

Moving with an old man's stately gait, Bubble led the way up a flight of stairs. Sam trailed behind with the youngster's shuffle that cries out for more speed. To look at them, no one would have thought Sam the elder, for all the injuries that time or war had inflicted on the pair. *We are wounded soldiers, coming to observe the battlefield*, Sam thought, and then chided himself. *We are who we are; don't try to romanticise a bullet in the back or the weight of age.*

At the summit of a long twisting stair, they made their way out on to a tower. A guard saluted sharply, but was waved away by Bubble, saying they didn't wish to be disturbed.

It was bitterly cold. Ice was already forming on Sam's wet hair, giving it the appearance of a strange helmet. The city of Gehenna was laid out below them, with every street corner marked by a burning fire. In the hills beyond, a pack of hunters riding their huge, shaggy beasts were returning from a kill, and watchfires burnt on the horizon.

'What is there to see?' asked Sam, peering over the battlements and shivering.

'There.' Bubble pointed. Sam followed his finger until his eyes settled on the castle's small forge. Through the darkness his eyes picked out a heaving mass of soldiers, talking loudly. Outside the smithy a clerk was handing out heavy shields and long swords. And now that Sam had detected this, his gaze automatically flew over the second curtain wall to the space between the gatehouses and the keep. Even at this late hour, now that he was listening for it, he could hear the clash of weapons. The deep roar of shaggy beasts being fitted with harness. The yells of instructors relentlessly drilling their men.

'Asmodeus is recruiting all across the land. A thousand men enrolled in the first week, two in the second. A raiding party captured a border soldier, who was tortured for information and publicly executed. Belial is screaming for blood. War has been as good as declared.'

'He's a fool,' growled Sam.

'There's more. The council tried to resist him. He's had two members arrested and the rest sent home. He told me you weren't coming back; seemed very confident of the fact.'

Sam turned on Bubble. 'His words. Give me his exact words.'

'"I am not as ignorant of the affairs of Earth as you think. Lucifer is never coming back."'

Sam realised he was trembling. He turned several times like a caged animal, staring down at the castle he had built so long ago, then looking beyond to the snow-

covered horizon. 'Bubble, I want you to get out of here,'
he said finally. 'You know the safest places to hide.'

'What will you do?'

'Have a little word with Asmodeus. Or even a big one.'

Beelzebub nodded. 'I know where you can find him
tonight.'

Sam's back was throbbing alarmingly by now, but he
ignored it. Striding through darkened corridors, fire in
his eyes and his face clenched with anger and suspicion,
he gave no sign that, only hours ago, he'd woken from a
long trance.

The doors to the soldiers' hall slammed back with a
suitably dramatic boom of wood on wood. The centre of
the floor had been cleared and there was Asmodeus,
cheering on a pair of demons stripped to the waist as
they wrestled for a prize. The prize was a girl, from the
desert judging by the patches of red scale across her neck
and face, huddled in a blanket by the roaring fire and
shivering in the unaccustomed cold. At Sam's appearance,
everything came to a stop. The wrestlers disentangled
themselves, the roaring of appreciative demons fell to a
hush and the thumping of mugs ceased.

'Everyone get out!' roared Sam, sparks flashing from
his fingers and his hair. In the grate, the fire leapt up in
sympathy for his magic. As the soldiers scuttled past
Sam, Asmodeus stayed seated, insolent in his chair.
When the last soldier had gone and only the slave-girl,
Asmodeus and Sam were left, Sam raised one hand and
the doors slammed shut behind him on the watching
faces outside.

'How kind of you to join us,' said Asmodeus, cool as
only a frost demon could be. 'Care for a drink?'

In a few paces Sam had crossed the floor, strode to the table where Asmodeus sat and seized him savagely by the collar, pulling him bodily over the tabletop. 'Tell me what you know and what you're doing,' he whispered, 'and there's just a chance I won't kill you here and now.'

To his surprise and discomfort, Asmodeus laughed. 'Don't threaten me, old man,' he said. 'Your power is dwindling, everyone can see that.'

'My power? Don't you dare lecture me on my power, *little* demon, else you'll discover exactly what it is that's given me my name.'

'Don't threaten me!' Asmodeus repeated, wrenching himself free from Sam's grasp and skipping out of his reach. 'I have more powerful friends than you.'

'Who? Who told you I wasn't coming back? Who was so sure I was going to die?'

'You try to hurt me and they'll hunt you down,' warned Asmodeus. 'I don't know how you escaped them this time, but if you do me the smallest harm they'll come after you. And they have no qualms about killing.'

Sam raised his hands again, palms towards the demon Prince. As Michael had been all those centuries ago, Asmodeus was picked up and flung through the air. He thudded against a wall, where he dangled, feet trailing a few inches above the ground.

'Tell me!' roared Sam. His voice softened, became menacing and low. 'I made your kingdom. With blood and ruthless war I made it, and if you think I'll be inhibited about calling on that same blood and ruthlessness you clearly don't understand the land you rule.'

'You can't touch me,' sneered Asmodeus. 'My friends will kill you if you do.'

Sam brought a hand slashing down, and the demon's

head was flung round as though punched. 'If I have to play by your rules to find the truth, so be it!' he warned, bearing down on Asmodeus. 'Tell me who your friends are! What man or woman has told you to go ahead with the war?'

'Seth,' whispered Asmodeus. He was bright with pride and glee. 'Seth is fighting for *my* cause, Seth will redeem me.'

Sam's spell trembled, faltered. Asmodeus fell sprawling to the floor.

Seth, Son of Night. So it was true what Bubble had said about Seth somehow sticking his nose into Hell business. Seth was doing what Sam had always dreaded – walking that last little step into *his* world.

Why isn't anyone interested in taking over the Earth?

You'd rather they did?

He hadn't answered Annette's question fully. No one takes over the Earth because it is a mere shadow of the glory of Heaven, twisted, transformed. And Hell is a crude shadow of Earth. If you cannot take Heaven, you reluctantly take Earth. If you can't take Earth, you are desperate indeed to be forced to Hell.

And now Seth, the ultimate recluse, suspected criminal, old-time friend of imprisoned mischief-maker Loki, was indeed interfering in Hell, in *his* Hell.

'What did Seth tell you?'

'He said his brothers were after you, that between them he and they would kill you. For plotting with a traitor princess. He said he would help lead my armies to victory.' Asmodeus was glowing with triumph, mistakenly believing that he had in pay his very own Son of Time.

'Why? Why the hell is Seth bothering with Hell? Hell

is *beneath* him, he cares nothing for it! So why bother? What's of value in Hell for him?'

Asmodeus didn't answer.

'For Time's sake! Do you want me to discharge the Light? And read the answer straight from your pathetic little mind?'

'He's . . . looking for power.'

'That's splendidly mysterious,' Sam growled. 'But now try being precise.'

'It's – he wants – a particular artefact.'

'There are numberless "artefacts", even in Hell. Some invented by bored witches to kill cockroaches, some devised by mad wizards to extinguish suns. *What* artefact could be so valuable that Seth would bother coming here, to wage proxy war . . . alongside *you*?'

When Asmodeus didn't immediately answer, Sam, losing patience, raised one hand. Light, not burning white, but gentle and warm, promising worse to come, sprang in his palm. 'I will do it,' he hissed. 'Don't think I won't.'

'The . . . fourth key.'

'Fourth?'

Asmodeus didn't need to answer. He could see the fear in Sam's eyes. But he spoke anyway, fascinated by the sudden terror that filled Sam's gaze. 'Cronus. He's going after Cronus.'

Sam took a seeming lifetime to answer. Several eternities, by the reckoning of his frozen heart. 'Cronus? He wouldn't . . . he doesn't *dare*.'

'We're going to find Cronus,' said Asmodeus softly, recovering himself at seeing Sam so affected by his words. 'To overthrow Time, overthrow Fate, Destiny, Death . . . And you can't stop it. You've nothing left.'

'Cronus's key . . . in Hell? That's it, isn't it? Cronus's key is hidden in Hell, and Belial has refused to help Seth find it. So you're helping him instead. That's why you're raising this army and going to this stupid war. You're not marching to try and overthrow Belial, you're out to take the key – that's why Seth's here!

'You fool! You're handing Seth the means to destroy us all! You're giving him the army he needs to uncover the end of everything!'

'Not everything,' hissed Asmodeus. 'The end of everything *as we know it*. Cronus is just another way of existence, another way of life, and he rewards his friends!'

'Where is it? Where in Hell is the key? In the middle of the desert, buried under a few thousand tons of sand? In the mountains? In the Whirlpool Ocean, in Tartarus, in Pandemonium – where is it? Don't think Seth's above feeding you to the wolves if necessary. So where is the key?'

'I don't know! Only Seth does!'

'You fool,' whispered Sam. 'You are going to die.' As if such a small thing counted, in the face of the horror that now threatened.

Asmodeus pulled himself upright, tilting his chin defiantly. 'You dare not hurt me.' Sam almost had to admire his stubborn stupidity.

'I am not the one who will kill you. Either Belial, Seth or your own hand shall deliver the blow.' It was a guess, not a prophecy, but Sam knew he was right. 'There is nothing I can do to prevent it.' Turning, he threw up his hands in despair, the doors opening before him at a silent command. 'I tried to build a safe kingdom for you, but now there's nothing more to be done! All I fight for now is my own!'

'Lucifer!' Asmodeus called, not knowing why as the dark shape stepped out of doors into the bitter cold.

Sam spun, an accusing finger levelled at Asmodeus's face, so that the demon almost ducked for fear that flame would spew from it. 'You fool, Asmodeus! You small-minded, primitive fool! You've sold your whole land out as mercenaries to a battle being directed from another world!'

'Lucifer!'

Sam laughed and turned away, striding through the thick snow that swirled around him. 'All those who would be safe leave this place!' he yelled as he went. 'Do not follow your Prince!'

'Lucifer!' Asmodeus shouted, running after him. Snow was falling more heavily yet, seeming to wrap itself round Sam as though trying to protect its master, until the only evidence of his existence was the voice resounding through the castle.

'Run while you can! The Son of Night wears your crown!'

'Lucifer!' screamed Asmodeus as the guards flocked around him, uneasy and confused. 'Lucifer, you've lost even your own battles! You're nothing!'

All that answered him was the gentle fall of snow, and when the guards broke down the door to Sam's locked room, the bed was neatly made, the wardrobe empty.

Even the fireplace was cold. Which was odd, for the fire had been burning only a few minutes before.

FIFTEEN

Defeat Revenged

The day before, in a large police station near Victoria where not much caused surprise any more, the senior officer on duty was asked to step into a room wherein the items of a travel bag had been laid out for his inspection.

One silver sword, extremely sharp. One silver band that under any other name might be called a crown. Some clothes. And five passports, two in the name of Sam Linnfer, two in the name of Luc Satise, one in the name of Sebastian Teufel.

A present to the law from an unidentified friend.

A few hours later and the arrest warrant for Sam Linnfer had been issued. Not until the following day would Sam himself walk boldly into the police station, and leave with all his possessions.

He had no more battles to fight that were not his own. Sam took comfort from that. In the past he'd sought company and friendship, and with these had come the responsibilities of help and caring. He'd even revelled in fighting other people's battles, riding the bliss of faith in his friends. Faith had been a luxury often denied him, and in companionship at last he'd found some.

But now that was over. The Moondance network was all but blown, Peter and Whisperer hostages against his good behaviour. Freya was dead. Seth, son of Night, was making his way, maybe with terrible intent, into the vacuum left too long in Hell by Sam himself.

Seth, Odin, and Jehovah are all chasing after those keys. One of them murdered Freya. Oh, Light! All three of them, playing with fire!

Yet, in this moment of loss, without his Earthly identities to hide behind, he had a reason to feel safe. Not happy or clean, but safe. Now all his enemies could do was hurt him – he had no weaknesses that were not his own.

No weaknesses, bar one, whispered a little voice in his mind.

There was a furious hammering on the door, combined with the buzz of a bell. Such scenes were not common in the quiet back streets of WC2. When, even so, there was no answer to his knocking, Sam moved into the middle of the street and tilted his head up to the window. 'Annette!' he yelled. 'Annette, please open up!'

No answer. He rushed back to the door and rammed his hand, palm-first, against the lock with enough force to send shudders up his spine. The lock clicked, the latch seemed to turn of its own volition and the door swung open. Sam took the stairs three at a time.

The door to Annette's flat was already open. Her servant stared accusingly down at him.

'How did you get in?' she demanded in her heavily accented English. 'The mistress doesn't want any visitors.'

'Piss off!' snapped Sam, shouldering past her and into the flat.

'Hey!' she exclaimed, trying to bar him by squeezing into successive doorways. Searching with the energy of a madman for Annette, Sam shoved by easily.

'"Hey" has never been a word of power, and if it were you'd never gain mastery of it.'

He burst through a door which she'd given away by guarding it too hard, and heard Annette's voice even as he saw her. She was sitting up in bed, blankets pulled high and her thinning white hair brushed around her face as though it were a mane of pure beauty, cast down to highlight her looks to a bewitched suitor.

'Leave us,' she murmured to the girl, eyes not straying from Sam.

At the click of the door Sam rushed to Annette's side, searching her face, her mind, for any sign of harm, taking her ancient hands in his and laughing out loud in sheer relief. 'I was afraid they might hurt you,' he said. 'I thought I might not find you after all.'

Her face became serious. In a motherly tone she said, 'What trouble have you got yourself into now, stupid boy?'

If anything he laughed even harder. Through the mirth of relief he managed to explain, 'I got shot, lost two battles at once and spent a week in a rubbish tip, regenerating.'

'Ah. Playing the old games, even though you yourself are too old for them by far!'

'I know, I know.'

'And now the police are after you.'

Sam's laughter abruptly faded. 'Say again?'

'The police, young immortal. The keepers of the peace, the bastions of justice. They came here asking questions about you, saying I was a "known associate" of Luc Satise. They have your passports, your mixed identities. They have your sword and your crown and seem to have been informed by unknown sources that you killed someone.'

His serious face matched hers perfectly, but where her eyes laughed and wept all at once, his held nothing but concern.

'What did you tell them?'

'Nothing. You were the nice young man who'd briefly dated my granddaughter, that was all I knew.

'Then the other men came, asking about you. They seemed very angry. Does he have any doctors as friends; what are his favourite cities, can you give us addresses? I told them nothing, of course. I was just the harmless old lady who rambles on about nothing.' She clenched her ancient fingers into a fist and with her free, trembling hand pulled his face towards her. 'What have you done?' she asked softly.

'What else did they say?'

'They said to tell you something, if you turned up here. To warn you that, though they had failed to kill you, they still had your friends in Kaluga. They said to tell you to keep clear.'

He said nothing.

'Luc? Luc, I loved you. When I go to Heaven or Hell, I'll be waiting for you. What have you done?'

He pulled away from her and headed for the door. 'I came to be sure you were all right,' he mumbled. 'I was afraid they might have hurt you.'

'We're all young in Heaven. We're all old in Hell. We can be old or young together. When you die. When you join me.'

Sam turned in the doorway, and motioned as if to speak. He wanted to tell her that, if she just said the word, he would die. Never once come into her life again, be as a ghost.

But he hadn't the guts. What if he needed her again? What if something, that in reason couldn't be predicted, forced the ghost to rise and fall like a yo-yo from the grave?

So he said nothing.

For her, he had said enough.

I was afraid they might have hurt you.

Annette smiled vaguely to herself, humming under her breath, and leant back against the mound of pillows as the door clicked shut. The immortal had been afraid for her life. She was content.

So now Michael had seen to it that the British police were after him. Sam was grudgingly impressed. Sure, he was master of the art of constructive hindrance. Mortal police forces were nothing that couldn't be dealt with by twenty years in another country or just a few burnt records. But he couldn't deny the inconvenience.

I'm being slowed down. The smart archangel can do the maths — say, a week regenerating, a day trying to get my bearings, another day trying to pick up my stuff, another day trying to find the trail again. Michael's doing everything he can to throw me off without actually killing me.

Good old Michael, I suppose. I can almost — but not quite — forgive you everything.

❋

The next problem was money. Sam had far preferred the days when he could wave his hands and produce the illusion of gold but, in these complicated times of machines and order, he'd found himself forced to open a bank account. And, to his shame, he had quietly tricked and coaxed his way into a fair fortune, which had been gathering interest for more years than Sam Linnfer's birth certificate would suggest was possible.

The account would be monitored, of that he was sure. But even in these days of machines and security, there were ways.

He went first to an antique shop in one of the by-streets near Annette's apartment. Waving away assistance from an odious young man who looked down at everyone who didn't share his passion for prodigiously expensive Regency chairs and tables, he fell to studying a small statue. It was priced at five hundred pounds, hardly more than a foot tall and about as wide as his hand, and represented an improbably shaped woman wearing a necklace and little else. Sam studied it until his eyes ached, recalling every feature and contour, picking it up, feeling its weight, turning it over and over.

When he left the antique shop empty-handed, the assistant openly glowered at this philistine – or miser – who'd been wasting his time.

There was something strange about walking empty-handed through London – Sam, forever on the move, was used to a weight on his back. London itself had always been a safe city for him – its small side streets and sprawling suburbs had offered numberless places to hide or run. The buses and underground system were complicated enough to lose any follower in, and the inner city of old, terraced houses was plain enough for a scry, no matter how skilled, to struggle when identifying any one address.

But now he was on guard against anything and everything, sending searching looks at passers-by and pausing often outside shops to check who might have stopped with him. Scanning the sky for ravens. Probing the streets for spirits. Never finding anything.

He turned the corner into yet another narrow street. Two hundred years ago this place had been covered with horse muck and full of filthy, illiterate children. But now it contained trendy shops selling incense, and paper lamps that cast 'authentic' light.

Somehow, while entering this byway, he had acquired his much-missed burden.

It was not his sword nor his bag; but where, a few moments back, his hands had been empty, he now held a large object wrapped in tissue paper. Singling out an antique store that had lost all character and charm in favour of flashy window displays and over-pricing, he marched through the door and up to the counter.

'You know anything about antiques?' he demanded of the woman sitting there.

'This is an antique shop, you know, and I'm in charge of it.' She had an offended tone that Sam disliked at first hearing. He was in the mood to harbour irrational prejudice.

'I want to sell this.' He unrolled his bundle, revealing the same statue that, whether or not she was wise to the fact, still stood in its proud place a few minutes' walk away.

'We're not a second-hand junk shop, you know!'

He had a feeling she used the term 'you know' a lot.

'Two hundred pounds, lady. And that's a good price.'

He relished the word 'lady'. If she was going to utter infuriating add-ons, then so would he.

Reluctantly, she spared the statue a look. Then another. Finally she took it in her hands and began turning it over, studying the base, running her hands over it, her angry face softening into a slight frown.

'Hundred and fifty, and that's my best offer.'

'I could get five hundred elsewhere.'

She hesitated. 'Where did you get the statue?'

'My mum just died.'

'Hum.' Condolences did not come easily to this woman. Her whole life was work, and work was the only way of convincing herself that her life was full. 'Do you know anything about it?'

'I know that my friend said I could get money for it.'

Again, a little 'hum', a pursing of her lips. 'All right. Two hundred, and it's robbery at that.'

Yes, he thought. *It's you who are robbing me. Only you're not. If you'd been someone else, if the time had been different, I would have felt guilt. But right now guilt is a luxury that I, devoid of all things, cannot afford.*

'Cash.'

'Are you mad?'

'Cash, or I'll take it to someone more cooperative.'

She hissed her annoyance but reluctantly counted out ten twenty-pound notes. He took them and made a hasty exit. Five minutes later and not only was he gone and well gone at that, but so was the statue. As though it had never been.

Sam followed his senses towards his missing weapon, as he'd followed them from Hell.

When he'd opened the Earth Portal he had focused on

no particular destination, but on the song that whispered inside his head – the one that all his weapons shared. He'd let that guide him, Waywalking towards it until he felt his lungs and mind would burst. To his surprise, the song had taken him to London. And now it had led him on to a bus heading south-west through the slow traffic.

A young mother yearned for sleep while her children squirmed and giggled on the seat beside her. The conductor was arguing with a man carrying two large bags of shopping. There's no room, sir. There's another just a few minutes behind, sir. A boy was listening to rap, far too loud. All Sam could hear was the regular thud, thud, thud of the beat, like the heartbeat of an elephant. A couple of women in suits were talking in high, self-conscious voices, delighted by the 'charm' of the bus. They were workers in the city. Buses were for other people, or when there were no taxis to be had.

Sam was remembering.

There had been someone else. Before his time, but back in Heaven Sam had heard all the stories. Someone else, the pride and joy of all Time's works.

He'd first been told the tale of Balder by a man both clever and good, who Sam would always call friend. Who'd never been twisted to anyone's false cause, by spirits or magic alike . . .

'They hate you, Lucifer.'

'Why?'

'Because you represent something they can't comprehend.'

Sam sat cross-legged on a table in a cool, dim library, watching the sunlight outside with desire on his face and a neglected book open in his lap. The librarian was sitting at the desk opposite him, cross-referencing between a pile of books that looked so old it was a marvel they hadn't fallen apart long ago. Sam could hear the sound of angels talking outside the window and the bellow of a dragon, and wished with all his heart to be somewhere else. But he'd promised his one good friend to help him, and in Heaven a promise broken was an especially grievous thing.

'Everything's in books, you know,' said Buddha suddenly. It was a favourite topic of the short, quiet Son of Wisdom. His skin was tanned, his ink-stained fingers worn by long hours working not only in the library, but in the garden and the alchemists' labs and by indulging in his favourite hobby of fishing. Sam had been drawn to him because, unlike his other half-brothers and sisters, Buddha didn't seem to want anything of Heaven, Earth, Hell or Sam himself. His half-brother was also endeared to Sam by the fact that he reminded him of a permanently startled guinea pig.

'There's always someone documenting things somewhere. Maybe not accurately, but at least they're trying.'

'What do you mean?' Sam was used to these sudden changes of topic, and was happy to follow Buddha's often confusing thought processes to some unseen destination.

'Well, here's an example. I have three books telling the story of Balder, and each one disagrees on every single point save the fact that he died.'

'Did you ever meet Balder?'

'Me? Good grief, no. I was still a child.'

'Tell me about him.'

Buddha shifted position, to be more comfortable. He sat straight at all times, as though someone had threaded an invisible string through his back and skull and was holding him taut.

'Once, there weren't eight queens, but nine. And the ninth was Light. She only had one son, and Time declared that if anyone was going to rule Heaven, it was this golden child. Balder. Balder was given a power similar to that which you possess. Like you, it appeared in the form of light, released when he willed it.

'It was, Time explained, the ultimate weapon. This Light would burn away all evil in the world, leaving only goodness behind. This Light would destroy everything impure. So one day Balder released it. And the Light burned through Earth and destroyed thousands of lives and made oceans into deserts. Balder was so appalled by what he'd done that he refused to release it ever again. So delicate and kind was this Son of Light that he would not harm a living soul.

'Time was furious, claiming that Balder had in him the ultimate weapon of goodness. But Balder resisted. He was no fighter, he said, and the weapon would never be used. Time raged, saying that he should have given Balder the other weapon. The cursed weapon that consumed its user as well as its target and made the world sing of darkness and impurity.'

Buddha was staring at Sam, but Sam made no move on hearing this. He went on sitting cross-legged, immovable as Buddha himself, until his brother continued.

'Even though he cursed, Time did not punish his child, but said he would still rule Heaven one day. Meanwhile Loki – true to his nature as father of lies and fickleness – grew jealous. He was jealous of this beautiful, honoured child with the incredible weapon inside him. Jealous of Time honouring him. So Loki slew Balder. And Light fled from Heaven in grief. And the ultimate weapon was no more.'

'If . . . Time loved Balder so, why didn't he warn Balder of this threat?' Sam asked.

'Time sees all futures, but he does not know until the present what future will become reality. He saw that there was a slim chance that Loki would kill his own brother, so he tried to keep Loki and Balder separate. The chance remained slight: most futures Time saw promised that Balder would survive. But Loki is unpredictable, and he made that slim chance reality. I dare say that, in the second before Balder died, Time saw all those thousands of future possibilities change, the possibilities where Balder survived die one by one, the possibiiities where Loki killed his brother increase in waves. The one improbable future where Balder died had become reality.

'There were rumours, of course. Rumours that Loki had been planning it all along and had somehow managed to blind Time to the real danger his son was in. Rumours of spells that kept Loki's thoughts suspended outside Time's reach, rumours of everything from the wild to the trivial, with little regard for the plausible. It was simply a case of Time misjudging his sons' capacity to use their powers against him.

'It was a mistake Time won't make again. Now, he uses people to bring about the futures he wants.'

Sam was silent a long while before he spoke again. 'He's using me, isn't he? The necessary one.'

'It seems likely. And to tell the truth, this other cursed weapon of which Time spoke . . . Well, if a Son of Light will not discharge it then maybe the son of a more ruthless element will.'

'Say it, brother,' warned Sam. 'Discharge the weapon,

and be destroyed in the process. Seth knows it. I know it. You know it. Our father knows it. The interesting question is whether Time has also misjudged me.'

Buddha smiled wanly, but there was something in his weary eyes that made Sam's blood run cold.

'Lucifer, weren't you listening? After Balder, Time won't give anyone a choice in the matter.'

SIXTEEN

Picking Up the Pieces

Michael had done exactly as Sam would have. He'd delivered the enemy's most prized possessions into the arms of a semi-enemy, one that he knew Sam would not harm.

To hurt mortals was to attract their attention, and, as Sam had often pointed out, there were a lot of mortals to become interested in one man.

So having followed his sixth sense to the steps of the police station where, only a day before, an arrest warrant had been issued with his photo attached, Sam was taking pains with carrying out his plan.

Over his back he'd slung another bag, as new as the items it held. He stared up at the yellow-brick building with 'police' on a blue light by its entrance and no ground-floor windows. As he did so, Sam's face began to change. Never seek to destroy with cannon where you can trick with a mirror.

He became, in a word, a policeman. Indeed, in that

moment a sharp observer might also have been startled
by exactly how like a copper he became. In his firm but
kind face that bore utterly no resemblance to Sam's own,
a stranger would have perceived, not the fatigued policeman of reality who'd seen several crimes too many, but a
casting director's naive interpretation of how a copper
should look – a good man trying to fulfil his duty.

But most significant was not the seeming authenticity
of Sam's new features, nor the uniform which must
surely have been there always, but the fact that he was
one and every policeman in the world. If someone were
asked to describe him after only a glimpse, all they'd be
able to say was that he had no distinguishing features.
Not the slightest hook of the nose, nor even a handsome
face. He was just . . . everyone.

Illusion's face impassive, Sam jogged calmly up the
steps and into the station. The trick was to look as if he
knew what he was doing. People are reluctant to question those who look purposeful, for fear that such
purpose rebounds on them.

Reception. The tired copper on the desk glanced up
but, seeing the uniform, looked away again. Sam padded
down as many easy-access corridors as he could find,
until his sixth sense informed him that to get at his precious belongings he would have to tackle one of many
door locks.

At the door to which his senses had directed him he
began punching in any old random combination.
Meanwhile his mind delved through the door to the lock
beyond, pressed against a dozen complicated mecha-
nisms, felt a spring push back against him and pushed
harder. Felt it click.

He was going to get away with it; he could feel it.

As he entered a small room lit only by harsh white lights, he almost laughed out loud at the sight that greeted him. Laid out neatly on the table were his sword and crown, the ultimate prizes of his journey. Just in time he restrained himself from rushing forward to seize them. A woman wearing a stained lab coat was turning towards the door. Her face was thoughtful.

'Who are you?'

A dozen answers occurred to him, most of them prepared in advance. Nonetheless Sam hesitated, long enough for her to question him again while peering at his face and trying to recognise the unrecognisable features. 'Been sent to pick these things up,' he answered finally.

'I wasn't told.' It was an accusation, presumably daring him to produce an official form that no amount of cunning illusion could manage. Illusions needed firm images as a basis, and he had no idea how such a form should look.

Buying time, he tried to change the subject in the first clumsy way that came to mind. 'Have you been analysing the metals? What do you think?'

She frowned, but he'd judged her right. A scientist, for whom being asked about her specialist field banished any other thought. Picking up the crown in her gloved hands and turning it over she said, 'It's no metal I've seen before. Some compound, I suppose, but what kind I don't know. It defies all standard tests. And look at this.'

Sam winced as she smashed it as hard as she could against the table. When she raised it again, it wasn't even scratched by the impact. A bunsen burner was alight nearby and she calmly held the crown over the flame. A large black mark quickly formed but when she removed the crown and rubbed, the mark came off easily.

'Indestructible. And the sword is exactly the same. Very light, too. And impossible to date.'

Still holding the crown, she smiled at a whimsical thought. 'Do you think it would suit me?'

'Don't put it on!' He'd spoken more sharply than he'd intended, and hastily added, 'You might contaminate the evidence.'

Her frown of surprise changed to one of suspicion. 'Who *are* you? I haven't seen you here before.'

He slung his bag from his shoulder and dug into it, seemingly oblivious to her stare. *Look like you know what you're doing . . .* From the depths of the bag he produced a package which, as he unfolded it with an appearance of concentration, formed itself into a slim golf bag. He turned to her, smiling apologetically.

'Sorry about this.'

She was suddenly aware of how quiet the corridor was, and how empty the lab. Instinct took her over and she opened her mouth to scream, not sure where the danger came from or why – but knowing that this man was not what he seemed. Before she could utter a sound, something hard and invisible, but rough as any arresting officer, caught her and flung her backwards. Her head met the wall, and she slid to the floor.

Sam had already slipped the sword into its anonymous case and the crown into his bag. He hastened to her side and checked her pulse; she was momentarily stunned, nothing more. Slinging the bag over his shoulder he hurried from the room, slammed the door behind him and began to walk quickly down the corridor. All he needed to do was keep moving, keep looking ahead, keep the illusion going. He was the faceless man.

Nevertheless, as always when alone in enemy

territory, there was the fright of an actor about to forget his lines before a massed audience. A single slip and he was done for; every move had to be perfect. Never let your fear show. In this place, fear stood out.

But the illusion showed no apprehension, even though the man beneath it was flushed with heat and could feel his heart pounding. For every mind that registered interest in him, Sam's own mind had a little image, a whispered thought that turned it away. He transmitted such images almost unconsciously, after so many centuries of illusion-making.

There was commotion nonetheless in the corridor behind him, people shouting. Sam kept walking, not turning his head. There was a fine balance to strike. If he marched ahead without looking back at what was happening, people might wonder why. If he turned and stopped, he might become trapped and his cover would be blown.

He strode on, eyes ahead, senses fixed on the doorway and freedom. Into reception again, where an officer was already taking a call from some unseen informer talking about 'assault' and 'theft of evidence'. Sam willed himself not to hurry his last steps to the door, danced down the stairs, turned from the police station, let his illusion fall and broke into a sprint, booty cradled under one arm as he ran and ran.

Andrew had whispered in that Moscow street a name which, at the time, Sam had deliberately ignored. He'd ignored it then because he had been busy distracting the valkyries and Firedancers. Now, when he knew his place, and what he was fighting for – now it was suddenly the centre of his world. Gabriel. Gail and Gabriel.

The two names, like Luc and Lucifer, seemed too similar for coincidence. Gabriel. Archangel. The kind of person who just might, on discovering the full horror of what Odin and Jehovah were planning, betray her master, and try, however vainly, to hide Andrew from discovery, as the one man who knew where to find the Pandora keys.

Sam didn't waste time. He went straight to the local pub, bought half a pint of Guinness and a packet of peanuts and, when they were both consumed, went to use the pub's toilets. They were small, grungy, and had space for only one man. But they had locks on the doors, and were dark enough for his purposes. He scryed.

Gabriel. Gail. Whoever you are. Whoever it was who must have tried, and failed, to protect Andrew. If they know where you are, then I need to know too. I need to get to you first, whatever the cost. Helllllooo, anyone out there, or must I discharge the Light and read the minds of men to get what I want?

Images, feelings, sounds, the scry picking out piece after piece and slowly assembling them into an image of Gail-Gabriel. Archangel. *Helllllooo . . .*

And suddenly, as he'd known there would be, a shield, barring his way, sending his mind back with a jolt, and cutting off all access to the focus of his scry. As in Moscow he searched for the markers, opened himself to them, whispered, *Here I am. I am a friend.* The shield parted. He passed through, felt life moving beneath him, soared like a bird, sped towards his target, and hit *another shield.* He hammered against it with futile strength, but it didn't break. He searched it for markers, felt them, heard them whisper, *Enemy.* Felt magic gather to repulse him, shielded, bared the storm, attacked, bared again. All to no avail. He knew it was going to be no use. He saw the way the inner defence had been constructed, just inside the primal, friendly shield and almost welded to its shape, so that anyone breaching the first would still be unable to penetrate the second.

He knew who'd made it too. The smell of the magic on it, the way it had been constructed, all fluid lines, traditional curves, no imagination, no spark, just stodgy laws of warding applied by a careful, well-trained practitioner. He recognised that structure. He could name the Waywalker who made it. Jehovah. Jehovah was keeping him out, Jehovah knew that he'd come, Michael must have told him . . . cutting off his way to Gabriel.

To Gabriel.

Archangel.

This time he didn't bother with aeroplanes. He had no passports and the money he'd conned would not suffice. He went straight to a Hell Portal and Waywalked calmly and at a steady pace to a Portal in an isolated cave near, but not in, Gehenna.

A flock of white bat-like creatures, all pointed teeth and hooded eyes, erupted from the cave mouth in a rush as he came out through the Portal. The cold hit him like a fist; his clothes were far too thin to keep him warm for the long minutes he stood there, heaving in great breaths and trying to forget the haunting voices from the Way that clung to him like spider's silk. He could distantly, oh so distantly, hear the sounds of the city, but he didn't go to investigate. Hell was not his concern any more. Maybe later, yes, but not now. Not with Seth on the scene; clever, cunning Seth.

When he turned again to face the Portal he was shivering, his breath condensing in front of his pale face. He

dug around in his bag until he found a second overcoat
to pull on over his first, a long scarf of the rag-tag variety
that he preferred, and a large hat. Hitching the bag back
on his shoulder, without further ado he marched straight
back into the Portal. He knew that if he stopped to stare
at the Portal and work out what he was doing, he'd never
go.

As the shadows tore at him and the mist filled his
lungs with burning fire, some part of Sam felt strangely
happy. He was at war again. Michael had shot him, Seth
had invaded his world. But somehow, through it all, he'd
found out who his enemies were. Odin, Jehovah, Seth.
He had purpose and direction at last.

Sam Linnfer broke from the Portal once more, into
Russia.

Maria was a strange spirit, as spirits went. Most of her
kind were restless, always drifting through the Way of
Fey in search of something to satisfy their eternal curiosity. But not her. She had long ago discovered that if you
sat in one place you could watch the world change
around you, rather than go searching for it. She found
this gradual change more interesting than wandering
around, rootless and uncertain. Maria had sat through
the revolutions of 1917, through the German invasion,
through the ending of Russian communism. She had
watched buildings rise and fall, known everyone who
ever passed down the small street outside her flat, and
even done the unthinkable – taken a part-time mortal
job. For two days a week she was an usher at the
theatre, and it was something she adored. Not only was
there a pageant of human life, as people went to and
from their seats, but by using some not-quite-mundane

inspiration she'd been able to sneak into almost any performance.

Maria was, as some said with disgust, a mortal-lover.

She lived in a small block of flats overlooking a road that never had more than two or three ramshackle vehicles on it at any hour. So she was surprised one cold evening to observe a new car, a red one, pull up beneath a street lamp and let out a passenger. His face was hidden beneath a large hat, and on touching him her questing mind encountered nothing. Not a shimmer of power, mortal, immortal or spiritual, but neither the open book that most mortal minds offered. Blankness.

She watched this strange figure move towards the block of flats, staying in the shadows at all times. Saw his dark shape stoop by her car and look at it with his head on one side, as though listening for something. He straightened again, and stared straight up at her window. She jumped back instinctively, pulling the curtains shut. Then chided herself for being a nervous fool. Tweaking the curtains aside again, she peered down into the street, but the man was gone.

Scared people often shrug off their fear as fantasy, and this was exactly what Maria now did. Returning to the kitchen of her cramped flat, she picked up the book she'd been reading and settled down by the small gas fire for a pleasant night acquainting herself with her latest hobby – mortal literature.

There was a knock on the door. She rose quickly, her spirit curiosity overcoming her nerves. At the door she peered through the spyhole. A man in a long black coat was standing with his back to her and his head turned away, as though examining the stairwell.

She opened the door – and wasn't sure what hit her.

One second the stranger was doing a good impression of a lost tourist, the next his foot was in the door and his face was contorted in a look of such ruthless determination that she nearly screamed.

In stunned silence she took in the black clothes, black eyes, black hair and black expression of the man she'd tried to lead to his death. Then she did scream, raising her hands in warding. Her element came to her aid: a sphere of water erupted from her hands and locked around Sam's mouth and nose – but he simply shook his head and it shattered.

As Whisperer controlled fog, so she controlled water, and the ease with which he'd destroyed her only good spell made her feel nauseous with dread. Her scream rose louder as he barged in through the door, kicking it shut behind him, grabbed her arm and threw her bodily into the nearest room, which turned out to be the bathroom. She kicked and punched but he was far stronger, throwing her to the floor, locking her knees in his own and pinning her arms to her sides.

A dagger was at her throat. She knew it was *his* dagger, the kind of weapon which would end any life, spirit or otherwise.

'Shut up!' he yelled in her face.

'I had to do it!' she wailed. 'They gave me no choice!'

He must have hit her, for she remembered feeling pain, real pain, delivered with a precision that a mere mortal fighter could never have managed. Sam knew where and how to hurt spirits.

'Where did they take them? Where is Whisperer?'

'I don't know,' she whimpered.

Pain again, this time of a mental kind as a spell flashed across her.

'Look,' hissed Sam. 'I am Satan, I am the Devil. I am everything that Heaven reviles, and I have been stripped of everything but the clothes I stand up in.

'Don't think that, bereft as I am, I'll let myself be bound by morality. I don't wish to be what they say I am. But if that's what works, then I'll be ten times worse than any story preached from a pulpit. Do I make myself clear?'

She nodded, terrified.

'How do you contact someone who *knows* where they are?'

'I was given a crystal. They'll come to me.'

'Good.' He reached for her face.

As she realised what he was going to do, she began to kick and struggle again, screaming at the top of her voice. But to no avail, as he laid his hands across her forehead and dived into her mind, tearing through her shielding as though it wasn't even there.

It was the ultimate shock of violation and she turned rigid as his voice spoke to her from inside her head. <You cannot fight me. Do not even attempt it, spirit!>

She felt her body relax beneath him, even as inside she fought and fought. But his grip was relentless. He didn't violate her memories or listen to her thoughts; nonetheless the horror of having any presence, however restrained, inside her, controlling her, made her want to shriek at the unmerciful fates which had allowed this insult.

She felt Sam release her, stand up. But she was still unable to move, so firm were his controls. He spoke carefully, syllable for syllable, as he struggled to keep his grip absolute on Maria's mind. He could feel her memories and thoughts calling to him, but firmly evaded them.

Few people, spirits included, recovered from having
their whole mind taken.

'Get up.'

She rose, expressionless, hands hanging limp at her
side.

'Get the crystal.' He followed her from the bathroom
into her bedroom – and marvelled at it. Pictures painted
by mortals, mortal books, even a television set and radio.
Most spirits recoiled at the mere idea of such things.

She unlocked a box, moving like a zombie, and held
out a small, palm-sized crystal.

'Call the contact. Tell him you urgently need to meet
him.'

Without a flicker, without a pause, she cupped her
hands round the crystal and closed her eyes. Between
her fingers he saw a brief, faint glow. Their communica-
tion lasted all of a second.

Wordlessly she returned the crystal to the box.

'When will he get here?'

'Half an hour.'

'What's his aspect?'

'He controls the fog.'

'What? Was he the one who summoned fog on the day
I arrived in Kaluga?'

'Yes.'

He looked thoughtful for a moment, but said only,
'Are there securities?'

'No.'

'He'll simply knock on the front door?'

'Yes.'

He nodded faintly, and raised his hand to her forehead
again. Her eyes flickered shut and with a faint sigh she
slipped to the floor. Sam hastened to gag and bind her,

before rolling her under the bed. He released the controls from her slumbering mind, leaving only a command
to sleep for five hours.

That done, he went into the kitchen and made himself
a cup of coffee, taking it through to her tiny sitting room,
where he pulled one chair up to the table and placed
another opposite, in the manner of an interrogator
preparing for his subject.

There was a knock on the door. Going over to check
the spyhole, he observed – both with his mind and his
physical eyes – the heavily coated figure, pale-faced like
Whisperer, whom he remembered from his last
encounter with Michael. Opened the door.

'Good evening,' Sam said politely. The spirit turned,
his mouth opened, raising his hands in defence just as
Maria had done. But Sam was already there, lunging to
catch the spirit in a grip of magic that lifted him off his
feet and dangled him.

With a click of his fingers Sam produced a fine flame
in the palm of his hand. Unnecessarily showy, perhaps,
but he wanted to impress.

'Make one sound and you become the latest case of
unexplained spontaneous combustion.'

The spirit wisely stayed silent.

'Shall we?' The spirit was dropped to his feet again.
For a second he looked like he might bolt. But Sam's
faint smile and the way he tossed a fireball from hand to
hand as though it were a cricket ball and he was about to
bowl a googly, made the spirit think better of it.

'Inside.' Sam's voice was harsh despite his smile that
never once flickered. The spirit edged through the door,
jumping as it slammed shut behind him.

'Into the sitting room. Sit down.'

Sam took the seat opposite the spirit and gently flicked the fireball on to the table between them, where it bounced then hung in the air, spinning slowly and giving off the occasional rosy spark.

'I really am so grateful you could come,' said Sam, reaching to take a sip from his coffee. The spirit shifted uneasily, still not saying anything. 'Now, let's get some rules straight, shall we? You call for help and you become a fireball. You get off that chair and you become a fireball. You use unpleasant language or attempt to lie to me and enough of you becomes a fireball so that you'll never heal the wound but never die either. You try to attack me and you become a fireball. You try to use your aspect and' – his smile widened – 'you become a fireball.'

He folded his hands in front of him on the table, fingers laced together and almost touching the still-spinning fire. 'So. Where are Whisperer, Peter and Andrew?'

To his credit, the spirit spoke defiantly. 'What have you done to Maria?'

'She's sleeping. You think I'd kill her? For what? Being forced into acting like an idiot with the rest of you? No.' He leant forward, and now there was no smile on his face. 'Look. I'm the Devil. I've had centuries of people telling me what it is I'm supposed to do and centuries of telling them no. But in this case I'm willing to make a small exception. Just for once I'm ready to prove those nice little stories about me are true. This is a fate which, if I were you, I would seek to avoid.'

The spirit hung its head. 'I can't tell you where the mortal is. Only the archangel Michael knows. I do know that he's very ill and might die. The Firedancer's poison is stealing his life bit by bit. The archangel is trying to save him, because he knows where the shield came from that protected him. But the others – yes, I can show you where they are.'

'Before you volunteer to show me anything, tell me how it's guarded. And remember, I don't like lying.'

'Three spirits and two mortal wizards. That's all, I swear.'

'Right!' Sam rose to his feet. 'And no tricks.'

'Who can trick a Son of Time?'

'Another Son of Time, since you ask, but yes.' Sam gulped down the last of his coffee and indicated the door. 'Shall we?'

SEVENTEEN

Immortal Avenged

The spirit drove. Sam watched, keeping his sword drawn across his lap. After half an hour of driving through the Moscow streets, made empty by the lateness of the hour, they pulled up in front of a night club with flashing neon signs and pounding music. A wall of muscle stood in the door, ready to repel unwelcome club-bers. Nearby a lorry was unloading crates of cat food for a supermarket. A couple of beggars slumbered on a doorstep. But it was to a flight of stairs leading to a base-ment that Sam's spirit guide pointed.

Sam could sense, as promised, three spirits and two human wizards. Beyond them, inside a warded room, he caught the faint tinge of dead leaves, and the smell after rain, sneaking through their shields. The humans felt asleep, but spirits rarely slept.

'Why did Michael keep them alive?' he asked softly.

'He doesn't like killing spirits. And though they're loyal to you, he thought you might not be alive for much longer.' The spirit was unafraid to speak the simple truth, knowing that Sam could feel it as such.

'Thank you,' said Sam. 'You fill me with confidence. Now tell me one more thing: Is the archangel collaborating with the Firedancers?'

'No.'

Sam was surprised, but he didn't let it show. 'How interesting,' he said finally. Then, 'Thank you, I think you've been a help.' He laid one hand gently on the other's shoulder. The spirit shuddered at Sam's touch, closing his eyes as he steeled himself for what he thought would be death.

'I do hope you have a nice day.' Sam triggered the spell. The spirit pitched forward, unconscious, head slamming against the horn. Hastily Sam moved him, to sprawl across the two front seats. Locking the car behind him, he walked, sword in hand for all to see, towards the club. The bouncer on the door stared at this figure in black with a mixture of disbelief and uncertainty. He looked almost relieved when Sam, with a pleasant smile, turned away from the door and jogged down a flight of slippery iron steps into the blackness of the basement area.

There was a large metal door. Sam knocked calmly, and waited, a blacker outline against the gloom. What little light caught his eyes made them glow, like a cat's.

There were footsteps, and the door opened.

'Good evening,' said Sam – and lashed out with one foot at a spirit, who crumpled forwards. Sam whirled through the door, bringing his sword in one movement across the spirit's throat. Two other spirits, who'd been playing poker with tarot cards, erupted to their feet, each reaching for a gun. A couple of human wizards had been snoring quietly on a pair of old mattresses. A pipe was dripping. Against one wall a bank of washing machines chugged round and round, opposite a row of neglected sinks.

'I know spirits are loyal to each other,' said Sam quietly, 'though you do not call it loyalty, for fear it makes you sound too mortal. I know too that most spirits are essentially good. I know you won't want to see your friend die.'

The spirits exchanged doubtful looks.

'I too am loyal to my own,' Sam continued. 'And this is the arrangement. You give me my friends, and I won't cut your friend's throat.'

'Two for one?' snapped one spirit.

On the prompting of instant dislike, Sam raised his free hand in a blur. His dagger flew across the room and paused, hanging in the air, spinning gently near the spirit's heart.

'No. Two for two and we'll call it quits.'

The spirits didn't move.

Sam sighed loudly. 'Gentlemen, I've had a bad week. A sister killed, mortal allies poisoned, friends kidnapped – these things do not make me happy. I'm sure that under normal circumstances we could talk this over like rational, civilised immortals. But these are not normal circumstances. Now, you give me two people, I give you two people. The balance of accounts is even.'

The humans by now were rising to their feet, all gaping mouth and confusion. Sam gave them a humourless smile.

'Glad you're up. Get my friends, else I'll blast the lot of you.'

Still no one moved.

'For Time's sake don't provoke the Devil himself!'
roared Sam. Anger at last broke through his self-control,
and made his black eyes flash with fire. The echoes
bounced around them, dwindling to fill the darkness
with angry whispers. *The Devil himself? To defeat a monster
you must become it first, know thine enemy. To beat a ruthless
man the winner must be ruthless too, the Devil himself?*

The third spirit moved, rushing towards the inner
door and dropping the keys in his fumbling haste to open
it. Sam's outflung hand stayed motionless, keeping the
dagger point spinning in mid-air, ready to strike the
second spirit at a moment's notice. The third spirit disappeared into the darkness of the room. There was the
sound of voices, of movement.

A few moments later and he emerged again, covering
Peter and Whisperer with a pistol. Sam's two comrades
were a mess, grimy and tired. He could see their shields
in tatters from too many interrogations.

'Lucifer,' murmured Whisperer disbelievingly.

'Oh, come on. You think a bullet in the back would
distract me from seeking out your company again?'
asked Sam lightly.

He turned to the others. 'All right,' he said, 'here's
what we do. Whisperer and Peter leave now. So do I,
taking any threats with me. No one gets hurt, no one
panics, no one tries any last-minute heroics. Are we
agreed?' There was a flurry of nods.

Sam indicated the door. 'Go,' he murmured.
Whisperer and Peter ran, Sam backing out behind them
with his sword still drawn. His free hand twitched, and
in response the dagger returned to his fingers. He
retreated further until he could feel the cold outside air
on the back of his neck. Then, taking a deep breath, he

let go of his dagger, which returned to hang in the air across the spirit's throat. Withdrawing his sword, he backed out of the door, eyes slitted in concentration at keeping the dagger where it was. Inside the room no one moved, no one breathed.

Sam backed up the stairs, feeling each step beneath his feet. He kept his eyes fixed on the hovering blade, one hand flung out towards it at all times to steady it. Halfway up the stairs he clenched his fingers. Narrowly avoiding the spirit's neck, the dagger flew into his hand. Sam turned and ran, taking the steps two at a time and willing the door behind him to slam shut.

At the top of the stairs he turned, expecting to see the door burst back open at any second, hear the crack of gunfire. But Peter was standing there, face contorted with effort as he held his hands palm out, keeping the door in place by willpower.

Sam tossed the car keys to Whisperer and pointed. 'Throw out the sleeping guy.'

At Peter's side Sam raised his own hands to double the magic against the door. Seeing Whisperer bodily heave the unconscious spirit out of the car, the bouncer started from his place in the night club doorway. 'Hey!'

There was a roar from the car engine, and Sam grabbed Peter's arm. 'Come on!' As the spell was dropped, the spirits and the two wizards exploded outwards from the basement. Sam and Peter thrust past the bouncer as if he wasn't there and barrelled into the car. The doors hadn't even closed before Whisperer was accelerating away.

In the car a breathless silence followed. 'Well,' Sam mumbled finally. 'I'm glad to see you too.'

❋

'Uriel did most of the questioning,' Whisperer said.

They'd pulled into a squalid service station where plastic-looking hamburgers were the only food available. Sam picked out the gherkin from his and tried not to think about how the burger itself had been made.

'She wanted to know about you, mostly. How much you knew, how much you'd told us.'

'Were you hurt? When you explained that I'd told you nothing?'

Peter shook his head. 'They could sense whether we were telling the truth.' He added, 'They were very interested in the Light. When you released it, were you just trying to stun the target? Could you control whose thoughts you heard? Did you hear thoughts within the radius the Light had covered, or could you hear everything at once?

'You were wise,' he went on. 'You kept everyone, including us, in the dark. There's only one person who can answer all these questions, and that's you.'

'And Time,' muttered Sam. 'Why don't they go and interrogate Time!' he spat with sudden vehemence.

The spirits said nothing, watching him. Sam went back to munching on his hamburger, slurped up a disgusting powdery milkshake from a paper cup, and wiped his mouth on the back of his hand. Finally he said, 'I'm sorry for . . . what has happened. I'll make amends, somehow.'

'There was one more thing,' Whisperer said. 'Uriel asked us what we knew of the keys. To the Pandora spirits. We denied all knowledge of them. Uriel grew angry, said that three were found, and all that remained was to find the fourth key. She wanted to know if you had it.'

Sam was staring at vacancy, remembering. 'I was once told, by a particularly clever man, albeit one who looked like a guinea pig, that the Pandora spirits were imprisoned because Time feared them above all the rest. Greed, Hate and Suspicion. Yet such spirits as Corruption, Envy and Jealousy freely walk the Ways. Time feared the Pandora spirits because he knew they could set son against father, father against son. And because Cronus wanted that to happen. Because Cronus, imprisoned by the fourth key, wanted Time's children to turn against their maker, and fight Cronus's battle for him. So the keys were scattered, and Time forbade anyone to free the Pandora spirits.

'But it is the way of men to desire all they cannot have. To want to break the rules . . . Oh, Light!' He put his head in his hands and sighed.

The spirits were silent, watching him. 'Look,' he said. 'I know where I'm going next, I know what I'm going to do. Lose yourselves in the Way of Fey. If you encounter any of the Moondance, tell them to lose themselves too. Freya discovered what was going on, and they know I'm close behind Freya's footsteps.' *Which is why they're trying to kill me.*

Peter and Whisperer didn't argue but drove with him straight from the service station to the nearest Fey Portal. At their departure they said not one word, but slipped into the Feywalk with all the reserve of kings, not thanking him for rescuing them, nor cursing him for endangering them. Such was the gift of spirits – they only felt what they intended, and proudly resolved otherwise to feel nothing.

Alone now, Sam drove through empty roads and emptier countryside, following his senses to a Hell

Portal. *Three of them, playing with fire. Surely they wouldn't be so unbelievably stupid as to try and actually* free *the Pandora spirits . . .*

He thought about the three of them. The clever, passionate Saviour, the romantic who'd never had any real name. Yes, Jehovah would want to leave his mark. Sam could imagine him greedily claiming the spirit of Suspicion as his servant, playing it against his enemies as part of those subtle games he revelled in.

Odin had been someone he'd quite respected. Father of Valhalla, head of his house, the clever, silent one who just about kept his loutish brothers out of trouble. It had been slippery Loki, and the death of Balder, that had started the decline of Valhalla, a failure that to Odin spelled shame. But who could have thought him desperate enough to stray this far from the path of Time? On the other hand, as father of his house Odin's dedication had always been shadowed by something darker. In a word, obsession.

And Seth. Quiet. Ambitious, without a doubt. The one whom everybody suspected of being a plotter with Loki, but who'd never been caught out. Was he trying to control Hate?

He pulled the car up on a muddy path. It led to an expanse of pasture, in which a pair of well-fed, if dirty, horses were grazing. He walked round the edge of the field, close to a tall hedge. After about fifty yards he came across a gap and pushed his way through. Inside the hedge was a small hollow. The remnants of a fire had blackened a circle of dead leaves. A child had nailed a sign in Cyrillic declaring 'secret den' in scrawled paint on to a wooden post. Ropes and supports had been erected around the hollow to keep it safe for the children to play in.

Sam smiled despite himself. If the parents had known what kind of secret place their children were playing in, they would never have gone to the trouble.

Stepping round the burnt-out remnants of the fire, he raised a hand and felt the Portal stir at his touch. Sam didn't go through it, but sent his mind scouting ahead into the mists, rushing through the shadows in quest of something he knew would be there. He found what he sought, winding his will around it and bringing it towards him, though it struggled in his grasp and tried to dive back into the mist.

Reluctantly the creature was pulled out of the Portal and into the real world, where it cowered at Sam's feet, shivering. Sam waved a hand, and the Portal collapsed again.

The creature before him was strange. Delicate wings grew from its back, but its face was twisted with hate, its clothes ragged and its eyes narrowed with passionate loathing for its captor. Its nails were shaped to a needle point, ready to gouge out its victims' eyes, and its teeth were small and sharp for tearing through meat. It was a Wayspirit, a twisted shadow of its Feywalker cousins. Where spirits like Whisperer and Adamarus had forsaken feeling of their own free will, the creature before Sam could feel nothing but the hatred of the Way, and its voice was the loudest and sweetest one that called to unwary travellers, luring them to their doom. It despised Earth, Heaven and Hell alike, and mewed piteously to have been so forcefully dragged from its abode between worlds.

'Look,' said Sam, as kindly as he could, though his gut twisted to think of all the beguiling whispers the spirit had thrown his way, 'do what I tell you and this'll all be over quickly. Find me Seth. Tell him to meet me alone on neutral ground. The traditional place.'

The spirit didn't move.

'Now, please.'

It snarled its hate but rose to its feet nonetheless, knowing itself tagged for death unless it obeyed, and dived towards the place where the Portal had been. There was a flash of white fire and it was gone. Wayspirits could move faster through the Ways than any other race. It was what made them so valuable to anyone who knew how to summon them.

Sam opened the Portal again, wondering with how much more anger those claws could tear at him now that he'd intruded on the spirit's privacy. Drawing himself up, he told the part of him fretting at such things that he was a Prince of Heaven and not scared of any mere shadow.

If he'd fully believed himself, he wouldn't have laughed to hear his own voice. But laugh he did.

Prince of Heaven, my foot. Prince of the unwanted lands, maybe.

But still a prince. And not scared of shadows.

Resolved in this way, he went in search of the neutral ground with the one thought that gave him strength. *Things are falling in place.*

EIGHTEEN

Falling in Place

Sam emerged from the Way of Earth in total darkness. His ears were overwhelmed by the rushing of water and his nose by the stench of algae. When he moved, his feet slipped on wet marble, and nearly went out beneath him. His cat-like vision quickly grew adjusted to the dark, and picked out an underground river that roared through a cave of white marble carved out to immaculate proportions by some long-dead dwarvern architect.

The Hell Portal had its own sculpted porch, in which carvings of fire and ice entwined each other in an intricate dance. Moving away from it, he picked his way along the slippery marble path towards the one faint source of light. It came from a small doorway, a faint white flicker of magical firelight that never died down. He paused in the entrance and took out the silver crown, putting it on with reverence for another crowned prince resting inside for all eternity. That done, he drew his sword and advanced.

The cave was huge. Somehow it was dry despite the rushing river outside and the unnaturally still lake at its centre. In the middle of this lake a golden coffin rested, on a platform of diamond that floated as though no more substantial than a feather. The walls were crystal and gave off infinite reflections of the cave's white magic light, banishing every shadow. From the roof a strange complex of crystals and mirrors was suspended, gently spinning. Where a stray beam of light was caught, it was reflected into the depths of the largest crystal and emerged rainbow-like at the other end, casting all the colours of the spectrum on to Balder's final resting place.

Sam bowed stiffly to the grave, the traditional mark of respect, and padded quietly round the edge of the lake, eyes never leaving the golden coffin. He felt that if he spoke, the whole shrine would crack and crumble, and he kept his silver sword drawn as much to convince himself as the guardian spirits here that he was a prince of equal measure to this sleeping Son of Light. No one would shed blood in this place. It was the ultimate sanctuary.

He didn't have to wait long. Playing his fingers along the cool crystal wall of the cave, he jumped when a soft voice said in the door, 'Well, look who wants to talk. How's the back?'

Seth, dressed with his usual vanity, stood in the doorway. He had a long, curved scimitar at his hip, and wore long black and gold robes that had been fashionable for about ten minutes during the late sixties, but now survived only in the wardrobe of eccentrics.

Uncomfortably Sam took in his laughing dark eyes, which somehow wore intelligence as a taint. Sam's own white face was steely. He sheathed his sword. 'I know what you're doing.'

'That's nice for you.'

'I know you're trying to take over Hell.'

'Only bits of it. I won't be there long.'

Sam's face grew warm and he felt his stomach tighten. He bit back on the words that rose with his bile. 'You killed Freya.'

'Not personally.'

'Then Jehovah did it, or Odin.'

'She was in our way. So are you.'

'You mean to free them? The Pandora spirits? *All* of them? *Cronus?*' Even now, Sam could hardly believe his own words.

'Yep. Given the chance, of course.' Seth sighed, as if bored. 'You know, I only came out of curiosity.' He stared thoughtfully at Sam. 'And to assess the enemy.'

'Why am I your enemy?'

'It's not who you are, Lucifer, it's what you are. The Bearer of Light. You're Father's tool, destined to die in his service. You've no choice. Not since we've been actively defying Father, and Father sent Freya to investigate us —'

'Did he?'

'Most probably, but I must admit' – giving a sudden, sickly smile – 'she bungled that thoroughly enough. The only reason I'm here, though, is to see exactly what Father will throw at us next. Let's face it, it's going to be you.' He cocked his head on one side. 'Why did *you* want us to meet? Why do you want to see me?'

'Perhaps it's because . . . I respected you once. I wanted to see what was left of that. I hoped we could stop this thing now.'

'My dear boy, you're several centuries too late. But then, you always were behind the times.'

Sam said nothing, feeling the hate rise inside him. *Seth had everything I never had, and look what he's doing with it.*

'No,' said Seth finally, still looking Sam over. 'I don't think you'll be a problem. It's a pity, really. You could have been a great ally. If Balder had been alive today, if he had been my enemy instead of you, I would probably have asked you to join the cause.'

'Oh, right. And thank you, my back is fine.'

Seth's eyes glowed. 'I wanted you dead. But Jehovah gave the job to that fool Michael. He should have remembered archangels don't kill archangels, however fallen.'

'And your so-called cause?'

'Will make us free.'

'I feel free enough right now.'

'Then you've never studied French philosophy. Nothing else goes on quite so much about the separateness of being and the imprisonment of the soul.'

'I prefer good old scepticism.'

'Did it get you where you are today?'

'You achieved that.'

'Nonsense! I've merely helped, over the past few weeks. It was Father who put you where you are now.'

'I have nothing to do with him,' said Sam coldly.

'But you're part of him. He's part of you. You can't get much more together.'

'The same great link connects you to him. Yet you defy.'

Seth looked scornful. 'Come on, Lucifer. You've spent your life defying Father. You've spent years trying to get out of his grasp, turn away his plots, be something he

doesn't want you to be. Your entire life has been one long
lone act! I'm simply taking it a step further.'

'How? What exactly are you going to do? Tell me!'

'Can't you find out? You have friends who can con-
struct tight, tight shields and know the game our beloved
sister, Freya, has finally stopped playing. You've been
shot, chased, fought, made to dance to any beat but your
own – can't you find out? Or do you genuinely expect
me to tell my greatest enemy?'

'I've never crossed you before. You had to kill my
sister to make me fight!'

Seth was unruffled. 'You'd fight me anyway. Time will
make you. You'll die, I fear, of an overdose. Of Time, I
mean.' He frowned, then laughed. 'I'm sorry,' he said. 'It
amuses me that I, the Son of Night, who's masterminded
this whole affair, from Freya's death onwards, am talking
to the one weapon that might prevent me from finding
freedom.'

A weapon. Not a person. 'What freedom?'

'Freedom from Time, of course. You see, Lucifer,
you're thinking in a mere four dimensions. That was
always your trouble. Just a little too pragmatic; a bit *too*
here-and-now. Time might be life. But he's also death.'

'You cannot defy Time.'

'You did. You were supposed to be the Bearer of
Light, Balder's glorious successor. But you spat at his
throne and dared him to make you discharge the Light.
You said you wouldn't be his servant. A risky policy, if
you ask me.'

'Believe me, I've paid the price. Banished to Earth for
thousands of years before they even invented toothpaste.
And Father, for my defiance, didn't stop his own children
exiling me, when I sabotaged the Eden Initiative.'

Seth was silent. When he did speak, his voice was serious, almost concerned. 'Join me.'

'No.' Sam fought the impulse to violate this place of sanctuary by hitting Seth hard in the face. 'You killed Freya.' His face was flushed with anger and bitterness.

'Why do you care? Surely she's just something you can't touch from a world you can never go back to. What did she matter to you?' Seth's tone was light, but he was watching Sam closely.

Sam's features had frozen over.

'Why,' murmured Seth, 'I believe that's it. What *did* Freya mean to you? What would you do for her memory, now that she's dead? Is that what you're fighting for?'

His voice darkened, even while it resounded with triumph. 'But she rejected you. She went to Thor. You meant nothing to her. Stop this stupid game, Lucifer. Not even you are powerful enough to win against us.'

'I did love her.' Sam spoke as much as anything for his own sake. 'But I see now' – looking pointedly at Seth – 'that loving someone is rarer than even I used to think.'

Seth ignored him. He moved suddenly towards Sam, who instinctively stepped back. 'Why don't you discharge the Light now? Balder would forgive you. You're his heir, practically his son, albeit not by blood. So read my mind, then destroy me. That's what you really want to do, isn't it?' His smile was immovable. 'Go on. Fight. You've always fought before, why not now?'

Sam said nothing.

'Ah.' Seth's grin widened. 'But you *are* fighting!'

Sam's eyes flashed, but still he didn't respond.

'Though it's not me you're opposing,' breathed Seth, growing more confident. 'You're fighting Time. You think he wants you to strike at me. So you won't. You're fighting inevitability. You'll lose, of course. In truth, you've always lost. Like Freya.' Sam's hands, hanging limply at his sides, clenched into fists. 'You know,' breathed Seth, 'it was Jehovah who killed her. He had his fun first, of course. Does that upset you?'

Just let me find another time, another place . . .

The look on Sam's face was not lost on Seth. 'How about poison? Much more efficient. Or the Light? Burn me to a cinder, feel your mind being dragged into a sea of a thousand other minds, forget your name, forget your troubles, forget —'

Sam's hand lashed up, and the silver dagger was in it. The tip came within an inch of Seth's face, and froze. Seth's own dagger was out, an inch from Sam's gut. The water around Balder's statue rippled in concentric circles. Sparks filled the air around their weapons. Neither could move their hand towards the other.

'Another time, another place,' Sam said out loud. He smiled grimly. 'Besides, there are things I need to know.'

They watched each other as both daggers disappeared. Seth demanded, 'Where will you get your knowledge? There's no one left.'

'Yes there is.' *Freya's diary. Gail. Remember me, Freya? I'm the one who treks around the world fighting other people's battles. Miss me, Freya? I'm nicer than I look.*

'But I might get there first,' said Seth. 'And I fear that unless you get yourself out of this affair fast, you'll never learn anything again.'

'No. You stop this.' Sam said. 'It's well known that a man with nothing left to lose will fight ten times harder. You legitimate children never really knew or understood the extent of my power. Magic was never made an official Queen of Time because the other queens feared her;

she was one of those powers that could defy all futures to
make the most improbable, the most lonely little pos-
sibility come to life. Miracles have always been an
unpredictable factor that defies prophecy and divina-
tion – that is why my mother was reviled. And that's why
you fear me!'

For once Seth's smooth manner was nowhere to be
seen. His eyes burned, but he looked at Sam with a face
as expressionless as a visor.

'Remember this. I'm the one worshipped as God of
Destruction.' He turned before Sam could speak and
strode to the door, pausing to look back like an actor
leaving the stage. 'As a Bearer of Light, fighting alone,
you may be interesting. But nothing more.'

He vanished into darkness, leaving Sam staring at
vacancy.

You meant nothing to her.
'Sebastian?'

He knew the second he heard her speak what she was
going to say. 'Sebastian' had told him all.

'Lucifer. I am Lucifer,' he replied quietly, knowing it to
be futile. 'Call me by my proper name, please.'

He had been sitting in front of the television, watching
man taking his first steps on the moon and wondering
what humankind would dream up next. Sam had been
waiting several hours for her, and when she'd knocked
diffidently on the door he'd known. She never usually
knocked. They understood each other too well for that.

'You know I have to go,' she said suddenly, desperately, wanting him to believe. 'I can't stay with you any
longer.'

'Why?' he asked simply.

'My house is dying.' She almost shouted the words at him, knowing he couldn't care less for Thor or Odin or any of the rest of her ancient, declining family. 'Valhalla is dying!'

Good riddance. 'And you must go and be Thor's companion princess. Yes, I think I know this story. It's the one about the princess, the prince and the pauper, where the fair princess is forced to marry for the sake of country and duty, right? And the unfortunate pauper is left to shovel the shit like all other *banished* peasants.'

'Lucifer . . .' she began, a note of pleading in her voice.

'Go,' he snapped, suddenly determined. 'Do the right thing. You know you must. Do it now, and don't look back. I'll honour our agreement; I swear I will. You won't hear anything from me. Not unless you want to.'

If anything this made it worse, but then hadn't he known it would?

'Sebastian! Lucifer! Look at me.' Freya could go through all emotions at once, and they would all be true to her. That too, was a gift of the Daughter of Love.

'No.'

'Why not?'

He shrugged.

As she approached, he stared determinedly at the black and white flickering screen, watching a man in a white spacesuit bouncing up and down on a rock a quarter of a million miles away. He wondered if it would be possible to Waywalk to the moon or farther worlds, or if Time had other children for that purpose.

He felt Freya, inches away, kneeling next to him. He felt her breath tickle his neck and closed his eyes.

'You can't turn a blind eye for ever, you know,' she said softly. 'I have to do this. You know I do. We've all

had to do things which at the time seemed rash or hurtful
or hard, but in the long term it pays off! We lead such
long lives. You can't always live for the present – sooner
or later you have to think of the future, because there's
simply so much of it. And when the future has wound its
way into the present again – why, then you can live and
laugh and be the creature of now rather than tomorrow
and have not a care in the world. But to make that future
become the present, you must do as Father does. Be a
child of necessity, do the hard thing. I want you to understand!'

'Understand,' he replied with a little laugh. 'You're
trying to teach the necessary, bastard Son of Time to
understand?' He turned, and stared at her straight in the
face. The action unnerved her, but she held her ground,
staring back.

'I love you. And though I can understand why and
where you go, I don't understand why I, who have spent
a lifetime understanding all too well, cannot let you go. I
have lived all my life by reason and logic, but now . . .'
He shrugged again and looked away. 'Your reason and
logic seem to have undermined all mine. I think there's a
limit on the amount of reason or logic in the universe.
The more one has of it, the less another has. It's a bal-
ancing act, trying to find that point where reason and
logic is the same in all parties concerned so that they can
finally see eye to eye.'

She smiled faintly, but there was no humour in it. Very
carefully she gave him a long, tender kiss. When she
pulled away she was smiling still, but all he could do was
stare at her in silent wonder and wish for more.

'I do love you, Lucifer. I want you to know that.'

'I love you too. I know it doesn't matter, though.'

'If you know that then you are truly ignorant.' She began to walk towards the door.

He turned, straining to see her retreating back, wishing for her to go as though she had never been, praying for her to stop and come back. 'Freya!' he called as she reached the door. He scrambled to his knees, holding his hands out like a beggar. His face was hot, his heart racing. 'Freya!'

She didn't turn.

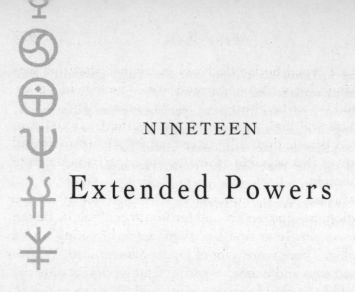

NINETEEN

Extended Powers

You never knew the extent of my power.

Even in Heaven, before his banishment, he hadn't shown them his powers. Even when he was fighting to survive, he had never fully let himself go. But now, with things picking up at such a frantic pace?

He walked straight into the Hell Portal, unhesitating, and strode through pleading shadows without a qualm. In Hell once more, he took a deep breath and turned about, spending not more than thirty seconds in that world. As when he'd tried to find his weapons, he gave no particular direction, but a target. Lights flickered in the mists ahead, multiple Portals vying for position near where he wanted to go. Sam kept the image strong in his mind, until just one Portal shone out in the mists ahead.

He broke through it, heaving in gasps of breath as he emerged into the cold light. Looking round he could find no immediate clue as to where he was, but heard a giggle of voices nearby. He'd come out behind a small building

where a typed notice declared in English that this was
the ranger's hut. Moving round from it he beheld a playground full of laughing children in hats and gloves. The
sun was still high in the sky; the weather was cold but
clear. A drastic time-difference then, between Russia and
wherever this was. He estimated anything from seven to
nine hours.

Refusing to be bothered by the uncertainty of his
situation, he quested around for his target. Felt it. Began
to move, slowly at first and then faster, breaking into a
light jog. There were a lot of joggers, he noticed. White-
teethed men and women wearing tight lycra that only the
incredibly fit could get away with and listening to teach-
yourself Spanish or music tapes as they loped along
paths beneath trees still not in full leaf. Sam jogged with
them, easily moving faster.

He saw the edge of the park, recognised the new-old
stone walls and the tall street lights, saw the yellow taxis
jostle against the huge gas-guzzlers of the suburbs. Saw
the densely ranged, many-storeyed apartment buildings,
their doors manned by gloved porters. Heard the young
men by the old lamp-post rapping unselfconsciously to
some unheard beat. Saw the station and the signpost.
Central Park West. Eighty-fifth Street.

What, he felt like asking, was the archangel Uriel
doing in New York?

If mortal commuters got jet-lag, so Sam quickly found
himself getting Way-lag. His body told him it was nearly
that late time of the night when the only things on television are repeats of last week's episodes and cheap porn
disguised as authentic drama or documentary. But his
eyes were telling him that the busy New York subways

were only just filling up with suited men and women, homeward bound but still talking urgently on mobile phones. New Yorkers, he had learnt a long time ago, never stopped working, even when on holiday. The golden word 'opportunity' hung before their eyes at all times and yes, they worked as Time worked – making small possibilities reality, making money, making their luxurious dreams come true.

Uriel's signal still felt distant – but he was locked on to it. Years in Jehovah's service had made him especially alert to the unseen auras of other archangels, and he followed his senses like a dog follows its nose. It was easy to find people in New York, if you knew what you were looking for. As the signal swung to your left or right like a compass needle, you simply kept going straight towards it, using the north-south, east-west grids of the streets for your guide. He walked, bumping into people and paying no attention to the roads around him save when he had to cross.

Going south down Central Park West, he felt the signal swing again. He crossed the road at the Natural History Museum and walked past the huge building, with the banners of dinosaurs and stars waving gently in the breeze, to Columbus Avenue. Twenty-four-hour supermarkets jostled against greasy cafés, and long single-decked buses roared north towards Harlem while limos sped south and west towards Broadway. A pair of tired Hispanic women carted their blond charges home to their playrooms, a couple flirted on a bench in a small fenced-off area where dogs were legally allowed off their leads.

Sam felt the nearing presence of Uriel swing to his east again, suddenly. Was she taking the subway? To be moving that fast, it seemed likely. He turned, padding patiently south and east as the sky turned blue-grey and the street lamps began to flicker on. He crossed Sixth Avenue where young shoppers in trendy suits forgot the hour and those who could not afford the luxuries on display pressed their noses hungrily against the windows. Here there was more traffic and, though the street was heaving with life of every kind and apartments ran into huge towers and the Empire State Building loomed over them all, there was little or no greenery. Sam found himself wondering what the anti-technocrat Whisperer would think of a scene that was such a dramatic, glamorous change from Russia, where . . . Hell, yes, where he'd been only three hours before.

Uriel was motionless again. Now that Sam was drawing nearer, the archangel's presence seemed to cry out to him, beckoning him on. He crossed Fifth Avenue, hardly noticing the heavy traffic or the landmarks that seemed to thrust from every street corner. He continued east, crossing roads where the glamour seemed to have run out, leaving only huge office blocks and dull arcades full of overpriced jewellers and specialist tailors. He struck glamour again, lost it, passed a restaurant where the director of one business flattered his hated rival over a glass of fine Italian wine on a red and white checked tablecloth. The sign on the door declared authentic Italian cuisine. Everything in New York was authentic, even those things which blatantly weren't.

It took a stranger's eyes to see through the web of illusion the city had woven around itself. As foreign journalists reported on the rat problem, and the spirits denounced the lack of greenery in these dense streets, so Sam's black eyes saw the lengthening shadows, the bins that hadn't been emptied and the falseness of the smiles. It brought back the phrase that had sprung to his mind when this business had started.

'Lord, what fools these mortals be.'

Sam had once heard Shakespeare performed in America, but had never repeated the experience. He'd seen the Bard himself appear in his works, and hearing Hamlet sigh of his misfortune with an American accent had jarred the part of him still haunted by the relief of living in the sixteenth century. As far as he was concerned, that had been the best century of the lot: after the Renaissance had begun, things could only get better. The dark and middle ages had lasted far too long for his taste.

'What crude, primitive fools,' he repeated under his breath.

And turned south again. The street plan was growing more complicated, roads lancing off at diagonals and even the occasional tree springing up through the tight pavement, fenced off from the public. Washington Square now, where cars and trees cast shadows in the never-dying lights around. Into the smaller, quieter residential streets with their airy penthouses, and small newsagents selling papers in half a dozen different languages, predominantly Spanish and English. A man and a woman, delighted with their perfect life in this perfect world, were walking a large grey dog that stopped at the sight of every stranger and won each heart by fondly licking the coldest hands. Uriel was nearby. Sam could sense her like a fire in the corner of his eye. Close enough so that he started shielding his own signal, as Uriel had not.

Turning on to another street, he stopped, craning his neck to stare up at a glass penthouse resting on the top of a white triangular building. A light was on, and his probe could sense only Uriel inside. Sam had walked miles, but hadn't felt it. He was going to find answers.

Marching across the street, he peered at the single door. There was an intercom, but he wasn't foolish enough to try and disguise his voice. He checked for wards, but there were none. Pressing his hand against the door and checking instinctively for pursuers with both eyes and mind, he triggered the locking mechanism on the other side and pushed it open.

Inside was a lift and a stairway. Sam took the stairs, watching every corner for the same attackers he'd encountered in Kaluga but knowing in his heart that they weren't there. He paused on a shadowed corner away from both window and doors, and took out his sword, wiping the sweat off his hand before taking a firm grip on the hilt. He continued up as far as a small landing with only one door. There was a skylight above, and a spherical light shone down on a deep, very clean carpet.

Sam knocked on the door, standing aside from the spyhole and keeping up his shields, projecting with studied ease the mental illusion of just another mortal. The door opened. Uriel, her red hair wet, and wearing nothing more than a dressing gown and pair of slippers, peered at him.

'I do apologise,' he said, ramming the butt of his sword up and into her chin. She fell back, and he swiftly delivered two more blows that sent her crumpling to the floor.

The apartment was just three large rooms – a bedroom and a bathroom, with a sitting room, dining room and kitchen blended into one. There were large sliding doors and a balcony on which well-tended flowers grew unnaturally well for the time of year. It was a matter of moments to turn out the cupboards and find some masking tape. With another apology to the stunned and helpless Uriel, Sam tied her to a nearby radiator and blindfolded her. He didn't want even the lesser power of an archangel employed against him. Meanwhile Uriel was recovering consciousness, turning her head this way and that and moaning.

Sam didn't bother with hitting; he didn't bother with yelling. He knew he couldn't read an archangel's mind as simply as he had Maria's. Not without aid. He turned his back on her and raised his cupped hands to his face, squeezing his eyes shut.

His fingers began to tremble, then he began to shake all over. Tears sprang to his eyes, and his mouth opened in a silent scream as white light surrounded him, expanded, rushed towards Uriel, filling the room, and stopped inches from her quaking form. Then it collapsed and Sam staggered against the kitchen table, eyes streaming, hands trembling as he clasped them to his ears.

'Lucifer!' pleaded Uriel. 'What are you doing?' She had felt the barely controlled discharge, known it for what it was.

White-eyed, Sam turned on her and his face was twisted in pain. 'I can hear your thoughts,' he said softly. 'And you are now going to tell me where Andrew is. Where I can find Gail. What's really going on.'

<No.> He could hear her mind, feel her fantasies, all her many fantasies, about what he might do to her. Her fear was his fear, and he trembled as it rushed through him. Her hatred was his hatred and he bit his lip to try and fight it down. Her thoughts were his thoughts <No. I will not tell. No. I must not tell.>

'Where's Andrew?'

And even as she replied, 'I don't know what you mean,' he heard her thoughts. <Dead. Seth got to him and killed him. Bastard.>

'Then where is the other accomplice? Gail.'

'Lucifer – no, look –' <She's in hiding, and very good at it she is too. Hiding behind her tricks and her shields. Oh, Saviour help me, he's in my head, he's reading my mind, that's why he's released the Light. Please, please help me.>

'Make this easier for me. Where roughly is she?'

Images flooded his mind, and he focused on Gail, refused to listen to the thoughts of the many, many other people around, focused on Uriel. Images of a map, a circle drawn around a small collection of towns. <She's hiding somewhere in there, shielding herself. She is a traitor.>

'Traitor? What do you mean a traitor?'

Helpless, Uriel grunted her futile rage and struggled against her bonds, but she could not silence her thoughts. <Gabriel has betrayed us, she has powerful friends and we cannot find her. He's in my mind, he's tearing through my thoughts and I can't keep him out. I must keep him out, please, please help me!>

'Who are her "powerful friends"? Who are Gail's . . . Gabriel's "friends"?'

<Wizards and spirits. Spirits and wizards, traitors. Bastards. Fools. No, I mustn't think, he can hear me thinking.>

'How many people are searching that area?'

'Get out of my head!' she screamed. 'Get out!' <Three archangels, ten angels. The Firedancers are afraid to approach. The Portals are guarded against us – we have to use mortal means to get in and out! No!>

'The Portals are guarded? You mean spirits watch them?' His eyes were burning, his ears ringing. He could feel something flowing through him like fire, but it made his head swim and his heart pump and the whole world burned in the darkest colours of the soul.

'You're going to die, Lucifer!' She was struggling ineffectively, trying to beat him by sheer willpower and fury alone. He ignored her, and kept on listening. He had no choice but to listen. <Whoever goes through the Portals is seen. To be seen is to become a target.>

'Jehovah is looking for the Pandora keys, yes? He and Odin and Seth?'

'No.' <Yes.>

'How many keys have been found?'

'None!' <Three.>

'Is Seth really planning to defeat Time? He wasn't lying to me? Out of envy? Or disdain? Or for whatever other reason that he can't be trusted?'

'Of course he was lying. You know it's in his nature!' <No – no, he really meant it. He really does mean to find it – Cronus's missing key, left in Hell!>

Sam's mind was filling with furious, burning images. Human thoughts, mortal thoughts were tearing through him, back-noise from the streets below. He groped blindly for the sword, but he could hardly see. Everything was etched in fire, blinding him. His head felt as though it were going to burst.

'Lucifer!' Uriel screamed after him as he staggered towards the door. He was vaguely aware that he'd managed to sling his bag on to his back.

He was receiving images from Uriel that he didn't want to see. Images of his own death a thousand times over in a thousand different ways. Others, too, of

Jehovah, smiling, talking of high things. <We are going to shape the world, my angels. We are going to prove once and for all that there is only one way to rule.>

He found the door.

'Lucifer! You can see my thoughts, and they are bloody for this!'

He whirled around, one hand flying out. 'Be silent!' he roared. Something that made the air ripple and the glasses shake on their shelf tore through the air and smashed into her, and he could sense Uriel's thoughts no more. Yet the fire in his eyes promised him that she was alive. Mortal thoughts, mortal ideas were tearing through him, suggesting things so profane and immoral that he wept to hear them.

Going down in the lift, he slipped to the floor, burying his tightly shut eyes against his knees and pressing his hands over his ears as the roar of the world assailed him. A couple were waiting for the lift on the ground floor. He heard their thoughts as the door opened to reveal him cowering inside it. If discharging the Light was power, it also brought him to this.

<A madman, a murderer. Ought to be shut away, quick, quick, call for help.>

Somehow he managed to stagger from the lift and into the street, and now the noises hit him even harder, a thousand deafening voices, all whispering the one, predominant word. <Me, me, me, me.>

He ran, not knowing his final destination but wanting to run, wanting to put distance between himself and the wall of human noise that threatened to drown him. People scattered before him, afraid. He wondered if they were looking at the drawn sword, or the whiteness of his eyes. Or the fear on his face. He was afraid of mortals,

mortals were afraid of him. They were afraid of the lies put abroad, he was afraid of the truths now open to his ears. He wanted to turn to the lady in the street and warn her, 'He's cheating on you, thinking of another woman.' He wanted to hit the old man who saw him and thought, <Another bloody mad Jew.> He wanted to comfort the terrified child who saw his nightmare rush towards him through the street. He wanted to slap the spiteful woman who saw in him another weak-willed failure who'd brought his own downfall on himself. But he didn't.

Sam ran on, into the deepening shadows.

He took a bus out to a Portal in New Jersey, keeping his eyes closed all the way and humming under his breath any tune that came to mind as the roaring, raging voices slowly faded. Painfully slow. He could still hear the distant whispering of the humans on the bus as they stared at him over their newspapers and briefcases, their little ignorant thoughts turning him into a monster. Or sometimes he caught their incidental thoughts – a man lusting over his secretary, a woman fuming in silence over the incompetence of hers and looking forward immensely to sacking the unfortunate menial, an old man thinking of the bloody kids next door and a pair of boys thinking of how they could next impress their friends with dirty anecdotes and reports of false conquests.

But gradually all this faded with the whiteness in his eyes and he was left clutching his bag on his knees and feeling nothing worse than ordinary revulsion at the thoughts that had briefly been his own.

Sam let the bus carry him right to the end of the route,

missing at least two Portals. He did not feel up to a Waywalk, not yet. When the bus reached its final stop and he was the last passenger left, the driver had to come and shake his arm. 'Hey, sleepy-head,' he said, 'end of the line.'

Sam opened his eyes and yawned. His eyes were still light grey and he could see in a second the colour of the man's soul. To his relief, the darkness on the outside was just an illusion, a projection of aggression crafted to hide a warm heart. Sam smiled despite himself.

'What's funny?' demanded the driver.

'I'm smiling at you.'

'So let me in on the joke, why don't you?' The man's voice was raised, but Sam could see that his abruptness was a fake.

'You're trying to hide the fact that you're a good man, for fear you'll get hurt again.'

The driver recoiled as if slapped, and Sam could hear his thoughts clearly. <He knows about Jenny, how does he know about Jenny and shit-head Carl?'>

Sam pushed past him, staggered down to the front of the bus and got off. It had probably been foolery to speak. But after a journey of listening to other people's voices, it was good to hear himself speak too.

Out here it was blissfully quiet – a small scattering of houses in leafy New Jersey, with clean cars on immaculate driveways. The roaring voices of the city seemed distant; most thoughts here were silenced, displaced by mindless evening television and brief flashes of dreams from sleeping children.

'Hey!' The bus driver again, calling after him. 'You need a hand?'

'I'm fine, thank you,' Sam called, half turning. His

voice seemed very loud and as he plodded down the empty pavement he began to sing again under his breath, focusing all his attention on the words to try and keep out the few thoughts that did crawl into his mind. 'Are you going to Scarborough fair?' A cat mewed piteously and brushed against his legs, sensing in Sam a fellow night-dweller. He stroked it absently and passed by. 'Remember me to one who lives there.'

A girl gang, giggling uproariously, bottles clutched in their hands, passed down the road. Sam heard their thoughts. <False IDs, whole new world of opportunity.> He kept on walking, looking away as they passed and refusing to see their souls, for fear that even in children so young there might be something black.

'She once was a true love of mine,' he sang to himself.

He could sense a Portal nearby. But his grey eyes swerved beyond the side street where the Portal lay to a small church, little more than a hall with a small wooden spire, and his feet began moving that way of their own accord. Outside the door he hesitated, glancing at the picture of Christ on the cross and the huge words around it – 'He died for us, brothers' – before knocking on the door. It moved under his touch and when no one answered he pushed it open, slipping into the cold, empty church. The only light came from a stand of candles, nearly burnt down, and the altar was plain and the stained-glass windows crude, compared to the old cathedrals of Europe. But it was quiet, with even the thoughts from the houses muffled. And there were no souls for the Light to examine.

He found a pew and pressed his hand against the armrest, leaving behind a faint silver glow that would warn him if danger approached. Pillowing his head on a hassock from the floor, he curled up on the bench and closed his eyes. It was blissful. No burning fire before him, no roaring voices inside. He would let his eyes drift shut for a few minutes, and then he would Waywalk. Waywalking was a dangerous business at all times, and he was going to do it with every safety precaution he could find.

And in the holy church of Jesus Christ, he slept.

When he woke, Sam no longer heard the voices. Weary, his bones clicking uncomfortably, he pulled himself up and opened his eyes. The world was no longer burning – after hours of fire the worst was past.

He could risk a Waywalk. Find Gabriel. End this battle once and for all.

TWENTY

Traitors and Archangels

He used the images he'd gleaned from Uriel's mind to set the destination. Striding through the Hell Portal he fancied he saw the face of the Wayspirit he'd enlisted to his aid in finding Seth. Scrying for Gabriel would have been futile – Uriel had made it clear that the archangel's shielding was something remarkable. Nor did he care who saw him emerge from the Portal. He was on the warpath now, ready to fight as he'd never been ready before.

For all he was tired, muscles and mind both aching from strain, he heard Uriel's voice again in his mind. *Whoever goes through the Portals is seen. To be seen is to become a target.*

That suited him. He wanted Gabriel to know where he was. He wanted to be a target.

He broke through the Earth Portal and looked around, searching for a clue as to where he was. It was dark. The Portal had come out in a backyard full of old

crates and smelling of beer. He heard the sound of
movement inside the large whitewashed house in front of
him and clambered quickly over the back wall to avoid
discovery.

There were houses with shutters. There was the smell
after rain. There were old corrugated iron rooftops,
rusting a little. Sam felt eyes watching him, felt alert
minds stirring all around and wondered who or what had
noticed his arrival. He climbed over a few more walls
until he landed in a muddy road, and looked up and
down it.

His night vision showed him that in one direction
there lay an empty landscape made only marginally
more interesting by distant hills and the odd thorn
bush that sprouted out of the dry land. The signs were
in Spanish. Turning to look the other way, he saw a
small town that boasted one garage with all of two
pumps on its small forecourt, one bar complete with two
old men on the step and the sound of pool balls hitting
each other, and one mini-market from which an old lady
with tanned skin and a flowery dress was emerging,
arms full. Five cars, old and battered. Three motorbikes.
One bicycle.

A quieter town he had never seen. And nowhere for
strangers to hide. The land around was entirely exposed.
*If someone took up residence here with a good sniper gun and
telescopic sight, nobody could get in or out.*

The perfect place for Gabriel to sit out a siege. Sam
went to the bar, ordering a beer and taking his bottle
outside to sit on the steps near the old men. He found
himself grateful that he couldn't hear their thoughts at
least. Equipped with his beer, and the squatting rights
got by it, he unsheathed his dagger and laid it casually at

his feet for all to see. The old men were quick to hurry away.

Sam hummed a little tune under his breath. He wrapped his coat tighter round his shoulders, leant his head against the wall and went on humming. He waited.

The town had little night life, save for the scratching sounds of insects and the distant murmur of the drinkers in the bar. There was the crack, crack of a boy playing a shoot em' up game on the bar's one machine. There was the clink of glasses. People saw Sam, saw his dagger, steered clear. Sam waited.

He spotted a battered old car heading towards him. Under normal circumstances he would have given it no attention. But this truck had spells inscribed on it – he could see them blazing out to his magical eyes even as he felt them trying to nudge his mind aside. He forced himself to look and study them, ignoring the magic which whispered that he should turn away. A general scry-shield, a distraction spell and a standard ward. The car had three occupants. All were spirits.

It came to a stop in front of him. Three pairs of eyes regarded him through the windows. A door opened and a voice called out in English, 'Put the sword in the boot.'

'Prove to me this isn't another trap, like Kaluga,' he retorted.

'We can't prove anything. You'll just have to believe us when we say Gail sent us. Keep the dagger if it makes you feel better.'

Shrugging inwardly, Sam did as they said and got into the car.

'Were you followed?' he asked.

'No. No one has been able to get inside the shield yet.'

'How come?'

'Gail isn't taking any chances. But it's good you came. We felt the release, you know.'

Sam said nothing. He was watching the empty landscape rush past his window. 'Where are we?' he asked suddenly.

'Mexico. Gail moved here fast when she heard that Andrew had been taken. She knew you wouldn't be far behind, though.'

'How?'

'You're not the only one with spirit friends, you know,' said the driver with a faint laugh.

Sam felt his fingers tingle. He knew that laugh. '*Adam?* What the hell do you think you're doing here?'

'Got recruited, didn't I?'

They'd turned off the main road and were now winding through muddy tracks barely wide enough to accommodate the car. Sam peered ahead through the gloom, and saw a small farmhouse. An oil-lamp burned on the porch and the windows were lit with a faint yellow glow. They pulled up in front of the house, and Sam quickly scryed the area before getting out. The place was loaded with magic. Spells casting the attention elsewhere, spells shielding huge swathes of land all around, spells to divert scrys, spells to warn of approaching danger – and all worked with such an expert hand that Sam found himself wondering if his mother hadn't been wrong and he didn't have an unsung brother or sister.

He retrieved his sword and bag and followed Adam up the stairs into the house. There was no electricity, but the dusty old rooms with their tattered sofas and moth-eaten curtains were lit by oil-lamps. Sam advanced, wary of treachery even at this late stage.

Three armchairs, their stuffing erupted out through

the ancient fabric, were placed before the fireplace with their backs to the door. Two were occupied. Sam took the third without asking.

'Evening all,' he said cheerfully.

'Well done,' said Gabriel. 'You made it.'

'You didn't make it easy. And whoever did your spells was truly brilliant.'

'Thank you,' said Buddha.

TWENTY-ONE

Open Conspiracy

For all that they smiled, and spoke to him in light voices that belied their fatigue, they were afraid. Sam saw it at once. Something in their eyes echoed his own fear and doubt.

'Why have you dragged me here?'

'We need you,' replied Gabriel. 'You are the necessary one. You're also the one who knows where to hide. We've not had your experience with either Hell or Earth.'

'Tell me what the hell is going on.'

Buddha gave a shaken smile. 'That phrase was better chosen than you know.'

In the end, it was Gabriel who told him. She hadn't changed since he'd last seen her, several centuries before. She had close-cropped mousy hair and an attitude of daunting pragmatism. Though she sat cross-legged on her chair, her slight frame hardly filled it. She met everyone's eye at all times, and when she spoke she gave

no inflection to her story, nor bothered to hide her
fatigue.

'At first I helped in the search for three of the Pandora
keys. I was not told by Jehovah that Seth and Odin were
also looking for them. I was told to find the key to
Suspicion's prison.'

'Why did you do it?'

'For the same reason that Michael tried to kill you.'
She shrugged. 'Same reason too that Uriel has blinded
herself to the real danger of this situation. Jehovah com-
manded it. And to us, Jehovah is . . . was . . . like a God.
There are some – Uriel, Rafael – who know in their
hearts that he's doing something foolish. But he is also a
Son of Belief, and after thousands of years' exposure to
his power, it's hard to turn away. It hurts more than
you'd think.'

She sighed, her mind far away, her voice on automatic.
'I didn't know much about the keys, back then. All I did
know was that they'd been lost, and were rumoured to
open doors to great power. I wanted Jehovah to have
that power, I really did. I thought he was good, so that if
anyone was to have it, it should be him.'

'Why didn't he tell you he was working with others?'

'For exactly the reason that I worshipped him, and
him alone. To tell me there were others would be, in a
way, to . . . *defile* the sanctity of our search. It would also
have increased the doubts already blooming in my mind
as I found out more about the Pandora spirits. Did you
know that the city of Atlantis, the one on Earth, not the
Feywalker kingdom, was sunk to the bottom of the sea
because Suspicion got loose in the minds of its sea
wizards?'

'No. What happened next?'

'One day I was recalled to Jehovah's presence, to describe to him how I'd sought high and low for the key, but so far in vain. He spoke more fervently than ever of the power that the Pandora spirits might offer. "We must find the spirits, Gabriel. And when we have them we must show the world what true justice is." He'd often spoken that way, but never had he seemed so close to achieving his desires.'

Sam could already hear the rest of her tale in his mind's ear. *Three of them, playing with fire.*

'You thought it was wrong,' he prompted. 'In your search you'd found knowledge about the keys, you'd began to realise exactly how dangerous the power was that you were playing with. You went to Freya, who called on her mortal allies. I imagine you were instructed to play it cool, pretend you were searching for the keys while in reality you tried to find out who the other two seekers were. At the same time, Andrew tried to forestall the others' progress by finding the keys first, by finding them and moving them, racing against the combined powers of my brothers. Am I right?'

She nodded. 'Andrew was to do my research for me. While I spied on my master he supplied me with cover stories as to where I was searching and reasons why, so that I would not be suspected, and, if possible, so we could get to the keys first. Meanwhile Freya tried to get Time to intervene. But Time would not. Time said that futures were spinning off in all directions at once and only one future could be allowed to happen, and that one must happen of its own accord.'

'So,' Buddha said, 'Gabriel turned to me. And I agreed to help her, even though I did not completely believe her tale.'

'In the meantime,' said Gabriel, 'I discovered that Seth and Odin were the others seeking the Pandora keys. But Andrew had beaten them to it. He'd found out their location – not Cronus's key, but the other three. He destroyed the book that held this information, but not before he reported what he knew to Freya. And she passed on what she knew to her other, able assistant. Her granddaughter, Fran.'

'Fran? But Fran denied all knowledge of the event, Fran was the one who—'

'Who betrayed us,' said Buddha. 'Freya had been careful, I give her that. She referred to Gabriel as Gail at all times. She didn't mention my involvement even once. When Andrew sent his last report she tried to get a message to you, to bring you in with us as discreetly as possible.'

'But it was too late,' murmured Sam, again ahead of the story. 'Andrew began to run, the librarian who'd helped him was killed. Fran had told whoever she told that Freya knew too much – knew identities, locations.'

'Freya was murdered, so involving you,' said Gabriel. 'Buddha and I began to shield Andrew from discovery until you could get to him and bring him to safety. You are, after all, the master of surviving in hard places. But we were unable to shield him completely. After he was poisoned and caught, he was revived enough for him to confess to my role. Again, he was not aware of the part played by Buddha. Freya had been careful enough about that.

'The dogs were now on my tail. Buddha came to my help again, lending his powers to my shields until such time as you were here.'

'You came,' said Buddha. 'That was the important part. To survive we needed you.'

'Why?'

'They have the keys, you know. Seth, Odin and Jehovah – each has a key of his own and is prepared to unleash the spirits. When that happens, you are the only one who can stop them.

'You are the Bearer of Light, you can destroy the Pandora spirits. Love targets Hate, Trust targets Suspicion, Charity targets Greed – and you are the only one with the power to channel these thoughts. The Light taps human minds, it feeds off their thoughts, the timeless concepts. If you enter the minds of other living creatures, and focus them on just one aspect – on Love, say – and then direct that power at its opposite – at Hate – then Hate itself becomes something you can destroy.'

'By the same principle I can destroy a Greater Power,' said Sam. 'But Greater Powers are spawned of *all* life. If just one person remained to feed Hate or Greed or Suspicion, it would have been for nothing. To do what you describe, I'd have to tap the mind of every living thing. And that' – he smiled, but his eyes could have frightened snakes – 'would not be pleasant.'

'Then we'll have to stop those three from freeing the spirits. Which is why the Light – and, unfortunately, you – suddenly become so important,' said Buddha.

Unfortunately for my sake. Thanks a million, brother.

'There's more,' murmured Buddha, seeing Sam's eyes go distant. He leant forward and spoke urgently. 'Cronus. If Seth releases Cronus, who besides you can prevent Cronus from overthrowing Time? Time defeated Cronus once before, but there's little chance of a repeat victory. He's too stretched; too much of his energy is focused merely on sustaining the universe. *If* Seth decides that the threat of Cronus isn't enough in itself – if he were fool enough to actually free him, you're the only person who might stop him.'

Sam was silent for a long moment. Then he said, 'I have been told as much, although I don't know how this might be. But if I've suffered near burn-out simply in repulsing Odin or in reading Uriel's mind, then fighting Cronus is likely to be the last battle. Cronus is anti-Time, anti-life. In order to destroy him I would have to channel *everything* that is life. Not just human thoughts but the life of ants and birds, trees and grass. Hell, there are a lot of ants around.' He stared at Buddha, daring and begging him all at once to deny it.

But the Son of Wisdom said nothing, and Sam's heart sank further. 'Seth surely wouldn't release Cronus?'

'He's mustering an army in Hell, isn't he?' said Buddha. 'He's going to march into Belial's territory, he's going to dig up the key, wherever it is, and he's going to say, "Hey, look, all my brothers and all my sisters, I've got the key, do what I tell you." And when they say, "Nah, you're bluffing, you'd never dare", how do we know he wouldn't free Cronus, just to spite them? All we do know is that he's done a lot to get this far. Who's to say his momentum won't carry him further?'

Sam opened his mouth to speak, then stiffened. 'Did you hear that?'

'I heard nothing,' said Gabriel.

'Nor I.'

Sam sat on the edge of his chair, craning his head up as though he might see through the ceiling. 'I heard something.'

Buddha was already on his feet, eyes closed. 'My shields are intact.'

'Mine too,' said Gabriel. 'There's nothing inside the shield that could move without our consent.'

Sam was also on his feet. He passed to a shuttered window, and hesitated. 'If I open this, I won't get fried by any spells, will I?'

'You're the master of magic,' said Buddha. 'You tell me.'

He opened the window and peered out.

His back was to the others, but they still saw him freeze.

'Sam?' demanded Buddha sharply, hastening towards him as Sam's mouth opened in a wordless cry. 'Lucifer!' He caught his shoulders, shook him hard, glancing only briefly out of the window to see what Sam had seen. But the night looked the same to him as it had before.

Gabriel was also by Sam's side, a frown on her face, and she was the next to stare out of the window. So she was the next to see it. 'Oh, Light,' she breathed. 'Look at the sky!'

Buddha glanced back out at the clear, star-speckled sky. He was not one given to showing alarm, not even to cursing, but his eyes grew distinctly wide. 'Well,' he said finally, 'you don't see that every day.'

Sam moved, pulling himself free of Buddha's grasp where before he'd been a statue. Staring wildly from one to the other, he almost tripped in his haste to back away.

'Can't you hear it?' he demanded. 'They're here! Can't you hear them? They're everywhere!'

'Sam, calm down,' said Buddha, reaching out to his brother.

Sam swatted his hand away. 'Listen! Just shut up and listen, won't you?'

Buddha obediently stood still, listening intently.

'I don't hear anything,' said Gabriel, impatient as always. She hadn't moved from the window, and stood framed in a sky discoloured by numberless blood-red stars and one louring, blood-red moon. Humans would call it atmospheric disturbance; they always did. But Sam knew better. Whether because of his magic, or the Light in particular, to him the voices were clearly audible.

Judging by Buddha's wide eyes, he could hear them too. He started forward, grabbed Gabriel by the arm and yanked her from the window.

'Move!' he yelled. 'Get everyone out of here! Tell them to Feywalk, tell them to get as far from this place as possible.' He turned back to Sam, who was standing motionless in the middle of the floor, staring at nothing with all-seeing eyes. 'You're hearing them through the Light, brother,' he hissed as Gabriel burst from the room in a confused run. 'How strong is their song?'

'Growing louder.'

'How fast?'

'Fast.'

Buddha grabbed Sam's shoulders again, and this time Sam didn't pull free. 'You're hearing the Pandora spirits. The Pandora spirits are free! They can affect anyone except *you*.

'The Light inside you is *created* by thoughts – without minds to tap, there would be no Light. From the first moment you discharged it you've been part of the Light, another mind drifting in a sea of thoughts. Part of you has been imprinted on every mind the Light has touched – and vice versa. So for the Pandora spirits to touch you is like saying they have to enter every mind in the universe. And they can't do that because, as they extend their power, it grows thinner.

'Listen to me!' Buddha almost shook Sam, who'd never imagined such an outburst from him. 'From the first moment you discharged the Light, you've been losing yourself in a sea of minds. *That's* why the Light has such a bad effect on you – you drown in other minds, while your own thoughts could be anywhere. How can Hate or Suspicion target a man whose mind is scattered beyond the corners of the earth?'

Sam stared wild-eyed at him.

'Don't you understand? For the rest of us, there's no ward in the world that can keep the Pandora spirits out, and if Seth or Odin or Jehovah has targeted this place then I am powerless to prevent them from entering my mind. And when they enter my mind I will be little more than a tool to our adversaries.'

'I don't understand,' said Sam, almost pleadingly.

'Imagine what will happen if Hate enters my mind while I stand so close to you!' hissed Buddha urgently. 'How easy would it be for me to slit your throat?'

Sam's eyes moved to Buddha's hands. They were trembling by his side, and though they bore no weapons he knew better than to trust that. He began to back away.

Buddha spoke low and urgently. 'Pandora spirits can see through shields and wards and magics. They can see me clear as day. They can see you also, but you are different. You carry Balder's power in you, and you have proven that you are willing to use it where he is not. You are still a good man, Lucifer. If Hate enters my mind and I strike out at you, then you will not strike back. How loud is the song?'

'Loud. It fills the room. I can hear . . . Hate. Yes. I can hear it clearly now . . .'

Buddha had grabbed a coat from a hanger and opened the door. Already Sam could hear the sound of retreating car engines.

'Don't trust anyone,' said Buddha in a low voice. 'If they find out who you trust, then those are the ones they'll turn against you. Find Seth, find Cronus's key. If the Pandora spirits are free I cannot stay.'

He was out of the door already.

'Wait! Where will you go?'

Buddha half turned, giving him a strange, lopsided smile. The area around the house was already empty and, but for the voices of the invading spirits singing their joy at freedom after being so long imprisoned, the night was unnaturally silent.

'Work it out, Lucifer! They will turn Greed on to Gabriel; she will say what part I had in this. They will turn Suspicion on to me; I will say what part I had. We are as good as lost. All that matters now is that you beat them.'

'Beat them? How? What do you expect me to do?'

But then it was too late. The song filled his ears and when he turned his head he saw the shadows moving. Buddha's eyes were wide, and glowing from inside. Then Sam saw Buddha raise his hands to his ears and with a hollow moan fall to his knees. Sam instinctively rushed forwards, but Buddha raised his head sharply at the movement. His eyes were white, and glowed brighter than the red moon.

'Run,' he hissed. 'Run now!'

Sam didn't hesitate. He was back through the door, had caught up his bag and sword and was running. The ground was uneven, the song filled his mind. <We are

here, Bearer of Light. You can destroy us, and you know
it. So we will destroy you first. We are here, there is no
place to run. We will find every one of your friends and
make them suspect, blackmail or hate you. Just because
your mind is blanketed in the Light, in all those other
minds scattered across all those worlds, it doesn't mean
we can't hurt you! You are all alone now. You've lost.
You've failed.>

He ran on, illuminated only by the red moon. Tall
grasses tore at his legs but he quickly set into a steady
pace, swifter and with more grace than the fastest mortal
athletes. He found that if he got into the rhythm of the
movement, actually counted each stride as a beat in a bar,
the noise of his thoughts drowned out the spirits, and it
was possible to ignore them. <There is no ward, no
shield, no magic that can keep us out, for we are
spawned of your minds . . .>

<Which is why my mind, one that has drifted into a
thousand other minds, is safe from you.>

<We are the Powers that Time never acknowledged,
the spirits spawned from the darker places in your souls.
We are a part of you, you cannot strike at us, even
though you hide your mind in all those others, losing
yourself with each passing day . . .>

<Shut up!>

The nearest Hell Portal was miles away, but he could
run miles.

<You are all alone. We will turn every one of your
friends against you because you threaten us. You are a
risk to us.>

<Huh – how?>

As he ran, the song grew fainter, or possibly the
rushing of blood in his ears louder, until it was abruptly

gone. Sam slowed to a stop and looked around. He was standing in the midst of an expanse of dry grass. The only light came from the moon above. He wondered what kind of creatures lived in the grasses, and how much persuasion they'd need to keep away. The night was still. Not even the cicadas dared play their usual scratchy tune.

An orange glow behind him caught his attention, and he peered in its direction. His sharp night-eyes focused on the house where, a few minutes before, he, Gabriel and Buddha had sat. He saw the flames rising from it. Was Hate such a powerful spirit, then, that it could make peaceful, temperate Buddha attack wood and nails as well as flesh and blood? He hoped not.

'Luc?'

He turned. Adamarus was standing there, unarmed, breathless from running, eyes wide.

'Light be praised,' muttered Sam, striding towards him. 'Are you okay?'

'Fine, fine,' he panted. 'But . . . the Pandora spirits? The stars and the moon, and then your brother . . .'

Sam said nothing, feeling shame in his family, and not for the first time. Then he frowned. His sharp ears were hearing whispers again, so faint as to be almost indistinct from the rustling of grass. Almost.

'Adam?'

'I'm . . . glad you're okay. I thought for a second we were gonners.' His voice turned disdainful. 'If I'd the spirits under *my* command I'd certainly have used them better.'

'Adam?'

Sam had in his hand the silver dagger. He saw that Adam was staring at it, almost hypnotised.

Adam smiled a cruel, unlikely smile. 'That's nice,' he said, in the same way a magpie might speak of a piece of shiny foil. 'You've got a silver crown too, haven't you? I've seen it. Is it powerful?'

'Adam, I think it might be a good idea if we split up for a while,' said Sam nervously.

'Can I look at it? The crown?'

'This is hardly the time or the place.'

'I'd like to have a look. I really would.'

'Sorry, maybe another time—'

'I'd like to have a look!' hissed Adam, suddenly angry. 'I really, really, *really* would!'

'Oh, shit,' said Sam, ever so softly, while Adamarus raised himself up to his full unimpressive height, spread his hands wide and sprang. And as he moved he changed. Nails lengthened, ears became pointy, eyes narrowed. He was a shapeshifter spirit, Sam remembered, but like most spirits his shifts were only partial.

And now he was shifting into . . . yes. Sam saw snake's fangs, wolf's claws, owl's eyes, dog's nose, lizard's scale and just a tuft of human hair and a few patches of human skin to suggest that this monstrosity could walk upright and even hold a conversation.

He rolled beneath the creature, and wondered if any of those claws or fangs could do him harm. Then he decided not to bother worrying, and grappled furiously to try and keep a combination of claw and fang away from his neck.

'Adam! Don't make me hurt you!' he begged, rolling over and over. A claw tore through his trousers and drew blood. He felt another claw run along his side and yelled out loud. But he didn't feel the heat or the dizziness of a fatal wound, and realized that, in his foolish, Greed-induced attack, Adam hadn't managed to create silver claws.

They rolled again, and in the darkness Sam saw a pair of fanged teeth lancing with perfect aim towards his throat. Instinctively he shoved both his hands up, palm first, to try and throw the creature before it could get to him. He heard a faint thud, as of a balloon filled with water gently puncturing. He felt a warm trickle down his wrist. Felt the silver dagger lodge against something hard.

Adam began to change, still hanging over Sam, teeth ready to bite. Sam pushed him off with a cry of alarm and dropped his blood-soaked dagger in dismay. The blood was a faintly translucent green that shimmered through all the pale colours of the spectrum as it flowed from the wound in Adam's gut.

Then Adam was in his true form. A little creature, barely five foot tall, with pointy ears and narrowed little eyes, clutching the bleeding hole. Sam felt a rush of magical wind as the spirit of Greed, seeing its subject fall, departed the body and looked round for more fit prey, before fading to nothing as though it had never been. Sam stared at the wound, tearing off the ruined, blood-soaked shirt around Adamarus's belly. 'No,' he whispered urgently. 'No! You are a spirit, you don't die like this!'

Adam gave a whimpering sound as Sam's fingers pressed too hard. He had been struck by a Son of Time, with a weapon enchanted by Time himself. Not even the King or Queen of the spirits would risk such a wound. Sam stared with his cat's vision at the wound, and finally Adam tried to speak.

'Just shut up and lie still,' muttered Sam, working

frantically to staunch the bleeding. Where the spirit's
blood fell, grass grew green and strong.

Adam tried to speak again, coughed blood, and fell
back. His breathing sounded like a child playing with a
grass whistle. Sam sighed, and wished that the real
world bore more resemblance to the operatic one – so
that Adamarus, though dying, might have the strength to
tell him what the hell he was supposed to do next. But
no. The blood was pouring slower now, but only because
the heart was weakening.

Sam reached a decision. He retrieved his dagger and
shielded it. He thrust his hair back from his face regard-
less of the trail of blood it left. Then he took a deep
breath and laid his hands over the injury.

He could hear the sound of the distant flames, and
wondered where Buddha was. *This is your fault, brothers
mine. Father, why don't you intervene? What is holding you back
from saving lives? Freya's life! My life! Why are you willing to
let your children die?*

He heard his own voice, younger, more hopeful,
addressing a father who refused to answer. *The miracle
makers are all Children of Magic, and miracles are not part of
your great scheme of things.*

*Watch your son make a miracle, Father. See why you are so
afraid of me! If your futures depend on this spirit dying now, and
since every future cries out that this must happen, then no wonder
the Children of Magic are banished from Heaven! For we are the
ones who make the impossible come to life, and if you cannot stop
my brothers then you cannot stop me!*

He closed his eyes and lowered his hands over the
wound. Light played around his fingertips. *I defy you,
Father. There is no such thing as fate!*

The wound began to close as the Light built in

intensity. Sam's black shirt darkened further as his own blood began to seep from different wounds. Old wounds, coming undone again as he poured his regenerative power into Adam. He felt blood trickle down his back from the bullet Michael had put there, and prayed that the process of natural healing had been at work for long enough to boost his failing powers.

Adam gave out a gasp, and breathed more easily. Sam fell on to his hands and knees over the fallen spirit. The world was spinning dangerously. Somehow he managed to find his bag and clutch it. He staggered up and began to run again, moving haltingly over the ground, leaving Adam behind and not even giving a thought to the unstable world or his bleeding back. There was no chance of entering a regenerative trance, of that he was certain. Adam had taken his healing gift for the while, and now it would need time to recover.

He didn't dare think of his own wounds. If he did he'd realise exactly how stupid he'd been and how near defeat he was, and that would never do. He thought instead of the thousand different futures that had just opened up. The chances of Adam surviving had been a million to one, and he'd created the futures that lurked behind that single one.

Eat dirt, Dad.

It was a long time before Sam stopped running. When he did, he was even more dizzy. He sank to the ground, put his head between his knees and tried to breathe.

From behind, he heard a slow, mocking sound. Someone was clapping. He turned.

Seth smiled. For want of a better reaction, Sam smiled back, all pride fading. 'Hi.'

'You're doing well, brother,' said Seth. 'Your friends are lost to you, aren't they? Quite driven away, now that the three Pandora spirits are at my disposal. What can you possibly do next, to stop me getting hold of the fourth key? To hinder me from reaching Cronus?'

Sam said nothing.

Seth advanced slowly towards him, a darker figure against the darkness. He was a Son of Night, he was in his element. Sam was already feeling drained, with blood, mostly his, sticking to his back and hands.

'Of course, the fact that you're the Bearer of Light is a mild inconvenience, but I don't think it'll be more than that.'

Sam eyed the other's scimitar. 'Why haven't you got hold of Cronus by now?'

'There's more defending him than just a few wards, you know. Time really doesn't want him free.'

'And if you die, does that mean nothing will free him?'

'And if *you* die,' agreed Seth, 'nothing will stop him.'

Sam rose cautiously to his feet, drawing his sword as he went, and looking for reasons to delay. 'Why are you trying to free him?'

'Oh, please. Don't go righteous on me.'

'I'm not righteous, I'm curious.'

'After all this? After running hither and yon, searching for a way to stop me, with the Pandora spirits now at *my* command, you're merely curious? Please.' Seth stepped towards Sam suddenly. Sam instinctively recoiled, staggering slightly with his own weight. He felt very, very tired.

'You should hear the spirits, brother,' whispered Seth. 'They can make the land itself hate, if they want to. They can turn joy to jealousy in the blink of an eye, make lovers hate each other and brothers suspect their own twin. But *you* . . . they can't touch you. You're dangerous. You're the Bearer of Light.'

'You killed Andrew.'

'He knew things. Where the keys were hidden. Where Cronus was, how to find him.'

'You fancy telling me?'

Seth gave a snort of disdain and began circling. Sam raised his heavy, heavy sword to a guard position and circled with him. 'I reckon he's got to be somewhere in Hell. Somewhere guarded. Otherwise you wouldn't need Asmodeus to get at him, since Belial is brighter than he looks, and refused you help. I reason you *need* an army of demons, to get to Cronus.'

'You reason well, for a fool.'

'Thanks. But not much. Why are you trying to free Cronus?'

Seth feinted briefly in, but Sam wasn't falling for it. 'Go on,' he said, trying to sound persuasive. 'If you're going to kill me you might as well tell me *why*. Cronus is anti-Time, the end of everything. What madness could drive you to freeing him?'

'You're so narrow-minded, dearest brother. Cronus isn't the end of everything, he's the end of everything *as we know it*. An end of Time – an end of death, an end of destiny, an end of the imprisonment we live with.'

'And you'd free him? You'd *destroy* your own father?'

'Father, brother, sister – haven't you learnt yet, dear boy? They're all the same. To Cronus, everything is just a part of himself.'

'You're not Cronus! You're Seth! You're a Son of Night and Time! You helped them *kill* Freya, you *killed* Andrew!'

'Andrew?' Seth gave a snort of disdain. 'He was a human, she should never have bothered with him. Of course it wasn't easy, keeping him conscious for long enough at a time. But he had knowledge that I wanted, and when it came to the end, he was weak. I could tear it from his mind, pull out everything I wanted to know and leave him empty. Far less messy than the Light. Not surprising, then, that he died easily.'

Sam said nothing. His face was set like iron. He desperately wanted to sleep. But he felt too detached even to imagine being touched by anything as warm or soft as rest.

Seth's smile widened. 'Doesn't that upset you, dearest brother? You trekked across the world for him, and he died on you. He gave me what I wanted, and he died. He told me where the fourth key was; he told me how to find Cronus. With the armies of Hell and the Pandora spirits at my back I *will* free him. I will end this stupid, pointless way of existence and create another.'

'Personally, I like this existence. So *you* have no excuse.'

'No excuse?' Seth lunged, and Sam parried clumsily to save his skin. 'You were lucky, Lucifer. You got full-out hatred and mistrust, you got to flee Heaven and hide away in Hell, you found comfort in mortals and weaklings.

'But not me. No, I'm the Son of Night, brother to Loki, murderer of Balder. I got the suspicion, the polite mistrust, the cold warmth, the terribly concerned conversations, the eager reassurances that no one held my brother's sin against me. I got the isolation in a crowd. I could have stood in a sea of people, knowing every one, and nobody would have answered to my call.

'We're very alike, in that respect. We're both lonely. But unlike you I have to live every day with the lies of my brothers and sisters, as they exclaim how pleased they are to see me but never invite me home.'

Sam considered. 'You're psycho, aren't you? Has anyone told you to actually do something about this situation? Or do you really think it justifies ending the universe?'

Seth snorted. 'You don't understand. *You* can lose yourself at any moment, throw all your worries to the wind just by touching the Light, burying yourself in the minds of others —'

'Oh, for Time's sake, this is too pathetic! You'd end the universe because you've had a bad century?'

'As we know it, Lucifer, as we know it! When Cronus rules we will never be alone — always he will be there, and all life shall be one. No death, no pain, no suffering.'

'No life, no change, nothing to indicate that there was anything else.'

'No more loneliness! Maybe not together, but not alone either!'

'Seth?' Sam had spoken so softly that Seth almost didn't realise. Sam was smiling ever so faintly, his eyes distant. 'Your shoelaces are untied.'

Seth glanced down. Sam brought his hands sweeping up and for a second the air exploded into light. As Seth shielded his eyes against the light, Sam dived forwards, bringing the butt of his sword around and across, hitting Seth on the side of the face.

One of Seth's hands came free from his scimitar and clawed up, closing round Sam's face. Coldfire burnt, and Sam's lips turned blue as it wormed its way into his skin.

Sam felt the sword fall from his numb, frozen fingers.

He brought his hands up and closed them around Seth's wrist. Fire – real fire, hot and orange and hungry – flashed at his fingertips and caught Seth's sleeve.

Seth screamed and snatched his hand away from Sam's face, dropping his scimitar and closing his free hand over the sleeve to extinguish the flames. Sam staggered back. Blood poured from his frozen nose, warming the icy skin as it passed.

He stared at Seth, who returned his steady look. Sam gave a painful grin, raised his hands slowly, palms together, and opened them.

Nothing happened. His palms were empty.

Seth frowned, hesitated, reached a decision, and brought his hands sweeping across and up. The darkness around Sam thickened to a black, living, suffocating mass.

Sam just kept on smiling, raising his empty palms higher and higher, as if drawing thread from the earth itself.

Seth looked down and yelled. Grass was knotting itself around his feet even as Sam was all but engulfed in darkness. He struggled to pull himself free, but the more he kicked the tighter the grass wove itself.

There was another blinding flash of light from Sam, and the darkness was dispelled. A flash of fire from Seth, and the grass turned to ashes at his feet. But Sam wasn't letting up. He swiped his hands, as if slapping someone, and Seth reeled. Before his brother could recover Sam did it again, back and forth, back and forth, sending Seth staggering with each blow. Seth caught himself long enough to ignite the grass around Sam's feet. But Sam ignored it and kept on hitting, eyes never leaving Seth's face, even as the flames lapped around him.

I'm the Son of Magic, you the Son of Night, but here we play by my rules, with magic, and I can win . . .

Seth fell to the ground, bleeding. He tried to crawl away. But Sam, with a cry of disgust, marched through the flames around him and up to Seth, drawing his dagger as he went. 'You bastard,' he hissed, 'you killed them both, you bastard!'

Seth rolled over, saw Sam and reached up. His hands passed straight into Sam as if he was made of mist.

Sam froze, eyes wide, a cry choking on his lips. Seth, blood-soaked Seth, bit his lip and held tighter, magic writhing throughout Sam as he sought to pluck out everything that made Sam himself. Lightning darted from Sam's frozen fingers and earthed itself. His eyes went from black to white, to black again; his mouth worked soundlessly. Seth's face was a mask of pain and concentration as, through the magic that joined them, Sam struggled to hit back, inflicting damage with every blow. But never enough . . .

'Father,' whispered Sam, 'for Life's sake, help . . .' His eyes met Seth's. Seth smiled, a tiny twitching of the lips that must have cost him everything. Sam smiled too, and his eyes moved to the dagger clutched uselessly in his left hand. The smile widened.

Seth's mouth opened in an 'O' as he snatched back his hands – too late. Sam's fingers opened.

The dagger fell, far too fast for anything but magic, in a straight line for Seth's belly.

At the last instant Seth moved, but his scream echoed off the hills as the dagger sliced through his side. Sam collapsed on to his hands and knees. Tears stung his eyes, every breath inside him was made of fire.

Seth was crawling away from him – him! Sam would

have felt triumph, if his brain wasn't trying to ooze out of his ears. Blood was seeping from his back and from where Adamarus had wounded him. Until now he hadn't realised how desperate his yearning for sleep had become.

'Pandora will do battle with you now, even if I don't,' hissed Seth.

Sam looked up. Seth had pulled himself to his feet and stood swaying. Blood poured from his side and he looked sweaty and as pale as the moon. Sam tried in vain to raise his hand to throw fire. Seth started towards him, one jerky step at a time. Again Sam lifted his head, and this time managed to hold up his hand.

Fire flashed round his fingers. Seth hesitated, then drew back slowly.

He didn't run – he was probably incapable of it. But Sam watched his every step as he hobbled away. Twice he fell, twice he pulled himself up again. Once more he stopped, face twisted with pain. A few hundred yards from Sam he collapsed to his knees, hesitated, then heaved himself up with the aid of a fallen branch lying in the field.

While Sam watched in exhausted silence, Seth must have pulled himself painfully along over that barren landscape for all of ten minutes, before he stopped and raised his hand. A Portal opened. Seth turned, clutching his side and peering through the darkness to get one last glimpse of his enemy, shook his head and stepped into the Portal, which closed behind him.

Sam laid his head down and closed his eyes. Gratefully, he felt his body brace itself for a full-blown regenerative trance.

*

Perhaps he slept for only a few minutes. Perhaps an hour. But when he woke, it was with his entire body in agony and the sensation that his skin was several sizes too small. He could taste salt in his mouth, smell grass and hear the gentle wind.

That, and the song. It was everywhere around him. He looked up. Nothing. But still it was there, the humming of the Pandora spirits as they wound their way around him. He levered himself to his knees. The stars were white again, but still the song went on. It was almost beautiful, he thought, listening closer. Horrible, terrifying, like the chant of the maddened crowd at a war rally, but beautiful. He stared at the sky and listened.

Something clawed at his ankle. He looked down. As the grass had come up around Seth, now it wound round him, slicing and tearing to create a maze of shallow grass cuts across his legs. The soil beneath him was growing hot, and he was beginning to sink into it. He gave a cry of dismay and staggered to his feet, but his feet were becoming ensnared.

Vultures were circling overhead. He saw them dive for him. He shielded his head as they dived, and struggled to pull himself free. Hot mud sputtered at him, burning his face and hands. He heard wolves howling and saw shapes running across the field towards him. Something hot and hard bit him in the arm and he screamed, falling on his face.

Rolling over he saw, standing on the edge of the field with their grim staring faces illuminated by torchlight, a long line of Mexicans. The song of the Pandora spirits was everywhere, triumphant, roaring in his ears. One of the Mexicans was reloading a gun to shoot him again. He tried to scramble away, but the land itself held him in

place. He had a bullet in his arm, and could hardly think
for the dizzying pain.

The land itself was hating him. The people had risen
up to destroy him, fuelled by the spirits. Every living
thing, be it bird, grass, wolf or human, was united in an
effort to destroy him. He had nowhere left to run. No
weapons left, no tricks up his sleeves, no allies and no
chances.

Except one.

Sam squeezed his eyes shut, and succumbed.

Sebastian . . .

For Time's sake! Do you want me to discharge the Light?

You meant nothing to her.

Sebastian.

Father, help me . . .

You never knew the extent of my power.

He wondered what thoughts were his own. He could
hear . . .

Little light, little fire . . .

. . . why do you run . . .

. . . why do you hide . . .

To come to this?

And the Light spread out from him, bending the grass
as it passed across the land, making the trees bend and
creak, making those creatures who could sense danger
better than humans bury their way into the ground and
cower from the blinding whiteness that made the stars
flinch. Touched the minds of men. Touched the minds of
every creature, mortal and immortal alike. Touched the
minds of the spirits. Drew them all in together.

I want . . .

I hunger . . .

Little light and little fire.

The Light, it comes, it comes . . .
Outrun dawn, outrun Light, run and he will not follow.
He is afraid.
We cannot outrun it . . .
Little light, little fire.
Is this me thinking? Or them?
I am . . .
But then so am I . . .
My name is . . .
But my name is . . .
And mine is . . .
And I like . . .
But I don't . . .
We can't outrun the Light, brothers.
He dares not destroy us.
He has not the power.
But then you never knew the extent of my power, did you?
Am I you?
Or you?
Who's you, then?
Or you? Or you? Or you?
Outrun the Light . . .
Or you? Or you? Or you?
Or me . . .
Or me . . .
Or me . . .

And as the voices grew too loud to bear, something else came with them. The Light riffled through the filing cabinet of a few thousand memories, isolated three factors, brought them to the surface, and sent them spilling across the land.

Hovering for miles around Sam, the Light slowed, hesitated for a second, then faded to nothing, leaving a sheepish darkness. Silence. If you ignored the voices of:

Me . . .

And me . . .

And me . . .

And me . . .

Am I you?

Or me?

Or me?

Is this me thinking?

Or someone else?

Like me?

Or me . . .

Or me . . .

Which one am I? My name is . . .

But then my name is . . .

And my name is . . .

Rising through the voices, came the memories.

Somewhere, in the darkness, a man who might or might not have once been Sam Linnfer:

Or possibly me . . .

Or me . . .

Or me . . .

Smiled. Love, Trust, Charity – he was surprised at how much of them was surfacing from the minds of the thousands of creatures he'd touched. A warm sphere, surging to the surface of a sea of never-silent voices, expanding to the same radius as the Light had encompassed and, like everything else, fading. Everything except the voices.

In the end, when his body was a thousand miles from his mind, which was itself just a tiny speck among thousands, he was grateful that he couldn't feel the pain.

A bubble of light, brighter than anything else in the night, rose up before Sam, split into three parts and rushed away from him, west, towards the sunset. The land below them was lit up for a second as if the sun had decided that eight light minutes wasn't nearly close enough to Earth, before they rose and became parts of the sky. A long silence. Far, far above, three spheres of burning Light containing respectively all the trust, love and charity that Sam – or what might be Sam, he wasn't sure – could find exploded against three twisted shapes trying to out-run the Light. Which, in the second of searing fire – Trust against Suspicion, Love against Hate, Charity against Greed – crumpled, and fell. In silence Earth consumed them.

Leaving Sam . . . somewhere.

Is this me?

Or me?

Or me?

Which one am I?

I hear you thinking.

But it might be me thinking and I might simply hear you thinking . . .

Or perhaps I'm all of you.

Or none of you . . .

Did I think that thought?

Did I?

Or perhaps I did?

Or perhaps I did?

Who am I?

You?

Me?

Him?

Her?

Me?
You?
Us?

Somewhere, in the middle of a field in Mexico, emptier still after the Light had scorched it, a small, dark man collapsed, white eyes staring at nothing.

EPILOGUE

Brief Victory

Sam could hear a kettle boiling. It was a strange sound, one that he hadn't been expecting. He'd been anticipating at least fire or screams. He lay very still for a long while, staring at the ceiling. It wasn't the most interesting sight, being blotched by leaks and decorated in a less-than-dazzling paint that had once been white. There was a spider's web in one corner.

He was lying on a sofa, blanket pulled up to his chin, wearing someone else's shirt. His back hurt. So did his arm. He raised the arm speculatively and examined it. There was a blood-soaked bandage, which he cautiously undid, to find a large area of dried blood. He scratched the blood away. Underneath was a pink web of scar tissue where the bullet had entered. There was no bullet, nor any injury, and the scar tissue was healing nicely.

He sat up, feeling the warmth of his face and hands as if he hadn't realised he could ever be well again. At that moment the door opened and someone backed round it,

carrying a tray. Sam observed the back in utter idleness
for a few seconds, then watched the tray approach him.
He found that the toast and coffee on it held his undi-
vided attention all the way across the room to his lap.

Adam sat down on the end of the sofa.

'Hey,' murmured Sam.

'Hey. Alive, then.'

'I think so. You?'

'Yes. The Pandora spirits seem to have gone.'

'I—'

'You attacked the spirits with the Light. You gathered
thousands of minds to your call, thought of trust, charity
and love – and bang. Hit them.'

'But . . . I didn't kill them.' Sam's comment didn't need
an answer. 'If I'd killed them,' he said slowly, 'I would
have had to gather every single mind around me in every
single world. The effort would probably have killed me,
as well as them.'

'You didn't kill Seth either,' said Adam. 'Though you
came bloody near. Nor, evidently enough, did you die.'

'But I came bloody near that too?' Sam asked.

Adam nodded. 'Seth's fled,' he added. 'The spirits are
severely weakened, and gone into hiding. You stopped
them, for a while.'

'A small, small while.'

'Time to breathe,' agreed Adam.

'What happened after . . .?'

'I woke up with your magic all over me and a vague
memory along the lines of, er, trying to kill you. There
seemed no sign of the spirits, so I went looking for you.
You were comatose – you've been in a regenerative
trance for almost a week. None of us could wake you. So
we packaged you up and flew you home.' Adam smiled,

nervously. There was awe in his eyes, bordering on fear. 'You won.'

'For the moment.'

'Still a victory. A battle, if not the war.'

Sam said nothing.

'What . . . was it like? The Light.'

'It was . . . almost peaceful. I heard the minds of everyone. Their combined love, trust and charity. And then – I felt Hate and Greed and Suspicion trying to flee the Light, and I didn't do anything. I *wasn't* anything – we were one.

'But . . .' Sam smiled faintly. 'But I don't know whether this is my own memory, or me recalling what someone else remembers.'

Silence. Then Adam said, 'What will you do?'

'I don't know. Seth chased Andrew halfway across the world, to tear the information on Cronus from his mind before he left him dead. It's fair to say Seth won't let that information rot for ever.'

'You really think he has the guts to go after Cronus?'

Sam thought. *Cronus isn't the end of everything, he's the end of everything as we know it. An end of Time – an end of death, an end of destiny, an end of the imprisonment we live with.* Seth had glowed when he spoke of it. There'd been a fanatic's gleam in his eye, much as Sam had often noted in Jehovah's. The look of a man determined to carry a mad scheme through to the end. 'Yes, I think he will. But not yet. He can't.'

'What about Fran?'

Sam shrugged. 'She betrayed Freya to those three. She told them what Freya had done, how Freya was going to bring them down.'

'Will you go after her?'

'She's a third-generation Child of Time. There are more convenient occasions for revenge. She'll meet her fate, just like Asmodeus and Seth. But Cronus . . .'

'If Cronus gets out.'

'Then I probably will be forced to use the Light again. Something which, I might add, I'm opposed to on principle.'

'What principle?'

'Lucifer's Principle of Survival, complete with foot-notes and a special illustrated edition for the dedicated collector. But Cronus won't get out.'

'Why?'

A grin. A faint memory of the boyish smile that had once gone before, a spark of the old Sam. 'Why? I'll be waiting with a big sword and a lot of motivation, that's why. The second someone moves, I'll be there. I'm dark-ness incarnate, after all. After thousands of years of being told that I'm inescapable, I'm almost ready to believe it.'

'You don't think thousands of years of hearing about your dark power has given you a case of egomania?'

'That's no way to address a man who's possibly saved the world from a minor apocalypse.'

'For the moment.'

'Yes,' agreed Sam. 'For the moment.'

There was a long silence. Adam broke it in a voice that, had it been human, would have been frightened. 'What now?'

'Now?' Sam almost laughed. 'Now I have breakfast. I'm starving. And there's a tomorrow, isn't there?'

'While there's life, there's hope?'

'While there's Time,' corrected Sam quickly. 'And even then the proverb needs an editor. "While there's Time, there's motion on a space-time graph," perhaps?'

'And hope?' persisted Adam.

'You're not becoming a romantic, are you?'

'Not yet.'

'But tomorrow?'

'I don't know whether there's such a thing as a romantic spirit.'

'Time changes everyone, Adam. You should have learnt that by now.'

Silence. 'And tomorrow?'

'There's hope,' he agreed. 'New threats, but hope.'

'For the moment.'

'Until tomorrow. And maybe beyond.'

Silence. Sam smiled vaguely and lay back, listening to the voices still buzzing around his mind. *Cronus isn't the end of everything, he's the end of everything as we know it.*

I know, brother. But things as we know them aren't totally bad, are they?

He slept.

Not so much a memory, but a dream. A dream of the past, and possibly the future too.

Dreams signified something, so he'd been told. But memories made you who you were. So, he remembered.

The Room of Clocks was empty, the only sound the steady ticking of timepieces. He stared around it, and his eyes lighted on the clock where, a few centuries before, he'd found a sword and crown. Then, for the first time, his gaze lifted to the huge empty throne at the far end of the hall. Behind the throne was the very largest clock, made of nothing but light. Its dial looked strange; he'd once been told that the second hand didn't measure the gap between one beat and another, but the oscillation of a wave of light.

Sam stood there, staring at the empty throne.

'No,' he said finally. 'You don't care, do you?' He sighed, and began pacing round the hall, talking as though to himself.

'It's very complicated, but I think the nub of the matter is this. You are the process by which we live and eventually die. You are the beginning and the end, and of course there *has* to be one of those. Alone, however, you are nothing more. But with life, especially sentient, self-aware life, you are something more. Every thought I think takes time, takes a little bit of you, so of course you remember it as though it were your own. So it is that every thought and every feeling is your own, jumbled up inside *you*.

'And yet you do not care.'

'Why are you here?' The voice exclaimed at him from all around, filled the room, deafened him.

He cowered away from it in fear, but when he spoke it was with defiance. 'You should know! You're in my mind!' he yelled over the echoes.

The room seemed to darken, its shadows lengthening and melding. Sam suddenly felt very cold.

'Insolent boy! You dare to come to me now? You dare to assume I will help you?'

'I am your son!'

Something ran across Sam's foot. Something else grabbed him from behind – but when he turned it was no more than shadow. Something heavy struck him across the shoulders, and he fell to his hands and knees.

To hands and knees, directly facing the empty throne, he realised. Then a hand, cold as ice, unyielding as marble, caught him by the hair and pulled his head up hard. He felt the pressure of a blade across his throat, and the pain of the cut as though it had really happened.

'No one has spoken to me as you have, boy. No one has ever taken such risks with my pleasure!'

'You brought me on yourself!' he yelled back, shaking with fear. It wasn't his fear, for at that moment he felt only calm, but an older dread drawn from his memories and being replayed across his mind by a furious father over and over again.

'Am I not your necessary child? Did you not make me to serve your purpose and your purpose alone? Was not Light too gentle for you and is not Magic the one power that can play your deadly games? Am I not yours?'

'You defy me! Me! With every breath you draw you defy me, and every thought you think is bent towards outwitting me. Me!'

Sam opened his mouth to speak, but the voice lashed across his ears before he could do so. 'Do not deny me, for I am in your mind and always have been!'

'Then you will know why I defy you! How can you be in my mind and not care?'

Pain shot through him like fire. Sam struggled weakly, but the grasp was impossible to break. 'You know I have no intention of serving you and yours! So if you don't care, why don't you kill me and save yourself the trouble?'

The grip was abruptly relaxed and he toppled forwards, gasping for breath. The fear was gone, so was the pain. But the shadows still danced around him. He looked around the room. There was no one there.

'Why do you defy me?' whispered a voice, and it seemed so sad and weary that he felt a pang of guilt for having contributed to this ancient power's woes.

'You don't even care for your own children, do you? They're destroying themselves, and if their destruction will make a certain future happen here instead of there, then so be it. The only reason you haven't destroyed me for the act of defying you is because you need me.

'So. I destroyed the Eden Initiative. Whooho. Good on me. At least your son can feel *something*, even if the father has the emotional competence of a brick. So what now? If you let me live you really ought to ask my nice brothers if *they'll* let me live. And if you let me live, let me live for my sake, not for yours. Father? You cannot have me believe that I was created as . . . as a machine, to perform a task and so die. At least pretend you care. Father?'

Silence. With a sigh, Sam clambered to his feet and gave the throne a frankly dirty look. 'You don't care, do you? You never have. You never will.'

'You will serve me.' It was a whisper, nothing more. 'Whatever you do, you will serve me. There is no escape.'

Sam's eyes turned to the light-clock beyond the throne. And he smiled a humourless, empty smile.

'You can escape from anything, if you know how to go about it.'

He got to his feet. He broke into a brisk trot, then a run. Magic rose around him as he moved. Shadows lengthened, clawed at his feet. The fear was back, and the pain tenfold. And the roaring voice that filled the room, filled the universe with its anger.

'You will not defy me, Bearer of Light! Not this time!'

Images were played across his mind in a blur, horrible images extracted from the memories of a billion other souls, but Sam ignored them. He knew who he was and he focused on that one identity amid all the others. As he ran he changed. Sparks flew off his fingers and when he opened his arms out wide it was as if a cloak of pure light moved with him, creating the effect of wings.

'Lucifer! You cannot defy me!'

With a laugh born of desperation and despair Lucifer plunged straight through the clock of light, and out the other side.

So he'd been right after all, and as he opened his wings of magic and felt the thermals catch them and pull him skywards, he wondered what his brothers and sisters would think if they knew how thin Time built his walls, and how much they took on faith.

Somewhere in London, a doorway of silver light opened, shimmered on the air for a few seconds, and vanished again. He knew who the enemy was, where to go, what to do. Three of them, playing with fire. Scorched, but still out there.

It was a million to one chance, but he'd make it happen.

Sam's story continues in . . . .

TIMEKEEPERS

The battle for Earth, Heaven and Hell has only just begun

And don't forget to look out for Catherine Webb's brilliant debut series. Set in the realm of dreams and starring the unforgettable sorcerer Laenan Kite, *Mirror Dreams* and *Mirror Wakes* are stunningly imaginative stories that sizzle with magic, mystery and fantasy adventure. If you've enjoyed *Waywalkers* you'll love these two books.

www.atombooks.co.uk

ABOUT THE AUTHOR

Catherine Webb wrote her acclaimed debut fantasy *Mirror Dreams* at the age of just fourteen, prompting extensive coverage in the national media and rights sales in France, Germany, Holland, Italy and Japan. Its sequel, *Mirror Wakes*, was published six months later, shortly after Catherine was named *Young Trailblazer of the Year* by *Cosmo Girl* magazine.

Catherine lives in North London and is currently studying for her A-Levels. As well as writing, she enjoys reading, badminton and chess. She likes cats, space (the stuff with stars in) and Fridays. She is less keen on drizzle, Hammersmith and the number 73 bus. Catherine is currently working on the follow-up to *Waywalkers*, titled *Timekeepers*. You can find out more about her at www.atombooks.co.uk.